FALL TO PIECES

BROKEN #2

CHLOE WALSH

Fall to Pieces,
Published by Chloe Walsh.
Copyright 2014 by Chloe Walsh.

Fall to Pieces,
Broken #2,
First published, April 2014.
Republished May 2020.
All rights reserved. ©
Cover designed by Sarah Paige.
Edited by Aleesha Davis.
Proofread by: Brooke Bowen Hebert.

DISCLAIMER

This book is a work of fiction. All names, characters, places and incidents either are products of the author's imagination or are used fictitiously. Any resemblance to events, locales, or persons, living or dead, is coincidental.

The author acknowledges all songs titles, song lyrics, film titles, film characters, trademarked statuses, brands, mentioned in this book are the property of, and belong to, their respective owners. The publication/ use of these trademarks is not authorized/ associated with, or sponsored by the trademark owners.

Chloe Walsh is in no way affiliated with any of the brands, songs, musicians or artists mentioned in this book.

ONE
LEE

I WOKE from my most disturbing nightmare yet, slick with sweat, and to a pitch-black room.

The memories of lying on the bathroom floor bleeding out – the knowledge of what I'd lost from my body – invaded my thoughts and I flinched, crippled with pain that was both mentally and physically debilitating.

Gasping for precious air, I felt around my nightstand until my fingers grazed the switch for the lamp. Flicking on the light, my mind immediately reverted to my nightmare, and I automatically grasped at my stomach.

I was fine.

I needed to relax.

But I couldn't go back to sleep.

Every time I closed my eyes, I remembered the blood.

Gushing.

Oozing.

Draining the life from my body.

I thought of the baby I would never hold in my arms.

My flesh and blood.

Torn from existence.

Stolen from me.

I saw the shattered look in those steel blue eyes I had become so accustomed to.

Gone.

Gone.

Gone.

I was lost.

So incredibly lost.

I felt as if I'd been cut apart and shredded, and I doubted I could put myself back together again.

I was heartbroken, I was grieving, and I was excited all rolled into a complicated flurry of emotions, swarming my mind, piercing my soul.

I wasn't sure if I should be happy. I didn't know if I *did* feel it. And then I felt guilty for *not* feeling happy.

Lord, I was so confused.

Grabbing the cell phone from my nightstand, I checked the time.

06:30.

It was officially Christmas Day.

This year would top the list of worst Christmases.

I would be spending my nineteenth Christmas in a hospital, pregnant and alone.

Pregnant.

Cam had left her phone with me before leaving the hospital last night with strict orders to call Derek's phone if I needed anything. I wouldn't call them, though. They had done more than enough.

I was alone in this now.

It was the way it had to be.

"Princess?"

That *word.* That single torturous, endearment had my heart catapulting around in my chest and my head swinging in the direction of the door of my hospital room.

"What are you doing here?" I whispered, trembling at the sight of him.

"I heard you crying from outside the door." Kyle closed the door behind him and walked slowly towards me.

I couldn't help but stare at him.

I looked at him differently now, not just because he had ripped my heart out of my chest, but because part of him was growing inside of me.

"I was worried, baby." He pulled a plastic chair close to my bed and sat down. "How are you feeling?" He sounded nervous.

His eyes roamed from my eyes to my stomach. I pulled the

blankets around myself self-consciously. "Confused," I replied. Confusion was my most potent emotion, especially now with him here.

Kyle shuddered and bowed his head for a moment. "Yeah, I can understand why. Are you feeling okay, physically? Are you sore?"

I didn't think I'd ever feel 'okay' again.

I nodded and peered up at him. He looked tired, no he looked shattered. I guessed he mirrored how I felt. His blue eyes were bloodshot from lack of sleep or crying…I couldn't be sure which. The pale blue hoodie he wore was creased. His jaw was dusted with a light layer of stubble, which was strange, because Kyle always kept himself clean shaven. His faded jeans were the same he had on the night of the party. I knew because I'd watched him slip them on moments before he left me. "Why are you here?" I asked quietly. "I told you to go."

He sighed, shaking his head. "I did leave, but I couldn't stay away. I've been outside your door all night, baby. I can explain everything. If you just give me a chance. It's not what you think."

I didn't want to know. I didn't want to hear his explanation. I knew what he would say.

He would try and worm his way out of what he'd done again. There wasn't a damn thing he could say to me this time that would make it okay.

Nothing could fix this.

Kyle had left me to be with Rachel and I really didn't know why I was so surprised. God knows, I'd had enough warnings. Cam, Mike, hell Rachel herself had warned me not to get involved with Kyle Carter. I should have listened. If I had, I wouldn't be lying here.

It hurt to think of Kyle in the same city as his evil ex-girl-friend, let alone together, doing god knows what, while I was miscarrying one of our babies on his bathroom floor.

Kyle took my silence as a means to speak. "I need to tell you about what happened two years ago with Rachel. You need to know all of the facts so we can move forward."

I flinched at the sound of her name on his tongue. "I don't want to hear this, Kyle…"

"You will hear this. You need to know the truth…all of it."

The truth couldn't help me now. I was too broken. I was torn apart and about to fall to pieces.

Kyle straightened in his seat. Taking a deep breath, he spoke. "I was seeing Rachel in my sophomore year at college. It was nothing serious, just a couple of dates. We'd only had..." His voice trailed off and he sighed before continuing in a gruff tone, "Been intimate once. I had no plans to pursue anything. I was barely twenty and enjoyed the life I had without complicating things." I watched his face as he spoke. It was obvious he was trying to give me a cleaner version of events. "When my grandfather died, I stayed at his house in Denver while his attorneys organized legal matters. I hadn't seen Rachel since school had broken up for the holidays, and I didn't care. She wasn't a priority to me, just another girl. I decided to crash at my grandfather's house after reading the will. It was two nights before Christmas and it was snowing. I didn't feel like driving home, and didn't want to deal with Cam and Derek's sympathy."

He shifted in the chair, his mind clearly reverting back to the night. "When I got to the house, Rachel was in the kitchen, having sex with my brother."

I sucked in a sharp breath.

I did not expect that.

My traitorous heart spiked for him.

He shook his head and rubbed his hand across his face as the memory of that night clearly played out in his mind. "Apparently, it had been going on for months," Kyle said. "So, technically she was cheating on him, not me."

"What happened?" I couldn't help but be interested. No wonder Kyle had issues. He'd been screwed over so badly in his life. It didn't excuse the way he'd treated me, not by any stretch of the imagination, but I could understand a little better.

Kyle sighed, rubbing his forehead. "I was pissed, Lee. Very fucking pissed. There was a lot of screaming and accusations thrown about. I was hurt and betrayed by my own brother. I hate my father, but my brother, he had been the one person I got along with in the family. I felt like I'd been duped."

"What did you do?"

"I left. After my brother threw seven kinds of shit at me for 'fucking his girl and stealing his inheritance,' I got the fuck out of there." He paused to look at me. "Rachel followed me, got into my car. I was so angry. I told her to get the hell out, but she wouldn't. So I drove off like a lunatic. I was trying to scare her into getting out of the car. She didn't have her belt on and I was going too fast. I ran a red light."

He shivered and rolled his shoulders. "We collided with a truck. The impact was on the passenger side. She was hurt so bad, Lee. She had to have emergency surgery."

Kyle was quiet for a moment. The next words he spoke were little more than a strangled whisper. "You remember, I told you my mom died when I was three?"

I nodded in confusion. "Yes, from a drug overdose. That's why you ended up in foster care. Why? What does your mom have to do with Rachel?"

Kyle nodded his head slowly. "Nothing and everything. Drugs were a contributing factor to my mom's death, but she died in a car accident."

I struggled to keep my face void of emotion. I could see this was clearly painful for Kyle.

Kyle frowned. "A car accident she purposefully orchestrated to end her life."

I sat up suddenly. The poker face I was wearing slipped away as my heart bled out for him. "Oh my god, Kyle...."

I cupped my hand across my mouth, afraid to say too much or worse, cry. If I started crying again I was afraid I'd never stop.

Kyle smiled, but it was more of a grimace. "Oh wait. You haven't heard the best part yet." I frowned at him, not under-standing how any of this could be interpreted as funny. His eyes moved from mine, focusing on the wall behind my head. "I was in the car when she did it."

I couldn't comprehend what he was saying. This was too much to take in, all in one night. He had been in the car when his mom crashed, the night she died? Did that mean she had tried to kill Kyle along with herself?

My god, he was only three years old at the time.

"Yeah," Kyle said quietly, interpreting where my thoughts had gone. "She tried to take us both out that night. I guess she fucked up though, since I'm sitting here." He laughed humorlessly. "Although, if she'd just jacked me up with a tenth of the shit she injected herself with daily, she could have finished the job."

I didn't know whether to hit him or hug him.

His mom had almost taken his life in her attempt to commit suicide and he was talking about it as if it wasn't the huge deal that it was. It frightened me that he could talk about such a terrible haunting experience without an ounce of emotion in his voice. The only hint of how he felt was when I looked in his eyes. Those sparkling blue eyes were troubled, they were clouded with such deep sadness.

I reached across and held his hand. It was all I could do. I guessed we had more in common than I'd originally thought. We both had some seriously dysfunctional parents.

I knew Kyle's dad was an ass. He'd been a married man when he impregnated Kyle's, then sixteen year old, mother before abandoning her pregnant and broke. Kyle had grown up in foster care and had been shoved from pillar to post, all while his father had been living it up, courtesy of his family's hotel empire. If it weren't for Kyle's paternal grandfather somehow finding him when he was twelve, and later leaving Kyle his entire fortune, Kyle's life would have turned out a whole lot different to now.

But his mom...how did someone get over something like that?

By pushing people away and never letting anyone get too close...

"So, you're telling me this because the accident you had with Rachel brought back bad memories for you?"

I wasn't stupid and clearly read where this admission was going. Kyle wanted me to understand why his and Rachel's car accident had affected him.

He squeezed my hand tightly. "Yes and no. These are the things I should have explained months ago. And I'm so sorry for that, baby, but you have to know that you're the only person I've spoken to about my mom since I was a kid." I squeezed his hand back. I knew Kyle found it hard to open up. It didn't matter much at this point in our relationship. He was right about that. This conversation should have happened months ago.

"I was a wreck after the accident," he whispered. "My head was completely messed up. The guilt, the memories..." He inhaled sharply before continuing. "When I was finally allowed to see Rachel after the surgery, she told me she lost my baby."

"She was pregnant?" I asked, astounded with the sudden irony of our predicament. I pulled myself up, listening intently now. "With your baby?" My blood ran cold at the thought and I dropped his hand as I stared at him bewildered.

"That's what she told me," Kyle said grimly. "Convenient, considering my grandfather had just left me a fortune. She played the baby card. I was young and I fell for it. I guess I was her meal ticket."

I flinched and he noticed.

Is that how he felt about me?

Did he think I tricked him?

He took my hand and covered it with both of his as he leaned towards me. "She was playing me, Lee– well, both of us. Me for kicks and my brother for what she could get. I guess she put her eggs in the wrong basket. She'd assumed my father or my brother would inherit everything." He sighed, shaking his head as he recaptured my hand. "I can't blame her for thinking that. Who would have bet money on me inheriting everything? Shit, even I questioned my grandfather's motives."

"Maybe it was his way of apologizing to you for his poor excuse of a son." I slipped my free hand over my mouth.

I shouldn't have said that.

"Maybe." Kyle smiled softly, looking down at our joined hands.

I was enjoying the way he stroked the back of my hand with his thumb far too much.

I pulled my hand away.

He frowned but didn't question me. Instead, he continued delving into the darkest parts of his past. The past he'd blocked me out of for too long. "She told me the impact from the wreck had damaged her, that she had a hysterectomy. I didn't question it. I was too absorbed in my guilt. It was so close to home, you know? I'd ruined my mother's life and then... I thought I had killed Rachel's baby and any chances of her having another. I felt so fucking guilty, Lee. I thought I'd destroyed her, ruined her whole life."

He looked at my face, his piercing blue eyes capturing me, pulling me in.

I was stupefied. "None of it was true?"

He shook his head. "It was all lies. There was never any baby and even if there had been, it wouldn't have been mine. I used protection with her. I always use protection."

Not always.

He hadn't used protection the first time we'd slept together. The night I'd given him my virginity and he in return had given me rejection issues and a seriously bruised heart.

God, I was so stupid.

I should have known that night. I should have walked away from him instead of going back and forth for months.

"It was Rachel's vindictive attempt at holding onto the affluent future she had planned in her head," Kyle continued. "She had surgery on her spleen, princess, nothing else. She knew I wasn't serious about her, so she laid the guilt trip on me, forcing me into submission, using my guilt as a means to trap me into the fucked up relationship you've seen over the past six months."

It was hard to hold onto my anger when I looked at the pained expression in his face.

His voice had a tint of desperation, as if he was begging me to understand.

I wanted to…but I just couldn't.

He sighed heavily. "At the time, I would have promised her anything she wanted. I thought I'd ruined her life. Giving up my freedom seemed the only redeemable thing to do. So, when she started crying about how no man would want a barren wife, I'd promised her I would stick by her. I agreed to an arrangement that when the time came for me to settle down…I would, with her.

"You have to remember, I wasn't born into the life of affluence either. I didn't understand what I was getting myself involved in when I met her. I didn't grow up encountering gold-diggers like Mike did. I was green and she knew it. I felt I owed her, so I made that promise. I didn't love her; I didn't expect to love anyone. I never anticipated you walking into my life last summer and turning it inside out."

Mike?

My mind was stuck on that one name. I couldn't believe this. "Mike is your brother?"

Kyle nodded, looking puzzled. "Yeah, I thought you knew that?"

No, I didn't. Because he didn't tell me. He never told me anything. This was another prime example of Kyle blocking me out. I shook my head.

Of course, it all started to make sense now.

Kyle and Mike's hostility towards each other had always seemed so...personal.

Mike's last name was Henderson.

Duh, The Henderson Hotel Chain.

How had I not put this all together sooner?

Because you're stupid, that's why. Too wrapped up in Kyle Carter to see or even think straight.

Different surnames because they had different mothers... Mike was claimed. Kyle had been abandoned. I'd been so freaking blind.

"I'm sorry, princess, I should have told you earlier."

Yes, you damn well should have.

Kyle should have warned me, and so should Mike. Mike and I were friends. It hurt me more than it should to think that I sat and ate lunch with Mike every day at work and he'd never once mentioned the fact that he and Kyle were brothers. I wouldn't have expected their whole life story, but a heads up would have been nice.

I blocked out my thoughts and tried to listen to Kyle, who was rambling on quickly. "When we got back from visiting your dad in Louisiana, after everything we'd been through... I couldn't take it anymore, Lee. I had you. Lee...you were more than I'd ever bargained for. I wanted you so damn much, but I was so fucking trapped. I needed a way out. I confided in Linda, told her everything. She dug around, contacted Rachel's mother and found out the truth about her surgery. If I hadn't told Linda, I would still be trapped right now. The night I left you at the party was the night I found out the truth. Linda had phoned me that day and told me that everything I had believed for two years, was a lie."

He stopped talking for a moment, leaned down and grasped my chin gently, forcing my eyes to meet his.

"I left the party with Rachel because I was desperate to finish things and for no other reason. I didn't lay a finger on her and I never will again. I wanted to be with you. I still do. It's always been you, Lee. From the second I saw you in my kitchen that very first night. You fucking broke me that night, baby. You took the air right out of my lungs, I haven't breathed since."

He was talking, but I couldn't hear what he was saying. This was not okay.

'If I hadn't told Linda, I would still be trapped right now.'

I suddenly felt cold to the bone.

Those words, that one simple admission of betrayal surpassed all his guilt and apologies.

Whether he intended it or not, that one sentence was the nail in the coffin for our relationship.

I couldn't be around him anymore. I didn't know the stranger in front of me. He knew all of the darkness inside of me. I knew nothing. "No." I blinked back the tears. "No, Kyle."

He leaned away from me, surprised, "No? What do you mean?"

He didn't get it, he didn't understand a damn thing. "I can't do this. With you. I can't." I whispered. I just wanted him to go.

He ran his hand through his hair almost roughly. "You don't get to push me away. It won't work. I'm yours. You're stuck with me. I won't leave you again." How could he say these things to me? Was he crazy?

I looked up at him; there was a determined glint in his eyes. "Well, I'm not yours and I'm not playing this game with you anymore, Kyle," I said weakly. "I always lose and I'm too tired to get back up again."

I needed to be alone, to think everything through. I couldn't do that with him pressuring me.

I knew that if he didn't leave soon, I would submit. I would cave and hate myself for it.

He had made a choice at the party and every other time he'd deliberately tricked me and lied.

I had one to make now.

"It's over. Whatever this thing is between us, I don't want to be involved in it anymore." The words tasted bitter on my tongue and my heart was screaming at me to stop.

Every instinct and urge in my body protested my decision. But my brain–the critical tool that had been absent for my previous Kyle Carter decision-making moments–was set.

My mind was made up and there was no going back.

He visibly shook at my words. "You can't mean that, Lee. She doesn't mean anything to me. I'm sorry I didn't tell you everything from the start, but you came along and...I didn't know... I've never felt..." he hissed. "Shit, it's all so complicated."

"It doesn't matter whether I know what happened this time or not," I sobbed. "I know what happened every other time, and all of the lies and secrets? I can't deal with it anymore. She told you terrible lies, Kyle, awful ones, but you did that to me. You lied to me, time and time again. Months went by where you could have told me the truth, but you didn't. How am I supposed to get over that? Our whole relationship was based on a lie. And the worst part of this whole mess is that you told Linda."

I stopped and sniffed away my tears. "You trusted and confided in Linda instead of me. I think that's what hurts the most. The fact that you thought so little of me. I'm in love with you, Kyle. It would have made my life so much easier to have known the truth. I would have understood. If you had just been truthful with me from the beginning...You didn't give us a fighting chance. I'd no idea what I was getting involved in, or whom I was getting involved with...and if Linda hadn't found out the truth, you would still be lying to me, hiding me. And the day would have come when you would have left me." I knew that was true. He had already done it to me many times over.

"You would have left me for Rachel," I whispered. "You would've had to because of your stupid agreement and I would have been cast aside like an old toy. Maybe it's only now because I'm pregnant that I can see it clearly, but it's wrong. We're wrong, Kyle. You led me on. I won't be that girl anymore."

TWO
KYLE

LEE PUSHED FURTHER AWAY from me in the bed, curling her hands around herself defensively.

This was not happening. No fucking way. I'd fought too hard to be with Lee, to have her walk away from me.

I stared at her pale face, tears were filling her eyes. "You're having my baby," I whispered.

I was going to be a father. Lee was having my child.

I had hope. She was mine. There was a part of me growing inside her that she couldn't deny and my heart swelled with hope. I felt like a bastard for thinking like this, but I was desperate. I was silently thanking god for my momentary blip in safe sex. It was my only way back to her now.

What could I say to her about the miscarriage to make her feel better?

Absolutely nothing.

Twins.

She'd been pregnant with twins for three fucking months and it'd almost killed her. I hadn't been there.

All those promises I'd made to her that I'd been so sure I could keep. The one fucking time she needed me, I hadn't been there. I was so full of self-loathing, I was afraid to be alone right now. My thoughts were tormenting me and the image of Lee's blood all over the bathroom floor was killing me. I didn't want to go home. I would never forgive myself.

For Christ's sake, I'd known she was sick. I'd fucking known and still I had left the party, too fucking intent on revenge that I'd been ignorant of my sick girlfriend.

She'd called for help. I remembered.

Some guy at the party had told me there was a girl calling for me...I had known it was Lee and I had still walked away. The dark sickened pain inside of me was suffocating. I didn't deserve forgiveness.

Derek had told me about Lee's condition. He'd called it a concurrent ectopic and intrauterine pregnancy.

I had no fucking clue what those words meant, only that the doctor had removed the baby that had died, and Lee's fallopian tube.

I was torn apart over the miscarriage, but I knew whatever I was feeling Lee was feeling it tenfold. I was so grateful she was still pregnant, but Jesus, I was terrified something else was going to happen. We had no goddamn luck. It was more than not having luck. It was as if there was a force determined to keep us apart; first Rachel, and now Lee herself. I watched the tears roll down her cheeks.

She was not leaving me.

Not now.

"I know," she whispered quietly. I waited for her to say something else, anything else, but she didn't.

What was I supposed to do?

Shit, I didn't know. I'd just told her everything, finally, but it wasn't enough. I balled my fists together. "Don't do this." I was begging. I'd get down on my hands and knees if it meant she'd come back to me.

"What can I do to fix this?" I asked, the emotion obvious in my voice. "Tell me what to do, Lee, and I'll do it."

She shook her head, her curls falling into her eyes. I moved closer to brush them back from her face. She gasped at the contact, she still felt something.

Thank God.

"You can't fix this, Kyle, you can't fix me... I need time on my own."

Like fuck I couldn't fix her. I'd spend the rest of my life trying to fix her. I didn't believe a word of her denial. I had screwed up phenomenally. There had to be a way back from this..."No."

"Kyle," she sighed, as I looked into her pale shattered gray eyes.

I guess it's true what they say. When you have everything, you have everything to lose.

That quote never had a truer fucking meaning than my life right now.

My heart sank. I knew whatever she was about to say would be bad. "If you care about me," she mumbled, pausing as she inhaled a wobbly breath. "If you've ever cared about me, you will leave me be."

"If you've ever cared about me?"

She didn't know the half of the depth of my feelings for her, but if I told her how I felt now she probably wouldn't believe me or worse, think I was lying to her. I shook my head and opened my mouth to respond, but she spoke first.

"I need to be on my own for a while. I need to make some decisions and I can't think clearly around you. I need you to give me some space while I recover. Don't come back here. Please."

I was torn apart by her words.

Did she mean it? Was she testing my commitment to her?

I thought about it and realized that she meant every word.

Lee didn't play games. She was the most honest person I knew. If she said something, she meant it.

But fuck did it hurt...

"I don't want you to be alone on Christmas," I said pathetically, holding back the tears. "Please don't ask me to do this, princess." Truth be told, I didn't want to be alone. Everything was slipping away from me and I was using anything I could think of to get her to change her mind. "Is this really what you want?" I asked when she didn't answer me.

She closed her eyes and slowly nodded. Tears slid down her cheekbones and there was a finality to this picture that I couldn't handle.

I jerked out of the chair, and paced the floor, unable to sit still any longer. I couldn't breathe.

How was I supposed to make my legs walk out that door and leave her and my baby?

"How much time do you need?" I asked, looking down at her.

Her body was tense, her eyes closed. "I don't know."

I went to her. Leaning down, I clasped her face between both of my hands. "I'll be here. When you are ready, you call me, I will be here." I kissed her lips, tasted the wetness of her salty tears on my lips. I pulled away too soon, afraid I would push her too far. "Do you understand me? I will be here waiting for you, when you're ready to let me back in."

THREE
LEE

I HAD A DECISION TO MAKE.

I had many to make actually. The first, and possibly most important one, I had already made when I placed that phone call last night. I was now hoping it was a decision that wouldn't come back to bite me in the butt.

I rubbed the skin covering my swollen stomach and sighed. I'd been through hell and back in the past six weeks, but I'd survived and most importantly, so had the child growing in my womb.

"You got everything you need, Lee?"

I smiled. It was a weak one, but it was all I could muster given the circumstances. "Yes," I replied, zipping my duffel bag.

Mike Henderson stood in the doorway of my hospital room, tall, handsome, and intimidating as hell, but he was offering me an escape. A temporary exit to this messed up life I had slipped into. When I phoned him last night asking for a favor, it wasn't to hurt his brother, or upset my friends. I'd just needed someone to talk to, someone who wasn't biased and who wouldn't judge me on my poor decisions.

It hurt to think of the reasons why I was standing in a hospital room. Losing the baby and losing Kyle all in the same night was something I didn't like to think about– I couldn't think about.

It had been over six weeks since that night. The night my life and everything in it fell to pieces. I'd found out I was pregnant and then I wasn't and then I was again, all in a matter of hours.

Twins, the doctor had said. One had died, one survived. And the man I loved, the man I trusted more than anyone in this world, had betrayed me.

For the sake of my sanity, I locked away those feelings and thoughts in a box, in the darkest part of my mind. The same box I kept the memories of my father's beatings and the petrified feelings that had engulfed me on the night of my high school prom, when Perry Franklin had tried to rape me.

Pretense was now my coping mechanism for carrying on. For surviving one day at a time.

So, for the past forty plus days, while I healed from the surgery and the medical team monitored my pregnancy, I'd closed off my feelings and tried to adjust to my new life.

I'd gotten a nasty infection after the surgery, which had delayed my discharge by a couple of weeks. It had been a gift from god.

Well, the infection was gross and that had sucked, but the relief of having an extra few weeks before I had to face my roommates—one roommate in particular—had sweetened the deal.

Dr. Ashcroft had warned me of the different complications and infections the baby was vulnerable to because of my intrusive surgery, but was delighted with how I was progressing.

The baby was perfect, developing exactly as he should be.

I had been offered to join a therapeutic group for teenagers who were struggling to adapt to motherhood, but I'd declined.

I was grieving the baby I'd lost, not struggling to adapt to the one I had inside of me. This sense of despair would pass. I just needed to give it time. Not talk. I didn't want to talk. I wanted to move forward. I thought that was a pretty mature response to the U-turn my life had taken. I was allowed to be sad. No one was going to tell me I wasn't.

I wasn't upset about being pregnant, even though, at my age and with my lack of qualifications and money, I should have been. Instead, I was excited and terrified in a good way, I think.

I had waited my whole life to have someone who I could love and would love me in return. The map of my life had shifted effortlessly and was now focused entirely on the baby growing inside me. Even If I could never have his father, I would have my baby. Yeah, I thought I was having a boy…that was my gut feeling.

Realistically, the thought of having this baby scared me to death, let alone having a boy. How could I raise a boy? I knew nothing about boys. Look at the man whose child I was carrying. I sure didn't know a thing about him. I hadn't seen Kyle since Christmas Day. For once in his life, he was doing what I asked him to do. He was leaving me alone and that depressed me deeply.

So much had changed. So many incidents and bad choices pushed me towards my decision to call Mike to collect me today.

I hadn't told my roommates, Derek Porter or Camryn Frey that I was coming home today. I didn't think my pride could take their pity and I knew they would tell Kyle. They'd kinda have to, considering the four of us shared a house – Kyle's house. It was bad enough I would be returning to his house. I didn't want an audience when I walked through that door with my tail between my legs.

So, last night when Cam came to visit, I'd told her I had tests all day today so there was no need to visit. Cam, Kyle and Derek, were seniors at CU and all three of them had classes on Friday, which gave me a few hours before I had to face them. If I had any other option, I would run as fast and as far from that house as I could. But I was broke and going home to my father was not something I could even begin to contemplate.

Daddy was recovering from a lifetime of alcohol abuse and the thought of arriving home, nineteen and pregnant, wasn't something that filled me with warm, fuzzy feelings. I had a pretty strong suspicion that my pregnancy would derail daddy's sobriety, not to mention my fear of what he would do to me. He had a nasty temper and the man could flip as quickly as a light switch.

No, I was just going to have to save up as much money as I could before the baby was born so I could get my own place.

Cam was my best friend though, and I knew it should be her bringing me home. She was the one who had sat with me day in and day out since I'd been hospitalized. Well, her and Mike. But I just couldn't face her…she wouldn't understand my calling Mike. In fact she would probably be furious. I understood why. Mike and Kyle were brothers, rather estranged ones.

Mike had played his part in the whole 'make a fool out of Lee' charade, but the difference was–and it was an important one–

Mike hadn't lied, hadn't hurt me and couldn't hurt me. Not like Kyle had or could. Mike didn't own any piece of my heart and I knew I could trust him. He was on my side. He had said as much when he arrived at the hospital.

I had screamed my head off at him when he'd showed up two days after I had the operation that removed my fallopian tube and my dead baby inside it. I'd told Mike to leave...but he didn't. Unlike Kyle, Mike had stayed and he'd taken everything I'd thrown at him—and I had thrown a lot.

I'd had a lot of dark moments in the first two weeks. Fear, doubt, anger and injustice were all potent emotions that had been swirling inside me at the start. When those feelings had lifted, a cloud of sadness took place. But Mike had stuck around on my worst days and then he'd kept coming back. He told me he was sorry he didn't tell me that he and Kyle were brothers, that the guilt was eating him. He said that he wished he'd warned me from the start about Rachel, but to be fair, he hadn't known I was involved with Kyle until I was so deeply devoted that even I had to admit I probably wouldn't have believed him. Mike hadn't known about Rachel's trickery and had been horrified over the lies Rachel had spun Kyle.

I had been, too.

It wasn't every day you met a girl who would go to the extremes of faking a pregnancy and hysterectomy to secure a man for money.

God, I hated that bitch.

Rachel Grayson would forever be on my shit list.

I'd accepted Mike's apology because he was my friend. He'd been my friend before I was ever involved with his brother. I accepted his comfort and friendship because I needed it. I needed one person in my life that was solely there for me. As good as Cam was to me and as nice as Derek was, they were Kyle's friends, too, and dragging them into the middle of this was unfair. A tiny part of my conscience protested that I was using Mike, but I needed him right now. Mike was mine, not Kyle's.

I had a lot to thank both Mike and Cam for. Even though they weren't overly keen on each other, they had both spent a ridiculous amount of time over the past six weeks visiting me.

"You sure? Have you got some papers you need to sign?" Mike asked, interrupting my reverie.

"I just have to wait for the nurse to return with the papers," I replied, tugging my overstretched t-shirt down over my thighs. It was embarrassing as hell that my jeans didn't tie. I'd been wearing pajamas for six weeks and hadn't noticed how much extra weight I'd gained, but my clothes had.

Earlier, when I was trying on my jeans, I had a 'fat moment,' they only tied half way. They were catching on my butt and my widely spreading hips. And if my hips weren't big enough before, they now seemed to be two inches on the wrong side of curvy. The swell of my belly was prominent now, but it looked like I'd gained a few pounds of fat more than the look of being five months pregnant.

Five months.

I still found it crazy to believe that I had sailed through more than three months of pregnancy without knowing. It was unsettling.

There was a knock on the door and I grimaced when a nurse rolled a wheelchair into my room. "Are you ready to go home, Miss Bennett?" she asked chirpily.

I zipped up my suitcase and smiled. I wasn't anywhere close to being ready, but I slapped on my brightest smile. "As ready as I'll ever be." Secretly I was petrified.

The thought of facing Kyle, and the possibility of seeing Rachel again made it hard to keep my breathing even. I didn't want to face him. Our last conversation had ended badly. But I had nowhere else to go and not enough money in the bank to last me longer than a week or two in a motel. As for returning to work, the idea made me light headed. I couldn't escape him.

"This is so cool, Lee. Do you think they'll let you keep this?" Mike asked, plopping himself into the chair and wheeling around the room. It was hospital policy to leave in a wheelchair, completely unnecessary, but unavoidable.

"Why? Are you planning on needing one sometime in the future?" I asked, amused at the excitement on Mike's face.

Men...

"You will need one, and a surgeon to remove my foot from your intestine if you don't get up and let your girlfriend sit down," said the unfamiliar nurse who was leaning against the door, along with another lady I didn't recognize.

I blushed and Mike jumped up from the chair, rolling his

hand out lavishly in front of him, gesturing me to sit. "I'm not his girlfriend," I muttered as I sat down quickly.

Ignoring my correction, the nurse introduced herself as Mary, and the lady with her as one of the hospital administrators–a short, frazzled looking blonde named Lizzie, with an alarming amount of paperwork in her hands.

My palms trickled with sweat at the sight of all those forms she was clutching. I had no freaking clue how I was going to be able to pay for over a month's worth of hospital bills. I was about to ask if they had a payment plan, when Lizzie handed me two sheets of paper from the bundle.

"Now, Miss Bennett. All I need from you is a couple of signatures. If you could sign under the patient signature line here and here, you'll be good to go," she said, dropping a pen on top of the rather intimidating forms in my lap.

I looked at her in confusion and then back at the papers. "What about my bill? Do you have a payment plan I can take on?" I asked, scrawling my signature under the printed version on one page and then the other.

"No need. Your bill has been paid in advance."

I snapped my head up to frown at her. "No, you must be confusing me with someone else. I haven't made an advanced payment. I don't have a credit card."

Lizzie was obviously confusing me with another patient, but the puzzled look on her face indicated that she thought that I was the confused one. "No, there is no confusion, Miss Bennett," she mused, flicking through her paperwork. "Yes, your bill has been covered in full by Mr. Carter."

She handed me a form and there it was, Kyle's signature and credit card details. My heart fluttered in my chest a little as reality smacked me straight between the two eyes. He'd gone behind my back again.

Son of a bitch.

"That's great," Mike interrupted, taking the papers from me and handing them back before clasping the handles of the wheelchair. "I'll take her from here."

I was still sulking when the car pulled up outside the familiar two story house on Thirteenth Street.

Goddamn Kyle and his stupid freaking money.

I wanted to pay my own way–I didn't have a clue how–but he'd just gone over my head on a decision that included me, *again*. He couldn't freaking buy his way out of his problems. I was so sick of him throwing his money around. I didn't want a dime.

Mike killed the engine and opened his door. I grabbed his arm quickly. "I'm not so sure that's a good idea."

Mike coming inside was a terrible idea. Kyle would freak. I was ninety-nine percent sure he wasn't at home, but I didn't want to take that one percent chance and risk another fight. I'd had, and seen enough of those to last me a lifetime.

Oh, I was going to speak to him about paying my hospital, but not right away. I needed to speak to him with a clear head and calm temper.

Right now, I had neither of those.

Mike frowned at me incredulously. "Are you joking? You think I'm letting you carry those cases yourself?" He scoffed and climbed out of the car. *Oh boy*. Moving around to the trunk, Mike swung my duffel bag over his shoulder and held my suitcase in the other. "No way are you carrying these bags, Lee. You've just had surgery and you're pregnant. Not a chance."

I reluctantly got out and walked up the driveway to open the door. My fingers shook as I placed the key in the lock and turned.

My key still worked, a small relief.

I hadn't been totally sure if Kyle had changed the locks or not. I didn't know where his head was at, or where I stood regarding my living situation for that matter. I knew that was my fault for banning him from the hospital and refusing to talk to him, but at the time it had seemed like a good idea, to give myself a chance to lick my wounds.

But now that I was away from the protective blanket of the hospital, and faced with the cold hard reality that was my life, I was thinking that I may have been ridiculous in my assumption that I could avoid Kyle.

Standing in the doorway of his house, it hit me that all I had been doing was delaying the inevitable.

I must have stood there for a long time mulling it all over because Mike walked around me and pushed the door open.

"You can change your mind, you know," he said gently. "You don't have to stay here, Lee. Come home with me. I have a ridiculously comfortable futon in my apartment."

I may not know where I stood with Kyle, but I wasn't stupid enough to take Mike up on his offer. Accepting Mike's invitation to stay would be as hazardous as moving home to Montgomery, except in this instance, it would be Mike's health in danger, not mine. I inhaled a shaky breath and shook my head. "I'll be okay."

I stepped into the hallway. It looked the same as it had the last time I'd been here–if not a little cleaner.

Yes, it was the same small hallway, the same red bricked house, just a different Lee. The girl I had been the last time I was here, was worlds apart from the woman I was now. Six weeks might not be a long enough transitioning time frame for an average person, but loss, grief and impending motherhood had certainly sped up the process for me.

"I'll just take your stuff up to your room," Mike said quietly as he headed for the stairs with my bags.

I made my way into the kitchen, amazed at how different everything looked when it was *exactly* the same as always. I filled the kettle with water and turned it on. I supposed the least I could do for Mike was give him a cup of coffee. Leaving the kettle to boil, I wandered back through the hallway to the living room. "Bruno?"

No barking, weird... I'd expected my old chocolate lab to greet me when I walked in the front door. Usually he had that sixth doggy sense and knew when I was close by.

Walking back through the kitchen, I slid the patio door open and stepped outside. The small, snow covered garden was empty. It was just as well since it was freezing outside. I would have been seriously pissed if my roommates had left Bruno outside in these temperatures.

They might be used to this weather, but Bruno and I were southerners. This amount of snow and ice was alien to us. I pulled my old green coat around myself tightly.

"Looking for someone?"

My heart stopped and then kick started in my chest, hammering furiously against my ribs.

I swung around slowly, trying to quell the sudden and extreme burst of emotion charging through me from the sound of his voice. It did no good though. The moment our eyes locked, I was a mess. A vicious tremor rolled through my body. I thought over a month away would prepare me, make me somewhat immune, but no, I was still every bit affected by him.

Kyle stood at the back door, legs parted, cheeks flushed from the cold. He looked every inch as handsome as I remembered–*more*–dressed in gray sweatpants and a blue hoodie. His sharp blue eyes were focused on me and his dark hair was hidden under a gray beanie hat.

I briefly wondered how he could stand the cold wearing only a hoodie. It wasn't exactly warm in Boulder during the month of February, but my thoughts were interrupted by the sight of what Kyle was holding. In his left hand was a leash connecting to the collar of my dog.

My eyes darted back to Kyle's face and I clasped my hands together in a bid to ease the trembling. He tilted his head to the side, eyes locked on mine, burning me. "Hey, baby."

His voice was like melted chocolate to a fat kid. I was a fat kid and he was my chocolate.

Dangerous chocolate, I needed to remember that, but all the anger I'd been feeling on the drive home had evaporated and all I was left with was an uncomfortable ball of nerves in my belly. Well, that and some serious appreciation for the sheer beauty of him.

Stop thinking like that, stupid.

"Hi," I replied meekly. Bruno whined as he pulled on the collar, trying to drag Kyle towards me, but Kyle held him back, his eyes never leaving mine.

I frowned.

Since when did those two get along? The last time I'd seen those two together, Kyle had been getting the 'I want to use your ankle as a chew toy' scowl from my dog. Obviously things had changed around here.

Kyle crouched down beside Bruno, wrapping an arm around his neck affectionately. "I know you're excited to see her, boy," he said to the dog, petting him. "So am I. But we gotta be careful with her. She's growing my baby in that belly of hers."

My breath caught and I turned away from him quickly to

wipe the tears from my eyes. How could he do it so easily? Rip down my defenses and tear my heart open with words.

"So, you and Bruno are walking buddies now?" I asked when speaking became manageable. My voice was thick with emotion, betraying the lightness of my question.

Kyle smiled crookedly. His eyes twinkled as he stood up and stretched. "Yeah, he's kinda growing on me." The dimple in his cheek deepened, softening his masculine features, making him look more his twenty-two years.

Jesus, he was so attractive.

I hoped the baby inherited those dimples.

Turning around, Kyle slid the patio door open and nudged Bruno inside while I averted my eyes from checking out his tight little butt in those sweats.

Oh, I was so doomed.

Closing the door on Bruno, he strode toward me, not stopping until his sneakers brushed against mine. I tried to take a step back, but I couldn't move a muscle. All I could do was stare up at the man my heart and soul were screaming out for, but my brain distrusted so vehemently.

His gaze swept over me lazily and it took every piece of my self-control to stand there and let him. His searing appraisal of my body affected me to no end. "You're back," he stated, looking me over once more, his eyes lingering on my midsection for a moment before returning to my face.

I let out a breath and nodded. "I'm back."

"You look good, Lee."

I hovered awkwardly. So we were going to make small talk? I could make small talk. "Thanks," I said, twiddling my fingers nervously. "But we both know that's not true."

The pregnancy glow that everyone talked about had skipped me. I was pale and washed out and swollen.

Maybe if I was as tall as Cam I could take the extra pounds more gracefully, but my five-two full figure already had enough cushioning. Adding baby weight to the mix made me look more like a small sausage, rather than a glowing first time mom to be.

And Kyle, he looked...perfect.

He stretched a hand out and brushed one of my wayward curls behind my ear. His touch burned me. "You're beautiful," he murmured, cupping my cheek.

I briefly allowed myself to lean into his touch. I missed this. I missed him. I hated myself for my weakness, but it was there, prominent and urging me toward him.

He let out a sigh. "I'm so fucking glad you're home, princess. I've missed you like crazy. I didn't know you were getting out today, I would've…"

"Lee, I put your bags in the second room on the right, that's yours right…oh hey, sorry, I didn't realize he was here."

Kyle's entire body stiffened at the sound of Mike's voice and I jerked away from him, moving towards where Mike was standing at the door. "What the fuck is he doing here, Lee?" Kyle demanded. He moved quickly, planting himself firmly between me and my escape route.

And so it begins.

"Kyle, calm down," Mike warned.

I stepped around Kyle, only to find myself sandwiched between the brothers. One cool and quiet, the other vibrating with angry energy.

"Is your name Lee, asshole?" Kyle shot back before focusing his attention on me. "Why is he in my house, Lee?"

I sucked in a steadying breath. I was not getting into this macho crap. "He is my friend, Kyle. He gave me a ride from the hospital. That's all. Don't make a big deal out of this."

Kyle's nostrils flared and hurt flickered in his eyes. "Why didn't you ask me to pick you up? Or ask Cam? You never said… told anyone you were being discharged."

I shrugged and stepped sideways, dodging both men. I went inside. If they wanted to freeze their butts off outside, well good for them. I caught Bruno's paws with my hands just as he jumped at my stomach. I staggered back slightly, the weight of Bruno knocking me off kilter. "I just didn't okay," I muttered. "I thought it would be better if Mike dropped me home."

"Better for whom? Goddammit. Bruno. Get off of her," Kyle cursed as he rushed towards me, pulling Bruno away.

"I'm fine, Kyle, I won't break." The look on Kyle's face said he wanted to argue that statement, but he wisely kept his mouth shut. I couldn't help but catch a glimpse of the pained look in his eyes.

"Well," Mike said brightly, closing the patio door. "The family reunion has been fun, but I gotta hit the road. I've got a shift at the hotel in an hour."

He wedged between us–I can only assume on purpose–as he walked out of the kitchen. "Call me later, Lee, if you need anything." I muttered a thank you and Kyle strung out an impressive array of f-bombs.

Kyle glared at me. "You are not calling him."

I felt my body stiffen. "I'm sorry, but was that a question? Because it sure as hell sounded like you were telling me what to do. You don't get to order me around, Kyle, not anymore. Mike is my friend. He is trying to be supportive."

Kyle stepped away from me and hissed. "He's not your friend, Lee. He is fucking with you to get to me. That's the only reason he's sniffing around you."

I shook my head and turned away from him. "Oh my god, can you hear yourself?" I walked away from him and headed towards the stairs.

"Where are you going? We need to talk about this. Lee?" Kyle shouted.

I swung around to face him. "My room. Is that okay with you, or do you want me to leave, too?"

Kyle stepped back like I'd just punched him in the gut. "Of course I don't. This is your home," he said in a shocked voice. I nodded stiffly and continued upstairs, stomping extra hard on the steps, childish, but it made me feel better. "I don't want him in my house again, Lee."

I paused at the top of the stairs and turned around. Kyle was standing at the bottom of the stairs with a pained expression. "And I don't want you to tell me what to do," I seethed. "We are not together. Oh and FYI, Kyle, I can pay my own damn bills. I don't want your money. Not one dime. You got it?" I didn't wait for his answer, I just stormed into my old room.

One hour. I was home less than one hour and the crap had hit the proverbial fan.

FOUR
KYLE

ONE HOUR.

Lee was home one fucking hour and I'd screwed things up.

What the hell was wrong with me?

When I saw her standing in the backyard, I thought I'd imagined her. She'd looked so fucking beautiful, fragile, mine.

I'd lost my shit when I saw that prick in my house, and dammit, I'd been making progress with her. I wanted to wrap her up and carry her straight up to my room, but I had no doubt in my mind that if I had tried she'd have kicked me in the balls. God knows, I would have deserved it.

Mike…

She'd phoned my fucking brother to collect her. That hurt like nothing else. My chest was still stinging from my gloomy awareness that Lee trusted him more than me.

I knew she'd allowed Mike to visit her in the hospital and that knowledge all but fucking killed me.

But what could I have done about it?

Not a damn thing, that's what.

She wasn't my wife, not even my girlfriend anymore. The only part of Lee's life that I had a say in was the baby, but up until this point she'd wanted nothing from me or to do with me. That left me kind of fucked.

At least she was home now, back under my roof where I could keep her safe.

Three hours had passed since she slammed her bedroom door and I was getting anxious.

Was she okay?

Should I knock and check on her?

I'd passed her door more than enough times to be deemed a stalker, but hell, I was worried.

I shouldn't have gotten so angry, not in front of her at least. She was just out of the damn hospital and of course, I had to go bat shit crazy in front of her. *Smooth*. I was jealous though. Jealous that she called Mike before me.

I pressed my ear against her door, hearing nothing but my own hammering heartbeat. I tapped lightly and waited. Ten seconds passed and still nothing.

Fuck this.

I eased the handle down and pushed the door inwards slightly. She could scream at me if she wanted. I'd prefer that to finding her sick...or worse.

I peered through the crack in the door and sighed in relief.

Lee was curled up on her bed sleeping. I opened the door fully and walked over to her quietly.

She was curled in a ball on top of the covers with her face resting on her hands.

My gaze flicked from her face to her rounded stomach. My chest filled with hope. I wanted more than anything to curl up on her bed and draw her to me. But I couldn't. She wouldn't want me to.

I slipped back to my room and grabbed a blanket from my closet. Lee didn't stir when I sat on her bed and set the blanket next to me.

After hearing about Lee's miscarriage in graphic detail from Derek, I was paranoid. I immediately checked the covers for blood. I was so afraid since that night. I wanted this baby. I wanted this for Lee. I wanted this for us.

I brushed a few tendrils of curls off her face. Releasing a sigh, she moved closer to my hand.

I placed my hand on her stomach, feeling for the first time the hard swell under her belly button.

Shit, it was harder than I thought it would be. I wasn't sure what I was expecting it to feel like, soft perhaps, cushiony. But her belly was hard.

My hand trembled and I felt guilty as shit for stealing this moment without Lee's consent, but I was desperate to be a part of this. To be included.

I pulled my hand away quickly, covered Lee's small body with the blanket before I rushed out of her room. It was too much and too fucking little.

Lee thought I'd stayed away when she was in the hospital. She'd all but begged me to keep away, said that she needed space and I'd given her what she thought she needed.

But I wasn't that selfless.

Every single night, I sat by her side in that hospital room while she slept.

Whether she needed me or not was debatable. But I needed her irrevocably. And I always would.

FIVE
LEE

I WOKE up in the same long, baggy t-shirt I'd worn leaving the hospital yesterday, with a nauseated pain in my stomach and a crazy urge to pee.

Throwing off the unfamiliar blanket, I jumped out of bed and rushed across the hall to the bathroom.

I needed to pee too badly to worry about where that blanket came from.

I reached the door of the bathroom and my hand froze on the door knob.

I couldn't do it.

I couldn't go there.

My stomach rolled at the thought of going back into that room. I turned around and hurried down the stairs towards Cam and Derek's bathroom. I didn't bother to knock, I just plowed in there. Thankfully, it was empty and I mastered the skill of peeing and puking at the same time.

"Lee, are you alive in there?" I heard Derek's say and the door opened slightly.

"Oh my god, Derek. Don't you dare come in here," I half screamed as I cleaned myself up quickly. I heard a nervous chuckle from outside the door, then the sound of his footsteps retreating.

I paused in front of the mirror and cringed.

I looked awful.

My gray eyes were red rimmed. My skin was pale, lips

cracked. Tugging the hair tie out of my untamed curls, I pulled my hair into a messy ponytail. I washed my hands and splashed some water on my face before heading towards the kitchen, not bothering to go back upstairs and change.

My days of modesty were over and even though the shirt I had on didn't completely conceal the scars my father had left on my thighs, I didn't feel the need to cover them up as much as before.

I grudgingly conceded that Kyle was the one I had to thank for that. All those nights he'd spent scattering kisses over every mark, welt and blemish on my body had healed the insecurities that used to batter my confidence.

Cam and Derek were huddled over the table, deep in conversation when I got to the kitchen. I cleared my throat before walking inside.

My presence triggered the end of their discussion.

"Coffee?" Derek asked me, rising quickly, not making eye contact.

"No thanks, Derek." I couldn't drink coffee anymore and it sucked. Dr. Ashcroft said the odd cup wouldn't hurt, but all those pregnancy magazines I'd read while in hospital red flagged it. "Where's Bruno?" I asked, sliding into the chair opposite Cam.

"Out for his morning stroll with Kyle," Derek replied without his usual punchy sarcasm. "You want some coffee Cam?" he asked.

Cam shook her head, keeping her eyes trained on her cup. I tried to catch her eye, but she seemed preoccupied, stirring the contents of her cup almost violently.

Oh boy…

"Hey Cam," I said quietly.

Her blonde head swung up and her eyes met mine. "Hey Judas," she retorted.

Yep, she was mad at me.

"I guess you're mad about Mike collecting me, right?" I muttered, struggling to keep eye contact with my angry best friend. Even when she was angry and snarling, Cam was stunning. Her poker straight blonde hair fell artfully down her back. She had an all-round tan, perfect skin and every feature on her face was enviable.

"Mike? Oh no, how could I possibly be angry with you about

Mike collecting you from the hospital? When I was the one who sat with you and held your hand every damn day for six weeks?" Cam said with a dramatic tone of voice. "No, I have absolutely no problem with that. *At all.*"

Okay, she was angrier than I thought.

It was always obvious when Cam was mad because she had that 'look' on her face, and used heavy sarcasm. The narrow eyed scowl she was directing at me and her sharp words proved I was receiving both.

"Cam, lay off her, she's just home," Derek said quietly. My head jerked towards where Derek was leaning against one of the oak countertops. His shaved head was turned in Cam's direction, his green eyes narrowed and focused on his girlfriend.

This was a first.

I had never, in all the time I'd known Derek, heard him say anything against Cam. I didn't want them to argue over me.

"Mike is not responsible for her, Derek. She shouldn't be relying on him for anything," Cam shot back glaring at Derek.

"No Derek, she's right," I said quickly, trying to ease the tension in the room. "I'm sorry, Cam. I didn't do it to hurt your feelings. That wasn't my intention."

Cam's tight shoulders seemed to relax, slightly. She sighed and nodded. "Apology accepted," she said as she stood up. "I have a shoot in thirty minutes, so I'll catch you both later." She walked out of the room without so much as a backwards glance.

The front door slammed loudly and Derek and I both seemed to blow out a breath.

I knew she was lying about the photo shoot. Cam was modeling on the side to pay for college and the bills, but never on a Saturday morning. Cam always went shopping on Saturday mornings. It was her version of church and she was completely devoted. And she always made me go with her. Obviously, I wasn't invited today.

I turned to Derek. "Have you any idea what that was about?" I asked, more confused by Cam's abruptness towards Derek than towards me. I deserved it, but what the heck had Derek done? Those two were the most affectionate couple I knew.

"This is the way she's been acting for weeks." Derek sighed, shaking his head. "I better go after her," he muttered, patting my shoulder before rushing out after Cam.

"Wait," I called out when I noticed Derek's keys on the table, but the sound of the front door slamming confirmed he hadn't heard me.

I took Cam's cup and busied myself with washing the breakfast dishes. I glanced at the clock on the wall over the stove. It was only nine thirty in the morning and the weekend was off to a crummy start. Filling the sink with water, I washed the dishes as I pondered over the realization that Cam and Derek were having problems.

Neither had mentioned anything when they visited.

Come to think of it, I hadn't seen much of Derek lately and Cam had been kind of standoffish the last few days.

Was she mad at him, or had I done something else besides piss her off over Mike?

What the hell had happened while I was gone?

I jumped at the sound of the doorbell ringing. Drying my hands on a towel, I rushed down the hall and opened it, expecting it to be Derek coming back for his keys.

It was Rachel.

Her groomed eyebrows shot up in surprise. Her face twisted into a scowl. I guessed she was as surprised to see me as I was to see her in Kyle's house, *again*. And what the hell was she wearing? I could see her boobs through the skin tight fabric of the white dress she had on.

"I'm here for Kyle," she sneered, brushing past me, confident and stunning as usual.

"He's not here." I closed the door behind her, standing as tall and fierce as I could. Rachel dwarfed my short frame. She towered over me in her neck-breaking thigh-high boots.

"I figured that, hick. I said I was here for him, not asking if he was here. I already know where he is."

Derek had said Kyle was out walking Bruno and I burned to ask Rachel how she knew that, but pride was impaling me, screaming at my common sense to shut the hell up and not give her the satisfaction. "Suit yourself, Rachel," I muttered, stamping down on the pain in my heart from my bitter realization that Kyle was still in contact with Rachel. I moved past her to the kitchen. She followed me, way too close for comfort.

"Packing a little extra weight there, Lee?"

Forcing myself to ignore her derisive tone, I cut her one of my bored stares. She was not going to draw me into an argument. Not now. Not ever again. "Yeah, I guess I am." My voice sounded light and carefree even though I was anything but. This bun Kyle had put in my oven was definitely super sized.

Rachel glowered at me. A look of pure revulsion encompassed her dainty features. She flicked her long red hair behind her shoulder. "I know what you did. He told me," she spat.

I had a fair idea who she meant by '*he*,' but I forced myself to shrug casually. "I do a lot of things, Rachel. I'm sure you don't know all of those. That would be creepy." I was sort of proud of myself. The girl I'd been a month ago would never have said a word to Rachel. Good thing I wasn't that girl anymore. I'd grown a spine and sprouted some nerve to go with it.

"I know you trapped him, but it won't work," she said nastily, leaning way too close to my face. She pointed a perfectly manicured finger towards my stomach. "That mistake isn't going to help you keep Kyle forever. Hell, it hasn't helped you keep him at all. Guess who he was with last night?"

My breath caught in my lungs.

Rachel seemed to know exactly what to say to press my buttons.

And it hurt, oh god, did it hurt.

Her words cut deep.

"You," I said, keeping my voice void of emotion, which was almost impossible to do when her words were slitting my battered heart open.

Rachel gawked at me, clearly surprised that I didn't take her bait. "How astute of you," she mused, recovering from her momentary speechlessness. "I had wondered if you'd come to your senses."

"What do you mean '*come to my senses*'?" I asked before mentally kicking myself for buying into her toxic game.

Curiosity killed the cat.

"I had wondered whether or not your little detox stent had helped you rethink your fantasy of a happy ever after with Kyle."

I gaped at her. "My little detox stint? You can't seriously consider what I went through to be a detox stent?"

Rachel smiled darkly. "Oh, that's exactly what I consider what you went through. But apparently, it only half worked considering you're still pregnant. I am disappointed that everything wasn't flushed out. That is what a detox involves, isn't it, ridding the body of trash?"

My whole body shook to the core. "You are one fucked up human being," I spat, fighting back the tears. "You are the most heartless, spiteful, vindictive person I have ever had the misfortune of meeting. But believe it or not, as much as I hate you and believe me, Rachel, I loathe you. I wouldn't wish what happened to me on you, or anyone else." I pushed past her to the hall, needing to get the hell away before I did something stupid.

Grabbing my arm, Rachel yanked me back towards her and I had a moment of pure fear for my baby. "If it weren't for you, Kyle and I would still be together. But you had to go and fucking ruin everything," Rachel snarled, digging her fingers into my arm. "He is mine. He doesn't belong to you. Keep your gold-digging fingers off him, you little fucking whore."

Jerking my arm free, I backed up a step closer to the door and shook my head. "He doesn't belong to anyone. Kyle is his own person and you are hardly in a position to call me a gold-digger, you freak," I shouted as I ran for the front door.

"Give up now, Delia. If you fight me on this, you will lose," Rachel threatened.

I opened the front door and stepped outside. "Goodbye, Rachel. I'd say have a nice life, but actually, I hope it's a fucking disaster," I said before slamming the door.

SIX
KYLE

I DECIDED to make a new plan. The last plan I had made sucked ass. Well, making good decisions and choices was never one of my fortitudes.

Those qualities belonged to the calm, rational members of society. No, my strong points went hand in hand with my flaws.

I had a temper, but I liked to think of it as being passionate. That was never going to change.

I was hot-headed, loud and fucking stupid as hell sometimes. All things I couldn't change.

But I could change one thing. I could open up. Let her in. Show her my vulnerability. She'd be the only one.

Yeah, that was my new plan.

Fuck, I hoped it worked.

But I couldn't sit at home all morning waiting for Lee to wake up. I'd been up since seven, waiting on her to get up so we could talk, but Cam and Derek's incessant bickering had driven me outside.

I'd had to get out of the house for a while, walk, fucking run, anything to clear my head of their drama and steel myself for the battle of all battles.

I was going to win Lee back, starting today.

No doubt.

"Come on, dude." I glared at Lee's brown Labrador that I was becoming fond of. Bruno cocked his leg for what had to be the fortieth time in an hour.

Jesus, when I got things settled with Lee, I was going to get him checked out. There was nothing normal about the amount that dog pissed.

I turned onto our street, slowed down by the arthritic crawl of Bruno. I'd walked her dog more times in the past six weeks than I could remember. Sad, I know, but by walking Bruno I felt like I was doing something for Lee.

Something was better than nothing.

It fucking hurt that she didn't want me near her.

Well, she had her time. I'd given her the space she wanted. Now it was time to fix this shit.

Approaching the house, my eyes zoomed in on the red Porsche parked on the road outside of my driveway.

No fucking way.

I quickened my step, practically running to the front door. Bruno must have sensed the danger because he galloped at a speed I hadn't thought he was capable of.

I'd never used physical violence on a female before, but this particular one was fucking pushing me. The door opened just as I reached it and there she stood. "What the fu –" Rachel grabbed the lapels of my jacket, pulled me towards her, and planted her lips on mine. Bruno growled and I pushed her away roughly.

Since Christmas, I'd tried futilely to avoid her. But the girl kept showing up everywhere. Last night, after I left Lee's room, I'd received a call about an emergency at the hotel, except it hadn't been so much an emergency as another one of Rachel's very crazy–very naked–attempts at winning me back.

I arrived at my office late last night only to find her draped over my desk, butt-naked. It hadn't been the first time either. Last week Linda, my hotel manager, had endured the same ordeal when she'd gone out to get some paperwork from my truck. Rachel needed to see someone.

This was getting too fucking creepy.

"Good. You're back. We need to talk." she purred, then turned on the heels of her thigh high boots and marched into my house, her skinny ass swaying in what had to be the most indecently skimpy white dress I'd seen a girl wear on a Saturday morning in February. I shook my head and followed her inside, but the damn dog pulled on his leash.

Bruno broke away from me and ran towards my truck. I glanced back at him. He was sitting beside the truck yowling.

Fucking coward.

"What the hell are you doing here?" I demanded stepping inside and closing the door behind me. I could hear the violent tone in my voice. Her eyes widened in surprise. "This has to stop Rachel. This is bordering on harassment. I could have you arrested for this. After the stunt you pulled last night I *should* have you arrested."

She had some nerve showing up at my house. The only reason I didn't have her ass hauled off by the cops, was my very strong suspicion that the girl was mentally ill.

"I'm not here to fight with you, Kyle," she said petulantly. Yeah, I seriously doubted that. But I refrained from telling her that as she continued spinning her yarn of lies. "I came to apologize to you," she said. "And to tell you what I've heard about your little southern belle."

Oh, this was going to be good. "What could you possibly tell me about Lee that I don't already know?"

She smiled and hiked herself onto the table, spreading her legs wide enough to give me a clear view of her bikini-wax. "I could start by telling you where she is right now?"

I shook my head and focused on her face. "I know where she is, Rachel. She's in bed resting. Now, if you value your freedom, you will get the fuck out of my house."

She smirked as she trailed her red-painted fingernails up the inside of her thigh. "Oh, of course. Well, I must have misheard things." She hopped down and strutted over to me. I stepped sideways before she could touch me. "Give us another try, Kyle. Please."

I gaped at her and moved to the other side of the table to put some space between us. "Are you kidding me?" I looked at her face and paled. "Oh my god, you're serious."

Rachel was unleashing a whole new brand of crazy.

She should bottle that shit up. She'd make a fortune. *Eau de delusional.*

"Just think about it," she said, prowling towards me. "We were good together once."

I flicked her hands off my chest in disgust. "Which part? The part where you were slapping the shit out of me? Or the part where you were blackmailing me? Because let me tell you, none of that was particularly *good* for me Rachel."

I strode out of the kitchen and opened the front door. "Now, this is the last time I'm gonna say it. Get out. Go and get yourself some help. Hell, send me the bill, but don't step foot on my property again." I held the door open widely and thanked Jesus that she got the hint.

Brushing past me, she paused in the doorway. "Just think about it," she crooned before kissing my cheek.

Sweet Jesus, she was insane.

I pulled away quickly and watched as Rachel pranced down the driveway.

Leaving the door open, I ran upstairs to check on Lee, praying to god that she slept through that.

I opened her door quietly. Her bed was empty. Shit. "Lee?" Running downstairs, I whistled Bruno inside. "Come on dude."

Lee's stubborn old dog wouldn't budge from the truck.

Goddammit.

I stormed over to get him.

"What the hell is up with you today?" I muttered. My last few words trailed off when I noticed the tiny figure with a head of brown curls hunched inside of my truck.

Aw hell.

SEVEN
LEE

OKAY, so storming out of my own house probably wasn't my smartest move ever, especially when I was barefoot and wearing nothing but a t-shirt. But I hadn't for one moment forgotten what Rachel was capable of and I had a baby to protect.

Freezing and mortified, I made a quick dash for the only vehicle parked in the drive. Kyle's truck. I tried the handle and almost cried out hallelujah when it opened. Kyle's carelessness for his property was my saving grace.

I made three ass in the air attempts to get in before making it on the fourth. I ducked low in the seat, my heart hammering in my chest as I tried to map out my options.

Going back inside the house was out of the question. I couldn't exactly take a stroll through the neighborhood dressed in a t-shirt in the month of February. Kyle's keys weren't in the ignition–which wouldn't have mattered either way because I didn't know how to drive. And I didn't own a cell phone. I settled on locking the doors and sitting right here, where it was safe and at least a little warmer than the driveway.

My mind was like a broken record, stuck on Rachel's disgusting words, repeating them over and over until the dam burst and my eyes flooded. I'd known cruelty. I'd suffered it for eighteen years at the hands and mouth of my father. But never, in all my life, had I heard anything so disgusting, or as unspeakably repulsive, as what I'd heard come from Rachel's mouth.

I hated her.

It was in that moment that I felt my first dose of pure unadulterated hatred towards another human being.

And I was angry, so unbelievably furious with Kyle for dragging me into their world.

Had Rachel been serious in what she'd said? Had Kyle been with her last night?

I didn't know what to believe. I wished I didn't care. But I did. The thought of Kyle with Rachel was excruciating.

A dog barked loudly and I watched in wide eyed horror as Kyle came running up the driveway. He rushed past the truck, pounded up the steps to greet a sickly smug Rachel who was now standing at the door. My heart plummeted into my stomach as I watched her kiss his mouth and even further when he followed her inside and closed the front door.

My brain went into overdrive as I imagined all the possible scenarios that were occurring between them.

Was he with her? Were they doing things right now?

My stomach churned at the thought and a deep swell of jealousy ignited inside me, burning through my veins.

Of course I was jealous.

I was freaking pregnant with his baby and he was in there, with her, doing god knows what again.

How was I ever supposed to trust him?

I decided to make a run for it. Screw the neighbors. I was getting the hell out of here. I put my hand on the door handle of the truck at the same moment the front door of the house flew open. Pausing, I watched as Rachel leaned over and kissed Kyle's cheek. I stiffened, biting down so hard on my cheek that I tasted blood.

Marching down the driveway, Rachel muttered, "Bye bitch," as she passed the truck.

It was then that I realized she'd done it on purpose; kissed Kyle knowing full well that I would see it.

What was her game?

She'd already won. She'd broken us up. So why in god's name was she continuing to torture me?

I sat silently, trying to calm myself down before I went back inside.

Dropping my head in my hands, I allowed myself to wallow for a few moments until the door handle of the truck jerked and I found myself looking through the glass, into those corn flour blue eyes.

EIGHT
KYLE

LEE UNLOCKED the door and I jerked it open. "What are you doing in my truck, princess?" *Nearly naked.*

Lee was crouched low on the passenger seat of my truck in nothing but an oversized gray t-shirt. My t-shirt, I realized and my pride swelled a little.

Lee glared up at me with angry, accusing eyes. "I was waiting," she said coolly, straightening up in the seat.

"Waiting for what? Wait, you got up yourself?" I asked grinning. Lee had never been able to get her short sweet ass in my truck before. Hell, she'd tried enough times and I'd given her more than enough shit for it. This was a first for her and I was oddly upset that I'd missed it. "Wait, did you strain yourself?" I asked, touching her stomach gently.

Fear climbed into my heart. Dammit, she shouldn't be stretching like that in her condition, should she?

Lee pushed my hands away as she tried to shimmy down the truck; an easy thing for a person of average height, but Lee was a short ass, barely reaching my shoulder in height. The drop from the truck's foot step to the ground was three feet more than I was prepared to risk. I ignored her protests and lifted her down with extra care.

"Yes, I got in myself. And no, I didn't hurt myself, you big douche," she snapped storming off towards the house. I trailed after her, thanking the heavens she'd missed the Rachel exhibit, whilst shamelessly enjoying the view of her swaying hips and peachy ass.

"Why am I a douche?" I asked following her through the front door and up the stairs.

"If you don't know why, you are a douche, Kyle Carter, by far the biggest douche I have ever met," she growled. Slipping inside her room, she attempted to slam the door on me and I had to stop it with my hand before it connected with my face.

"Leave me alone. Why don't you go chase after Rachel? I'm sure she'd be more than thrilled for you to run after her," she spat before adding, "it's not like it's uncommon for you to chase after her."

So she had seen the Rachel exhibit...Perfect.

"No," I said calmly. "I've left you alone long enough. I'm not leaving you anymore." I stuck my head through the small gap in the door, forcing Lee to relinquish her death grip on the handle. Thankfully she did, because for a brief moment she looked tempted to slam the door on my head. "I'm sorry about Rachel coming here. I'll talk to her and make sure she doesn't upset you again."

That must have been the wrong fucking thing to say, because Lee backed away with her palms held out in front of her, shaking her head in disgust.

"Uh, don't do me any favors, Kyle. Bring as many girls as you want back here. After all, it is your house and I'm just your room-mate. Well, that and an incubator for your child, but who's counting?"

"What the hell are you talking about?" I asked, trying to rein in my temper. "I haven't done anything wrong."

Today at least.

Lee snorted, actually fucking snorted at me, as she stormed over to her bed. "Go screw yourself, Kyle."

I tried to rein in my temper, I really did, but she had this way of driving me insane and drawing it out of me. "What is your fucking problem, princess?" I spat, losing my hold on my self-control, words spewing from my mouth before my brain had a chance to filter them. "I said I was sorry. Jesus Christ, you're over-reacting. You need to calm your shit down and breathe."

Lee bent down and started rooting under her bed. "You make me sick. The both of you do. Go, Kyle. Run along and chase her because I don't want to be near you right now," she screamed, pulling a duffel bag out and standing again. "This was a bad idea. I knew it. I *knew* I shouldn't have come back here."

"Whoa baby, what are you doing?" All the anger I'd felt moments ago sizzled out at the sight of Lee throwing her clothes inside that bag. I knew exactly what she was doing, but I was praying she'd prove me wrong.

Lee moved towards her wardrobe and I stepped in front of it. "Get out of my way, Kyle."

"Would you stop for a second?" I asked, for once trying to calm the situation down. "Tell me why you're doing this."

Lee tried to push past me, her movements wild and frantic. "I'm leaving. Get the hell out of my way so I can get my stuff."

I grabbed her shoulders, trying to hold her still. Getting this worked up couldn't be good for the baby. "Lee, will you just stop for a second and talk to me?"

Turning her head away, she stared out the window refusing to look at me. Her body stiffened. "There's nothing to talk about," she spat. "I have nothing to say to you."

I exhaled sharply, the air leaving my lungs in a rush. "There's nothing to talk about, really? Lee, you're packing your bags and trying to walk out of my life and you have nothing to say me. Are you serious?"

"Stop trying to make me feel bad," she said in a defensive tone.

Releasing her, I staggered over to her bed and sat. "I'm not trying to make you feel bad. I'm trying to make you explain," I said, running my hands through my hair, before leaning over and resting my elbows on my knees.

"Do you agree with her?"

I sighed in exasperation as I looked up at her. "Lee baby, I have no idea who you're talking about."

Lee folded her arms over her bump, her stance defensive. "Rachel. Do you agree with her?"

I fucking knew this outburst had something to do with Rachel. Everything bad always led back to her.

"What did she say to you?" I asked tiredly. I was so sick of the drama.

"According to Rachel, she was with you last night." Her voice cracked and she shook her head as if she was angry with herself for showing emotion in front of me. "Though, I really shouldn't be surprised, all things considered," she added before turning her back on me.

I stood up and strode over to Lee and turned her to face me. "Listen to me clearly," I said, staring down at her face. "I am not involved with Rachel, or anyone else for that matter. She showed up at the hotel last night because she's a sick little freak that doesn't seem to be able to take no for an answer."

Her eyes narrowed, and I watched the flurry of emotions flicker across her face. Anger, distrust, hurt, settling on confusion. "I saw you kiss her on the porch earlier."

I shook my head. "You saw her kiss me."

"She wants you."

Pulling her closer to me, I ran my hands up and down her arms. "Well, that's too bad," I said. "Because I want you. Just you." Unable to resist, I bent down and brushed my lips against her forehead. "You're mine, baby. I don't want to look at anyone else."

Her body sagged in my arms as she drew in a ragged breath. "I'm not… I don't want…"

I cut her off before she could finish. "Don't say it. Please. And you are mine, or at least you will be, when you forgive me."

Lee shivered. A deep frown wrinkled her cute forehead. She seemed to think about what I had said for a moment before speaking. "Why should I believe you this time? You, Kyle Carter, are a big fat liar."

She looked so cute, sounded so prissy that I couldn't help but smile. I knew this was a serious situation, but for the life of me I couldn't wipe the smirk off my face. Pulling back from her, I lifted my shirt and pretended to inspect my stomach. "Fat, you think I'm fat?"

Lee sank down on her bed and burst into tears.

"Are you okay?" I demanded, crouching down in front of her. "Are you sick?"

Jesus Christ, I was about two seconds away from calling 911.

I shouldn't have gotten in her face. Goddammit. I reached for my cell in my pocket.

"I'm the fat one, not you," Lee hiccuped, pointing at herself and then me. "You…you're all ripples and sexy grooves and I'm…I'm a cow."

I laughed and Lee threw her hands over her face, crying harder.

Shit, I was not good at this.

"Are you serious?" I asked as I tried to coax her hands from her face.

She swung her face up to meet mine. "Do I look like I'm joking?" she growled before continuing her sobbing. "And now you're laughing at me."

Christ, she went from angry to sad to angry in sixty seconds flat.

I tried to smother my smile and pulled her towards me.

"Don't hug me. I'm mad at you," she whispered even though she had a death grip on my shirt. She clung to me like a little monkey.

I could get used to this.

"I know, baby. I'm a horrible, selfish bastard," I crooned, stroking her head and rubbing her back slowly.

I could feel her nodding against my shoulder as her body slowly relaxed.

"You are," she agreed, sniffling, as she slipped her hands under my t-shirt.

"And fat. I'm fat, too," I coaxed, hoping she wouldn't stop touching me.

"So fat," she breathed, as her hands roamed up my chest.

Holy shit.

I moved to sit beside her and without breaking contact with her, I pulled her onto my lap. She straddled me, snuggling into my chest as she cried and felt me up at the same time. "Don't forget ugly," I added leaning down to kiss her cheek.

She seemed to warm from insulting me, so I was all for it. I'd say just about anything she wanted to hear.

Lee turned her face towards me at the same moment I did and our lips brushed.

I froze and Lee sucked in a sharp breath.

"You're a very bad man," she murmured.

I wasn't sure who moved first, but suddenly our lips were welded together.

My hand trailed up to cusp the side of her face. "So bad," I agreed, fucking thrilled from the sensation of Lee's mouth against mine. Her lips were soft, swollen and melted perfectly against mine. I knew this was probably going to come back and bite me in the ass, but Lee in my lap, with her lips on my mouth, after six weeks of doubt and insecurity, made it totally worth it.

I shifted back on the bed, pulling her closer, deepening the kiss. Her mouth opened as she sighed, so I slipped my tongue inside, desperate to taste her. Jesus, she was even more delicious than I remembered. It had been a long fucking six weeks, and I wanted what was mine. She was mine. She just needed to realize that.

I could hold her forever…

Our tongues collided, brushing against the other, taking slow swipes and licks that were driving me out of my mind and loosening what little hold I had on my self-control.

I groaned into her mouth, unable to conceal my excitement, or my desire. I was fucking hard and pressing against the softest part of her body.

Lee's hands tangled in my hair, tugging eagerly, as she was grinding her hips against me.

I slipped my hands under her shirt and caressed her bare skin with trembling fingers. I trailed my hands down her spine, over the curve of her hips, her waist and back up.

She moaned deeply when my fingers trailed over the swell of her breast. I cupped her softly, my dick straining against my jeans as her nipple hardened in my hand.

The sound of a door banging downstairs, and then Cam and Derek's angry voices filled my ears.

"All I'm saying is stay out of their business. Lee and Kyle are adults." I heard Derek shout.

Their voices quickly doused the fire of desire building between us. Well, I was still hard as a rock and raring to go, but Lee jerked off my lap, scrambling away on shaky legs.

"Oh god," she gasped, covering her mouth with the back of her hand. I stood up and moved toward Lee, but she held a hand out warning me off. "That was a mistake," she whispered, her gray eyes wide and unblinking. "I shouldn't have done that."

I clenched my fists at my sides, trying to keep a lid on my frustrations. I didn't expect Lee to take me back easily, but I'd felt her hunger, tasted how much she'd wanted me. It was all in her kiss. It was all in the way she was grinding her hot little pussy against me. "You're wrong, princess," I said, stepping towards her. "You're so fucking wrong. That was right. It felt right. You can't deny that."

Lee shook her head. "It was a momentary blip. I'm sorry."

I narrowed my eyes in disbelief. Lee could shake her head all she wanted, but her flushed cheeks and rapid breathing proved how turned on she was. Not to mention how hard her nipples were. They were straining against her top…

"Momentary blip?" I asked in disgust. "You wanted me, princess. I could feel it. I could taste it. Christ, your p…"

"Ahhh, stop. I am not doing this again," she shouted, covering her ears.

"I know I messed up before, Lee, but if you just give me a chance…"

She waved her hand in front of me. "I can't afford to give you any more chances. You throw them back in my face. Coming back here was a mistake." She stopped speaking and pinched the bridge of her nose in an attempt to calm herself. "Rachel being here…I can't deal with her, Kyle. I won't live in a house where at any moment she could show up."

"I had…I have no idea why she showed up here, Lee. I have nothing to do with her anymore," I urged, hoping like hell she believed me.

"Whatever, Kyle, it's not my business anyway."

I ran my hand over my face roughly. "Like hell it's not your business. I fucked up by withholding from you before. I won't make that mistake again. You need to trust me."

Lee walked over to her wardrobe and pulled out a pair of jeans. Jerking them on she muttered, "Trust is earned, Kyle. It's not something that can be handed out recklessly. I know enough, I have experienced enough to understand that. I know we aren't together anymore, but I can't handle Rachel coming around here gloating and flaunting your relationship in my face."

"I'm not having a fucking relationship with her. Lee, I can't stand her. I can assure you that she won't be back here. I promise. I'll make sure of it."

"I don't want you to feel like I'm dictating your life. I can stay with a friend if being here is too much?"

I watched wide-eyed as she slipped on her jeans. She didn't tie them. She couldn't by the look of it. "Tell me," I begged in a hoarse voice. "Tell me what to do and I'll do it."

Slipping on her converse she walked over to her door. "I shouldn't have to tell you. You should just know."

With that she slipped outside, closing the door behind her softly.

I threw myself back on the bed and held in a scream. This was going to be much harder than I thought. And for the first time since my talk with Derek six weeks ago, I had doubts as to whether I'd win.

NINE
LEE

I HAD to get out of that house, but as I walked, I wasn't sure where to go.

Everyone I knew in Boulder lived in that house. I racked my brain for possible places to go, but I was coming up with a very small list.

I supposed I could visit Mo and Dixon. Technically we were friends…Well, friends through friends. But then again Dixon was very full on and to be honest he kind of freaked me out. No, I scratched that notion from my mind.

The only other two people I knew were Linda and Mike. Mike was working today so I knew he'd be at the hotel and Kyle wouldn't since I'd left him in my bedroom less than an hour ago.

Oh god...

What the hell had I been thinking? Kissing Kyle, feeling him up? I was home less than twenty four hours and had nearly fallen into bed with him.

Disgust and anger coursed through my body. Disgust with myself for being so weak and anger towards Kyle for being the source of my weakness.

I couldn't deal with Kyle, or my feelings for him. I was holding a lot of bitterness inside of me and I was afraid of what would come out of me if Kyle pushed me too far.

———

It was bitter cold as I trudged down 11th street towards The Henderson Hotel. The impressive eight-story building stood proud in the center of 11th street, dwarfing the other buildings around it. The light coming from the modern glass paneled walls on the ground floor ricocheted off the traditional limestone stonework, casting out an almost majestic ambiance.

Stepping inside the foyer of the hotel was like stepping back in time. Memories flooded my mind. Memories of Kyle…

I pushed them down and went in search of Mike.

There were two restaurants on the ground floor of the hotel and Mike served in the larger one. I slipped through the glass doors and my eyes circled the restaurant in search of his familiar blonde head.

When I spotted him sitting at a table in the far corner of the room arguing with a leggy blonde, I had to take a double look. My feet moved towards their table as my curiosity got the better of me.

What the hell…

"Hey, Cam," I said, when I reached their table. "What are you doing here?" *With Mike*, I wanted to add.

Cam's head swung up. "I'm here because I'm warning your little friend to back off," she said in an agitated tone. "What are *you* doing here?"

"I…Uh, I was looking for Mike," I muttered guiltily.

I wasn't sure why I was feeling guilty.

I wasn't doing anything wrong, was I?

Cam shook her head in disgust before turning to look at Mike. "You need to stay away from your brother's girlfriends'," she growled. "Lee has enough friends. She doesn't need you interfering and causing problems."

Mike shrugged, smirking. "Wow, Cam, if I didn't know better I'd think that you were jealous."

I watched, mouth open, as Cam shoved her chair back and stood slowly, glaring at Mike. "It's a good thing that you know better," she seethed. "Isn't it?"

Mike shook his head. Ignoring Cam, he turned to face me. "How are you doing today, Lee?"

"Fine," I mumbled, thoroughly embarrassed and confused as hell. I knew those two didn't exactly see eye to eye, but they'd seemed to have called a truce while I was in hospital. But after this display it looked like they were back to the trenches.

"Do yourself a favor, Lee," Cam said, fixing her glare on me. "And open your eyes. Running to the father of your baby's brother is sick. He is bad news and you are looking for trouble."

Cam stormed out of the restaurant before I had a chance to respond, which was just as well because, quite frankly, I wasn't sure I could.

"Ignore her," Mike said, patting my back. "She's being irrational."

"Huh?" I said, still in shock over Cam's outburst. "Does she think something is happening between us?" I asked, appalled.

What she had said made me sound like a whore.

Mike shook his head. "No, I don't think so." He frowned. "I think she's making sure that nothing does happen between us."

Dropping into Cam's vacated chair, I shook my head sickened at the thought. "That's disgusting."

Mike chuckled. "Ouch Lee. Way to hit a man when he's down."

"Mike," I warned, not in the mood for jokes. There was nothing funny about what Cam was accusing me of.

"Relax, Lee," Mike said smiling. "I know a lost cause when I see one. You're in love with my brother, I get it. I'm not looking for anything more than friendship. I thought you knew that?"

"I did. I do," I assured him. "It's hurtful that other people don't."

"Screw Cam," Mike muttered. A frown creased his brow. "She's interfering in your life when she should be looking at her own."

"What do you mean?" I asked, staring into Mike's troubled brown eyes.

"Nothing," Mike muttered before smiling broadly at me. "So, how's my little niece or nephew?"

I smiled and sighed in relief as I rambled on about my baby, glad to change the topic of conversation.

TEN
KYLE

I WAS WATCHING a movie and eating Chinese food with Derek when the front door opened, then shut quietly, and Lee's curly head hurried past the open living-room door. Bruno, who had been still as a statue staring down our food, bounded out of the room after her.

"Don't," Derek said quietly when I went to get up. "Just give her time, dude. Don't chase her off when she's just in the door."

I didn't want to listen to Derek, but he was right.

Lee had been avoiding me since our kiss yesterday. Obviously, she wasn't ready to deal with me and I sure as hell didn't want to chase her away. I had enough odds stacked against me. I didn't want to add my stupid ass to the equation.

Lowering myself back down, I resumed my position of staring at the door. "That's all I seem to be giving her," I muttered as I took a slug of beer from my bottle. I didn't taste it. It wasn't doing anything for me tonight. "I'm walking on eggshells around her when I should be sorting it out."

"And what exactly do you think will happen if you chase after her right now?" Derek asked in an agitated tone. "Do you think Lee is just gonna forget all the shit that happened to her, and no offense, Kyle, but most of it you caused? Do you think she's gonna roll over like a dog? Dude, she is hurt and hormonal as shit. Keep pressuring her and she'll run."

"I get that," I groaned. "But she is carrying my baby. My baby whose life I want to be a part of. I *need* to be involved. Derek, you've seen the relationship I have with my father. I will not have my kid growing up all fucked up like I did."

"Yeah, you are pretty fucked up," Derek agreed, swallowing a mouthful of noodles. "But Lee will come around. She's a good girl…too good for your ugly ass. She'll do the right thing. Give her time."

"I hope so," I muttered while opening another beer.

"Besides, I don't know why you think you've got it so bad? You have the peace of mind of Lee being at home. I haven't seen Cam since she tore off yesterday. All I get is a fucking text from her saying she's staying at a friend's house. Lee's pregnant. What's Cam's excuse for being a hormonal antichrist?"

"Maybe Cam's pregnant?" I tossed out since Derek had brought it up first. It had crossed my mind more than once in the past few weeks and would explain a whole lot. Derek was right in what he said. Cam was acting weird lately.

"Nah man," Derek chuckled, tossing down his carton of noodles on the coffee table. "You're the only sperminator in this house. I've totally got that shit zipped up."

I laughed so hard I started to choke on a string bean. "Have you any filter on that tongue of yours?" I spluttered, hacking.

Shrugging, Derek grinned and slapped me between the shoulder blades. "I'm just being real, man."

"Oh, you're authentic all right," I laughed. "You're one of a kind."

ELEVEN
LEE

IT WAS LATE, well after midnight, and I couldn't sleep.

I was wide-awake, stretched out on my bed in the dark, staring at the ceiling.

My gut was clenched and my heart was thundering in my chest. I was scared. I hated the unknown.

The front door had banged loudly twenty minutes ago and Cam and Derek were still downstairs shouting. Well, Cam was shouting, Derek sounded like he was pleading.

Logically, I knew that I was worrying for nothing and should ignore them. But I found it impossible to shut my brain off and go to sleep when I'd experienced eighteen years' worth of nights lying in my bed afraid of the shouting and banging coming from downstairs. The only thing that had kept me alive on those nights had been staying awake and being prepared.

The soft knock that sounded on my bedroom door had my heart catapulting around in my chest.

Turning my head, I watched, paralyzed on my bed, as the door opened inwards.

Kyle stood in my doorway. The soft glow coming from the light in the hallway illuminated his body. He looked deliciously disheveled in gray sweatpants and a white muscle vest. His hair was ruffled, his eyes wide.

Relief poured through me first, only to be surpassed by a surge of heady desire that was quickly snuffed out by wariness. I settled on wariness.

Wariness was safe.

Wariness was smart.

"Hey," he said quietly.

"Hey."

He hovered in the doorway. "Can I come in?"

I shrugged. "It's your house."

Kyle sighed. Shaking his head, he came and sat at the end of my bed. "Can we talk?"

Pulling myself up I sat facing him, legs crossed. I nodded. "I guess."

Kyle leaned forward and braced his hands over his knees. I waited for him to speak. Finally he did. "I'm not perfect, Lee," he said quietly, staring at the ground. "I've never claimed to be. I fuck things up. Repeatedly. I say the wrong things. I never seem to get it right with you." He turned to face me and I gasped when I saw the flurry of emotion in his eyes. "But seeing you hurt," he croaked. "Knowing that I'm responsible? It's killing me. It is killing me, Lee, and my heart keeps beating."

"I don't want to hurt you," I whispered, locking the muscles in my legs, holding onto my pajama bottoms for dear life. If I didn't, I had a feeling I would throw myself into his arms. "I'm sorry."

Kyle turned and stared directly into my eyes. "Don't you ever apologize to me, you got it?" He sighed heavily. "I talked to Derek tonight. He gave me some advice."

He stood up and walked to the door. "I won't pressure you, Lee. I'll back off. You can have your space."

Kyle closed my door and I fell onto my back as his words churned around in my head and tore strips off my heart.

TWELVE
KYLE

IT NEARLY CHOKED me to say those words to her, but Derek was right.

I needed to give Lee time. If I kept pressuring her she would crack and most likely run.

What other choice did I have?

It was either back off and watch her from a distance or lose her from my life?

One choice would kill me. The other would be elongated torture.

I could live with the torture, so long as she stayed.

I took the stairs two at a time and didn't stop until I rounded the kitchen door. Stepping inside, I closed the door and glared at the two idiots in front of me. Cam was swaying as she held onto the countertop, obviously smashed. Derek was pacing the floor. They both turned and froze when they noticed me.

"Listen to me, dipshits," I hissed. "There are other people in this house besides you two. Some of us would actually like to sleep at night."

Derek's face reddened as he tried to pull Cam towards the door. "Come on, Cam. Let's get you to bed."

Cam shook her head and pushed Derek back. "Nope, not going…anywhere with you." Her words were almost inaudible; they were so slurred. She took two steps towards the door before falling flat on her ass. "Don't touch me," she screamed when Derek tried to pick her up.

"What the fuck has gotten into you?" he demanded in a shaky voice, clearly upset at her rejection. "I can't touch you now?"

"You'll hate me...and won't want to touch me," she screamed, then burst into tears. "I'm making it easier for you."

Derek ran his hand over his head. "I can't deal with this, Camryn. I can't."

He pushed past me and stormed out of the room. Seconds later I heard the front door slam.

"Whoops," Cam giggled, still crying. "You'll hate me, too," she slurred at me.

"Who says I already don't?" I grumbled as I bent down and picked her up. She folded into my arms, her long blonde hair spilling over her thin body.

"Touché," she mumbled, snuggling into my chest as I carried her down the hall.

When I sat her down on her bed, she automatically fell sideways. Pulling back the covers, I picked her up and placed her back down on the bed before covering her up. "Jesus, Cam. How much did you drink tonight?"

"Not enough to forget," she whispered, covering her face with her hands. "Never enough to forget."

THIRTEEN
LEE

THE TENSION at the breakfast table was palpable. I felt like I was about to walk into a war zone.

I hovered near the door, uncertain as to whether I should go in there. I needed to get my purse, but dammit I was tempted to go without it.

Cam and Derek were sitting on opposite sides of the table, shooting daggers and throwing insults at one another.

Kyle was sitting quietly in the middle, looking extremely interested in his corn flakes.

Bruno strolled past me, brushing against my leg, before trotting off to find solitude in the living room.

"I said I was sorry," Cam snapped. "Let it go."

"You mean you're sorry until the next time?" Derek shot back.

"Will you both shut the hell up for two damn minutes," Kyle growled.

Shoving her chair back, Cam stood up and stalked past me without a word.

"Sorry," I muttered, leaning across the table to reach my purse.

"Its fine, Lee," Derek said in an apologetic tone.

"Are you going somewhere?" That was Kyle. He was staring at me, his gaze intense and unwavering.

I blushed and nodded. "Yeah, I'm meeting a friend for lunch." The doorbell sounded, causing me to jump. "That's for me," I muttered. "I better go."

"What are you doing here?" Cam's voice boomed from the hallway, followed by low whispers.

I craned my neck around the door and groaned.

Mike and Cam were talking quietly at the door. Cam's face was flushed, her features angry. Mike looked untroubled. "I'm collecting Lee," Mike said calmly. "Can you call her for me?"

I rushed into the hall, but Kyle moved quicker. Pulling my arm, he turned me to face him. "Mike?" he seethed. "That's who your lunch date is with?"

I pulled my arm free. "It's not a date and you said you'd back off."

Kyle hissed and ran his hands through his hair. "I'm not okay with this, Lee."

I turned around and walked towards the door, stepping past a furious looking Cam. "Well, Kyle, luckily for me it doesn't matter whether you're okay with it or not."

Mike smiled when I joined him on the porch. "Hungry?"

I returned his smile. "Starving."

FOURTEEN
LEE

MY ALARM CLOCK SOUNDED. I got up and put on the only thing that seemed to fit me. A black, full length maxi-dress.

The weather was too cold to wear dresses, but I wasn't going to go to the hospital wearing jeans I couldn't tie.

I had an antenatal check-up this morning and wanted to look somewhat respectable.

Slipping out of my room, I went downstairs and waited on the porch for Mike to collect me, not daring to risk another pissing contest between the two brothers by having Mike knock the door.

I didn't want Rachel in our house and even though it was a totally different circumstance, I had to accept the fact that Kyle didn't want Mike in the house either. Thankfully, I hadn't seen Rachel since last week and if I had any luck I'd never see her again. Forever wouldn't be long enough as far as I was concerned.

I'd been home a week and the tension in the house was mounting. I didn't know if it was because of me and Kyle, or me and Cam, or Cam and Derek, but no one seemed to be getting along.

It was horrible.

Every argument seemed to have my name in it and it didn't take a mathematician to figure out that I was the root of the problem. The only person inside that house that was in any way approachable was Derek.

Good old Derek…

"What are you doing outside, Lee? It's seven-thirty in the morning." Cam asked as she stepped outside with a cup of coffee in her hand, shutting out the front door behind her.

"Waiting for my spin. I have an appointment at the hospital in thirty minutes," I replied, groaning internally, knowing that she was going to go off on me again.

Cam nodded as she wrapped her purple dressing gown around herself tightly. "You want some company? I can be ready in ten."

"No that's okay," I said quietly, hating the rift that was widening between us, but unsure how to fix it. "It's just a routine checkup. Nothing serious."

"Lee," Cam sighed, stepping towards me. "I'm sorry for the way I've been treating you lately…" Her words trailed off as her eyes slipped from my face. "Wait. Is that Mike?" she demanded. Her eyes locked on the silver saber pulling up at the end of our driveway. "I can't believe you, Lee."

"He's just a friend, Cam," I muttered while picking up my bag. "You're making a big deal out of nothing."

"No, Lee, you're being deliberately cruel," she shot back. "Stringing them both along like this, not caring about anyone else's feelings in the process, especially Kyle's. You've changed, Lee."

"We are just friends," I growled, thoroughly offended by her harsh accusation. "And how in the hell have I done anything to hurt Kyle's feelings?"

"Well, this is a pretty big example," she shouted pointing at Mike's car emphatically. "How do you feel about him? It's a pretty simple question. You either love Kyle or you don't. You either want him or you don't. He's trying his best and you're punishing him, prancing around town with his brother, taking Mike with you to appointments when it should be Kyle."

"My feelings for Kyle have nothing to do with you, Cam," I snapped, blinking back my tears. "You need to stay out of my business."

"And *you* need to get your act together, Lee, and stop moping and pining. Your grief is blinding you. Decide whether you can forgive Kyle or not, because leading him down a dead end road is fucking cruel. Set him straight or set him free." Cam slammed the front door and I slowly made my way over to the car, willing myself not to cry.

Cam's opinion hurt me deeply, it cut through me. This was my life, not hers. It wasn't as easy as just forgiving Kyle, even though I wished it was.

But the betrayal, the lies...so much had happened– it pushed us apart. There was no quick solution to this mess. Why couldn't she understand that?

Kyle and Rachel had destroyed me.

It wasn't a question of whether or not I loved Kyle. I did, deeply. It was a matter of trust.

"Morning sunshine...hey, what's the matter? Lee, why are you crying?"

I fastened my seatbelt, wiping my eyes with the sleeve of my sweater. "Nothing, Mike. We better go or I'll be late."

FIFTEEN
KYLE

I WATCHED from my bedroom window as Lee climbed into Mike's car and had to hold onto the window sill to keep myself from rushing outside and causing a scene.

Looking at her through the glass; that's all I ever seemed to be doing...

Pain like I'd never known enveloped me in that moment. I knew where she was going. Of course I fucking knew and a piece of me died inside as I watched her drive away with my brother.

"What time is it?" Derek mumbled from his makeshift bed on my bedroom floor.

"Seven-forty," I replied, not in the least bit surprised to find him in my room. This was the third morning this week. "You guys have another fight?"

Derek stretched his arms out and yawned. "Yeah, she went nuclear last night. It was safer to come upstairs than risk a pillow to my face," he muttered miserably. "I don't know what to do anymore, Kyle. She's been a different fucking person since Christmas."

I nodded. We were all different people since Christmas, but I knew what Derek meant. Cam had changed. "What are you gonna do?"

"Hell if I know man," Derek grumbled, as he slid on his jeans and stood up. "At the rate we're going, I doubt I'll have to worry about it for much longer. We haven't had sex in two weeks, Kyle. Two fucking weeks. That's like a year for us."

"Yeah, that must suck," I muttered, finding it hard to muster any real sympathy for Derek's two week drought.

That fact that it was late February and Lee and I hadn't been together since before Christmas being the main contributing factor to my lack of sympathy.

Jesus.

My bedroom door swung open and Cam glowered at both of us from the doorway. "Where's my phone?" she asked Derek in a cold voice.

He pulled her cell out of his pocket and tossed it to her. "Sorry, I forgot to put it back...how are you feeling this morning, babe?"

"And why haven't you put a stop to this Mike and Lee fiasco?" she demanded, ignoring Derek's question, glaring at me. "I know you were watching her from the window. Your curtains were moving."

I felt myself stiffen. "Why don't you walk your ass out of my room, Camryn, and keep your fucking nose out of my love life."

"You are a joke, Kyle," she hissed. "Letting your brother take Lee everywhere. Grow some balls and man up, will you? Mike shouldn't be taking Lee to her doctor's appointments."

"Did you get a lobotomy while visiting Lee in the damn hospital?" I spat, tugging on a shirt and pants. "Because you should go and get yourself a refund. This new version of yourself that you've got going on doesn't suit you. New Cam is a ratty bitch."

I didn't wait to hear her snide comeback–which, of course she'd have. Instead, I picked up my shoes and brushed past her into the bathroom. Brushing my teeth, I tossed some water on my face before slipping my shoes on. "Derek, do you want a lift to school?" I asked as I buckled my belt and headed for the stairs. I didn't have any classes today, but I wasn't about to throw Derek to the wolves.

And right about now, that's exactly what Cam reminded me of.

A blonde, snarling, cranky she-wolf.

"Yeah," Derek muttered, joining me in the hall and tugging on his hoodie and sneakers.

"What about me?" she demanded as we walked down the stairs.

"I'm sorry," I called out as I opened the front door and stared up at her. "New Cam can walk her own ass to school. But let me know when old Cam resurfaces. Old Cam can have a ride."

SIXTEEN
LEE

I SENT Mike away after he dropped me at the hospital. He'd argued with me about walking home, so I'd told him I'd catch a cab.

I'd needed space to think, to be alone with my thoughts.

I walked for hours recapping the fight I'd had with Cam.

Maybe I had changed?

Maybe Cam was right in what she'd said this morning. I was moping and pining...

But was there supposed to be a time limit on grieving?

Like, 'It's been months since you lost your baby, Lee. It's time to get over it.'

I felt so frustrated. So misunderstood.

I wasn't sure where I was going until I found myself standing outside the hotel.

Even then, I wasn't sure who I was looking for until I was standing outside his office door.

Taking a deep breath, I knocked and waited. Kyle's door opened and I gaped at the person in front of me.

"Mike? What are you doing here?" If I sounded suspicious, it was because I was.

Mike stepped past me, moving into the corridor, smiling at me. "Don't worry," he said. "Lover boy is still in one piece. We had our big boy pants on today."

Huh?

What the hell was he talking about?

I was about to ask him when Kyle stepped into my vision, standing in the doorway, silent and brooding, blowing my previous train of thought out the window. I looked at one brother and then the other before shaking my head. I was momentarily stupefied.

"Did you want me, or him?" Mike asked casually.

"Him," I croaked out. I shook my head. "I want Kyle. Uh...I want to talk to Kyle."

Mike smirked and saluted me with a hand to his forehead.

I heard Kyle sigh loudly and turned to face him. He opened the door out further, still silent, eyes wary, lips pressed tightly together.

I stepped into his office and Kyle closed the door behind us. I turned to look at him. He had his back to the door as his eyes gave my body a slow appraisal. The silence grew thick and muggy. I muttered his name at the same time he said mine.

"You first," he encouraged, waving a hand towards me.

I sighed, walked over to his desk and leant against it. "I don't know why I'm here," I said honestly. I watched his face. It gave nothing away. "I had a fight with Cam."

Kyle shifted, moving from the door, stepping closer to me. "Are you alright? What did you fight about?"

I decided to go with the truth. "You."

Kyle seemed surprised by that. His brow rose, his eyes widened slightly. "Am I allowed to ask why?" he asked in a quiet, unsure tone of voice.

Moving away from his desk, I paced the floor aimlessly. "Cam seems to think that I'm being a bitch to you," I said, sounding agitated. "That I need to get over myself and my grief. She feels I am leading you down a dead end road and thinks that I am being deliberately cruel to you."

Kyle didn't move a muscle, but his nostrils flared and his jaw ticked as he swallowed loudly. "I can understand why that must have upset you."

"Can you?" I stopped pacing and stared at Kyle. "Can you really understand what I'm feeling, or are you filling me up with more of your lies?" I wasn't sure why I was challenging his answer. I didn't understand why I suddenly felt furious with Kyle, or why I was overreacting like this. I didn't know what I had come here for. I only knew that right now I wanted to scream at him. I wanted to hurt him.

Two months of anguish was brimming to the surface. I had so much pain inside of me, so many unsaid words inside my brain and inside my heart, bursting to come out.

Kyle walked straight up to me, his blue eyes piercing me, his body crowding me. "Yes, I can," he said in a hoarse voice. "I know how much I hurt you. The decisions I made, good or bad, they affected you in ways I can't fix or redeem. I know how deep your wounds are, Lee. I'm not that much of an obnoxious bastard that I can't see the scars I've embedded in you. I fucking broke you, Lee. I want to be the one to fix you."

I could feel my body trembling. I tried to catch my breath, but it got stuck in my throat. My eyes burned. "Don't," I whispered, silently begging him to stop. "Please, I don't want to talk about this."

I couldn't hear this. I needed to get away from him.

I loved him and hated him all at once.

I wanted to hurt him and I wanted to hold him.

I wasn't thinking straight. I needed to think clearly. It was an impossible thing to do with Kyle's piercing blue eyes boring into mine and his words drumming in my ears.

"I miss the baby, too, Lee," he continued, ignoring my plea as he stroked my cheek. "It ruined me when you lost it. A part of me died that night as well. The grief…I know how it feels. I'm feeling it, too–living with it. Every day."

"Don't talk about it," I hissed, tearing my eyes away from him. I couldn't deal with his words. They hurt so much. I didn't want to hear about his grief. I had enough of my own.

This conversation was dangerous to my soul. I didn't like the darkness stirring around inside of me waiting to attack.

Kyle groaned loudly and stepped away from me. Now he was the one pacing the floor. "Get it out Lee," he said, pulling at his tie. "Say it. Get it off your chest. I know you want to."

Shaking my head, I closed my eyes. "No, I don't."

I felt Kyle's hands clamp around my shoulders, but still I kept my eyes closed. "Come on, princess. Do it," he urged. "You need to get it out. Tell me how you feel."

"I need to go," I cried, trying to pull away from him, not wanting to do this.

I didn't want to go there.

Kyle held my arms tighter. "You wanted space. I'm giving it to you. You wanted time. I'm giving that to you, too. You come here looking for me to comfort you and that's what I'm trying to do. But it's not fucking good enough for you, is it?" he demanded. "It will never be good enough until you tell me how you feel. Say it, Lee. Fucking say it."

"All right," I screamed, tears pouring from my eyes as emotions I thought I'd dealt with burst to the surface. "You want to know how I'm feeling? Well I'm devastated. I'm hurt. I'm fucking crushed." I pushed at his shoulders. "How could you do that to me with Rachel? All the lies, Kyle…how?" He tried to pull me into his arms, but I pushed him away, wiping my eyes furiously. "I feel tormented. You are tormenting me and I hate you for it."

"I'm sorry," he rasped, his voice torn. "I'm so sorry."

"Don't say that," I screamed, banging on his chest with my fists. He didn't stop me—didn't even try to protect himself—and he didn't stop saying it.

He grabbed my face with his hands. "I'm sorry, baby. I'm sorry."

"Shut up," I roared. Pushing him back, I slapped him across the face.

He dropped his hands to his sides. His chest heaved. His voice broke. "I'm so fucking sorry."

Disgust filled my body as I realized what I'd done. "Oh god," I cried as my legs gave out.

Kyle caught me before I hit the floor and pulled me into his arms. "Shh baby, I got you," he whispered as he sat on the floor rocking me in his arms.

"I'm sorry," I sobbed, clinging to his shirt.

Kyle stroked my back and kissed my hair. "Shh princess, I deserved it."

I shook my head. "What I said…." I paused, biting down on my lip in shame. "I didn't mean it."

He hugged me tightly. "I know. It's okay, Lee. It's alright, baby."

"I don't hate you," I whispered. "That's the problem." Turning my head so I could see his face, I stroked his reddened cheek. "I love you and I can't seem to stop loving you. I can't stop. "

Kyle's eyes flickered closed. His chest rose and fell raggedly. "Don't stop," he whispered. "Please don't stop loving me."

I watched as a tear slipped from his thick eyelashes and I stroked my thumb over his eye to clear it away. Kyle's eyes opened and fixed on mine. Common sense abandoned me and in a moment of madness I placed my thumb in my mouth, tasting his salty tear.

Kyle's mouth fell open.

Placing his hands on either side of my face, he kissed my eyelids and my cheekbones as he wiped away my tears with his lips. I twisted my mouth up to his, a mixture of desperation and desire pushing me forward.

Claiming his lips, I thrust my tongue into his mouth and tasted him. Kyle groaned. His thumbs traced my cheekbones as his tongue stroked mine. Twisting in his arms, I swung one leg over him to straddle his lap as my fingers attacked his shirt buttons.

"What are you doing, princess?" Kyle breathed against my lips.

I had no idea what I was doing.

I only knew that if I stopped now, I would never forgive myself. Maybe I was delirious, but for now I wanted him. "Take me," I begged as I pushed his shirt from his shoulders. "Make it all go away."

Kyle groaned and slowly pushed me back. "I can't do this," he whispered. "It's wrong."

My eyes jerked open. Reality crushed over me like a tidal wave as Kyle whispered words of rejection in my ear. I gasped as I dragged myself off him and scrambled away.

"Lee, wait," Kyle hissed, climbing to his feet.

I didn't.

I ran out of his office before he could hurt me further.

SEVENTEEN
KYLE

WELL, *I really fucked that one up*, I thought to myself as I watched Lee run out of my office.

I needed the coldest fucking shower I could handle.

I felt dirty, like I'd done something wrong. I'd never felt dirty over anything I'd done with Lee in the past except for now.

Jesus Fucking Christ.

What the hell had just happened?

My head was in pieces, but I didn't regret stopping her. She wasn't thinking clearly. She would have regretted it and that would have killed me.

We hadn't spoken in a week and I couldn't...I couldn't just take her on the fucking floor like she was some sort of fuck buddy.

'*Make it all go away*,' she'd asked me – begged me.

I knew I couldn't, not with sex at least.

I wanted to make it go away for her, but shit, I didn't want to take advantage of her vulnerability and I didn't want her to feel used.

For the first time in my life, I found myself questioning the power of the opposite sex.

I'd always been a firm believer that women had it harder than men when it came to pregnancy and parenting. My own mother's experience was always the driving force behind that concept.

Sarah Carter had been alone in the world. A teenage girl

brought up in foster care, duped by a married man, impregnated and then abandoned to grow, give birth to and raise me alone.

As a child my mother's drug induced suicide had almost destroyed me. But as I got older, I'd learned to accept it and eventually understand it.

She had me when she was just a kid herself and I knew exactly what it felt like to be utterly alone in the world and it fucking hurt like hell. I didn't blame her for her choices. Those were hers alone.

And every foster family I'd lived with throughout my childhood had not only proved but reinforced my belief in the concept that women were infinitely been dealt the shittier hand. I'd always believed and respected that.

But for the first time in my life I understood the other side.

I was living it.

What happened to the men who wanted to be involved? No one ever talked about those guys.

If Lee pushed me out, would my son or daughter grow up feeling the same abandoned hatred towards me, which I had towards my father?

I knew I couldn't live with that, which left me with the ultimate question.

If Lee didn't forgive me, could I fight her?

Fight the girl I loved more than life itself, for a child I wasn't sure I deserved?

Or walk away from an innocent baby I fathered?

I had two choices and I was ashamed of myself for considering either one.

EIGHTEEN
LEE

I RAN until my legs grew stiff and breathing became difficult.

Slowing to a walk, I made my way back to the house.

It was dark when I reached the front door. Turning my key in the lock, I quietly walked upstairs to my bedroom.

Mortified didn't come close to expressing the way I was feeling.

Appalled, embarrassed and humiliated weren't enough of a definition either.

Shame encompassed me.

Throwing myself onto my bed, I screamed into my pillow. It didn't help so I did it again.

"I need to talk to you." *Oh god, why?* I slid my pillow off my face slowly. When I saw Kyle towering over me I covered my face once again. "Come on, get up," Kyle said, pulling my pillow away from me.

"No," I moaned, covering my face with my hands. I was too ashamed to look at him. "I'm sorry, okay. Can we please just *not* talk about it?"

Kyle snorted. "Oh, because that's your answer to everything, isn't it, princess?" He pulled my hands away from my face and pulled me to my feet.

"I'm embarrassed, Kyle," I growled. "I'm not in the fashion of begging men to have sex with me." I cringed, hanging my head.

"Okay," Kyle said, clearly agitated. "First, I'm not just any man, so get that bullshit out of your head." He sighed and paced my modest-sized bedroom. "And second, don't think for one fucking second that I didn't want you." He stopped pacing and ran his hand through his hair. "Christ, Lee, I'm still fucking hard thinking about it."

"I said awful things to you. I *slapped* you," I whispered guiltily, addressing the worst thing I'd done.

"And I lied to you repeatedly. Kept you in the dark and fucked up with Rachel. I think I outweigh you in the prick count."

"So what are you saying?" I asked, utterly confused.

"I'm saying, I'll give you that one, princess." Kyle strode towards me. Grabbing my hand, he pulled me up against his chest. "You only get one get out of jail card from me, baby." He stroked my lip with his thumb. "The next time you ask me to fuck you, I won't say no."

I gaped at him, speechless as he sauntered out of my room.

NINETEEN
LEE

I POTTERED around the house bored out of my mind.

I cleaned my room, vacuumed the downstairs, did two loads of laundry and took a ridiculously long shower in the downstairs bathroom before trudging back up to my room depressed.

I was irritated.

I phoned Linda this morning about coming back to work and after a long and assertive grilling–from me–she had eventually confirmed my suspicions that Kyle was the reason I wasn't scheduled back on my shift.

Kyle had told Linda and I quote *"I don't give a fuck how you do it, Linda. Keep her out of there. I mean it. Lee is not to go back to work. No exceptions."*

Damn jackass control freak.

He had some nerve. I needed to be earning. My belly wasn't getting any smaller. I was starting to look like I was expecting twins.

You should have two. But you couldn't keep them safe...

Would I look at this baby and wonder–always be reminded of his sibling? I wondered if Kyle thought about it. Maybe he did, probably not though. He was too busy running around the place, ordering everyone about…

"Are you even listening to me?" Derek's voice startled me and I jumped from my bed.

"God Derek, you scared me. What did you say?"

Derek grinned widely, poking his head fully inside my

bedroom door. "I was wondering if *preggers* might be interested in some bacon and blackberry sandwiches."

I flung my pillow at the door, narrowly missing Derek's smirking face. "Don't call me preggers," I growled walking towards the door.

Derek grinned. "Oh, come on, my little ball of hormones. Maybe your favorite sandwich will improve your mood. And you can wash it down with a nice mug of steamy coffee. Oh wait, that's right, you can't."

"You're enjoying this, aren't you?" I asked, glaring at the back of his shaved head as we made our way down the stairs.

Derek chuckled. "I'm only teasing you. I do enjoy Kyle's reactions best. Shout 'labor' and he's close to fainting."

I followed the smell of greasy bacon to the kitchen.

Mmm, I knew there was a reason I liked Derek. He was the messiah of food.

I dug into my bacon and blackberry sandwich. If I didn't think about the combination, the taste was mouth-watering. Kyle and Cam both left the room when I ate these, but Derek was a trooper. Besides, he was the one who introduced me to the concoction. I was pregnant. What was his excuse?

"What are your plans for today?" he asked, sitting down next to me, pouring some milk in his coffee.

"The usual," I grunted. "Absolutely nothing."

"You say that like it's a bad thing," Derek chuckled as he gazed at the wall dreamily. "Man, what I would give to sit at home all day and be kept by some millionaire chick."

Kept?

Is that what was happening to me?

I was being kept?

"Do you think I want to live like this?" I asked thoroughly offended. "Do you think I aspire to be some millionaire playboy's *kept* little mistress?"

Derek snorted. "You are reading way too many trashy romance novels, Ice."

"Don't call me Ice," I growled.

"Besides," Derek said, batting his hand at me. "Kyle's a *reformed* millionaire playboy. And he sent you flowers on Valentine's Day a few weeks back."

"Yes, Derek, he sent me flowers. As in he was too lazy to go and buy them himself. He had them delivered by a florist."

Derek dropped his sandwich on his plate and frowned at me. "Did you ever consider that Kyle might have been scared? Christ Lee, for a smart girl you are seriously slow on the uptake. "

I raised my brow. "Come again?"

Derek rolled his eyes, but didn't reply.

"Anyway," I said, moving swiftly past his offensive comment, wanting to discuss a far more annoying topic. "You have classes today. Why aren't you at college, Derek?"

Derek shrugged and swallowed a mouthful of delicious coffee. I think I drooled a little bit. "I'm not missing anything important."

I doubted that.

Derek had a couple of months left before graduation. He needed to be in class.

"I don't need a babysitter, Derek," I snapped, addressing the real reason why he was skipping class. "Kyle is being a control freak. I'm pregnant, not dying."

"Don't," Derek muttered, flinching.

I knew he was remembering the night I miscarried. I almost died that night. I would have if he hadn't found me. "Sorry," I mumbled.

Derek attempted to smile, but it was forced. "You can't blame Kyle for being overprotective, or me and Cam for that matter. We nearly lost you that night, Lee. We lost one of you. Kyle…he won't ever get over that, you know. The fact that he wasn't there. That you… and he…he lost something as well that night. I think he'll carry that blame for the rest of his life."

This was too much. I couldn't think of that night. This was exactly why I needed to get out of this house. This was why I needed to be working, not sitting around overthinking.

I hadn't stepped foot inside that bathroom since I was rushed out of it on a stretcher. I could barely stand to walk past the door. Thankfully Kyle kept it closed at all times.

I couldn't go in there.

I wouldn't.

"You know what, if you're sure you'll be okay, I think I'll head in and catch my last couple of classes," Derek said standing up, ending the conversation that had become too heavy for both of us.

"Good idea," I agreed, wondering when it would get easier.

The memories and images of that night hung over the four of us like a black rain cloud.

Would that night ever fade from our minds? Would it ever leave?

Well I could forget, for a few hours at least.

I rushed upstairs and changed quickly. It was time I did something productive and I owed Kyle a long overdue visit.

Grabbing my purse and keys, I headed outside. I couldn't take Bruno with me because, just like my shifts at work, his leash conveniently disappeared when Kyle left the house, this morning–and every other morning for the past month.

It was hammering down with rain when I stepped outside and the coldness in the air had me yearning for the warmth of the house, but I trudged on.

If I could drive my life would be so much easier...

At nineteen years old, I should have my driver's license. Dammit, I should have my high school diploma.

I didn't have either.

I walked to the end of the street pausing to mentally map out Kyle's schedule on a Friday. I glanced down at my watch. It was two-thirty. He'd be in class.

I smiled darkly to myself and I headed left.

Let's see how he liked it when people interfered in his routine.

Oh, Kyle and I were going to talk.

It was on.

TWENTY
KYLE

ECONOMICS SUCKED ASS.

I leaned back in my chair and feigned interest.

Man, I needed a career change. I couldn't see myself in this suck-ass lifestyle for the next forty plus years.

Econ was mandatory for my degree though, so I sucked it up and made it to most of Professor Peterson's classes. I didn't feel the need though. The dude was sprouting out shit that I dealt with every damn hour of the day in the hotel.

Hotels, plural…thanks Frank.

It would have made my life a hell of a lot less complicated if my grandfather had left the hotel chain to Mike, or our father.

But no, he had to give one last lash of the whip and I was the fucking whipping boy.

He'd checked out and left me to deal…

I looked up when the door of the classroom burst open and my eyes locked on a petite brunette wrapped in a green coat standing in the doorway, cheeks flushed and dripping wet.

"Whoa," the guy sitting next to me muttered and I stiffened in my seat. "Holy fuck, Carter. You see that chick? I'd like a piece of that ass."

I clenched my jaw shut and gripped the edge of my desk, trying to ignore the very strong urge I had to rip his fucking head off.

Fighting in class was one thing. Fighting in Peterson's class was a first class ticket to expulsion.

"Can I help you?" Professor Peterson asked, frowning at Lee.

She blushed crimson as she clasped her hands over her stomach. Her coat hid the swell of her pregnant belly, but I knew it was there and she was getting bigger by the day…"Yes, I'm sorry to interrupt your class sir, but it's important. I need to speak to one of your students."

There was a lot of shuffling coming from the seat next to me. "Please be me. Please be me," the guy beside me muttered.

He was going to get a fucking fist in the face.

Christ, the feeling of possessiveness reared up inside me.

I glared at the side of his face, but he wasn't paying attention. His and the other guys in the room's eyes were fixed on my girl.

What the hell was she doing here?

Was she sick?

She didn't look sick?

In fact, she looked pretty pissed. Her eyes found mine and narrowed in promised violence. I lowered myself further in my chair.

Yep, she was pissed.

Fuck, if it wasn't hot as hell though, seeing her all cute and flustered like that. Pregnant Lee had claws.

"I'm sure whatever melodramatic emergency you're having can wait until after my class. I don't appreciate disturbances in my classroom, young lady."

Oh, fuck no. He did not just talk to her like that…

I tossed my books and shit into my bag without taking my eyes off Lee. I expected her to run out, or cry. She did neither.

Instead, she straightened her back and glared at Peterson. "While I appreciate your superficial ability at categorizing female emergencies professor, I need to speak to my '*baby daddy*,'" Lee replied using air quotations for the last two words.

Holy shit.

Did she just say that? Did I hear that right?

"Please don't be me. Please don't be me," muttered the guy beside me.

I snorted.

Peterson's cheeks pinked as he gaped at her. Lee stared straight at him, unflinching and I was so fucking hot for her in that moment. Wow.

Clearing his throat, he loosened his tie and looked towards

the class. "Okay, whichever one of you is responsible for this girl, out you go," he ordered.

No one moved.

You could hear a pin drop in the room as every guy in the class paled.

I stood up slowly and grabbed my bag. "Dude," the guy beside me said. His tone was sympathetic.

I smirked. If Lee was trying to get revenge by embarrassing me, then she'd failed. I was proud. I'd never deny her.

There were a lot of loud whispers and even some wolf whistles as I shuffled past the other desks in my row and made my way down the steps towards her.

Her gray eyes were bulging, as she worried her lip with her teeth. Why was she nervous? Did she think I was pissed?

I walked straight to her and wrapped an arm around her, pulling her close to me. Her entire body was tense and I couldn't help but lean down and kiss her wet hair. She smelled amazing. Fresh air, mixed with peaches and strawberries or some shit. Glancing at Peterson, I smirked. "Excuse me, Professor. My *baby momma* needs a word with me."

Peterson's eyes widened, then he shook his head slowly, clearly disappointed. "We'll talk later, Kyle."

"Looking forward to it, Larry," I replied, holding the door for Lee.

———

"Kyle, I'm sorry, I...I don't know what came over me. I was angry about work and Bruno's leash..." Lee looked green as she rambled outside of the Business building.

I smiled.

She looked incredibly fragile as she stood in the rain, oblivious to the fact we were getting soaked. *Beautiful.*

"I really am so, so...wait, why are you smiling?" she asked brushing her plastered curls back off her face. My grin widened and Lee's frown deepened. "Is there something funny?" she growled, planting her hands on her hips.

It took a lot of my self-control not to lean down and kiss that pout off her face, but I really didn't want a repeat of the last time.

I didn't think I could handle another one of her rebukes. "You're adorable when you're feisty, princess. I like it. I like it a lot."

Her jaw dropped, her lips curving into a perfect circle before snapping shut. "I'm not trying to be cute. I'm furious with you. You should be afraid."

I made a half-assed attempt at masking my grin, but it was hard to wipe the dopey grin off my face. I was so fucking happy that she was here. Angry or not, she was here. "Oh, you scare me, princess," I said. "You're the only one who has the ability to do that to me." I clasped her hand in mine. She pulled her hand away and I pretended not to notice.

Stung like a bitch though.

"And why is that?" she demanded, glaring at me.

"Because, you're the one person in this whole damn world who can hurt me," I replied honestly.

It was the truth and it seemed to stump Lee.

We stood a foot apart in the pouring rain, staring at each other, and I swear she'd never looked more beautiful. Her eyes were wide and soul bearing. I could read every emotion she was feeling in those gray pools. "Come on," I said, clearing my throat. "Let's get you out of this weather."

I placed my hand on her lower back and guided her across campus to the coffee dock.

She didn't shake my hand off this time.

TWENTY-ONE
LEE

I WAS the world's biggest jerk.

Whether I was annoyed or not, Kyle didn't deserve to be humiliated like that in front of a classroom, full of his peers and professor. I sat numbly in my chair, waiting on Kyle to return from the counter with our order. I couldn't keep my mind from drifting back to what he had said.

'You're the only one in this whole damn world who can hurt me.'

Kyle had a way with words. I couldn't believe everything he said. That was the rational side of my brain thinking. My heart on the other hand was banging around frantically in my chest.

"I got you a decaf because…well, you know," Kyle muttered, placing a cup of black decaffeinated coffee in front of me.

I smiled as graciously as I could, eying his strong kick-ass mug of coffee.

Men had all the luck in the world.

"Thanks," I muttered, adding a sachet of sugar to my mug and a good dollop of milk.

Kyle slid into the chair opposite me and picked up my spoon to stir his coffee. "So, was there an emergency? Or were you just pissed with me in general?" he asked, unzipping his coat and tugging it off.

My gaze drifted down to the fitted black sweater he was wearing. The rain had soaked through his coat and his sweater was molded to his chest, emphasizing every sculpted muscle…

"There was at the time," I muttered, dragging my mind out of the gutter and lowering my eyes from Kyle's body. "Now I feel kind of stupid about it. I was over dramatic."

He chuckled and I felt his fingers nudge my chin upwards. "You're pregnant, princess. You can be as overdramatic as you want."

His blue eyes were snaring me, and I had to look away or I'd be in trouble.

More than I already was.

"I need to go back to work, Kyle," I urged. "I'm smothering inside the house. I have to earn a living. I have things to pay for. I have stuff I need to get for the baby."

Kyle sighed and clutched my hand in his. "You don't need to pay for a damn thing, Lee. Not a penny. You…the baby, I will provide anything you both need. Let me take care of you, of both of you."

I shook my head at a loss. He'd paid for enough. Kyle had taken care of my hospital bills and the letter that had arrived in the post the other day confirmed that I now miraculously had medical cover and not the cheap kind either. "I don't know what I'm supposed to say to that, Kyle."

He clutched my hand tighter, stroking my palm with his thumb. "You're not supposed to say anything, baby. This is what I'm here for. You know I have the money, I'll pay for my responsibilities."

"I'll pay for my responsibilities."

Disgust filled me. I jerked my hand away and stood up quickly.

"Wait Lee, I didn't mean it the way it came out."

I shrugged on my coat, buttoning it quickly. "I know what you meant, Kyle." I wrapped my scarf around my neck with a vengeance. "Why don't you just say you'll pay for your mistakes? That's how you really feel. Well, I don't want your money. I never have and I never will. I am not Rachel. I was never with you for what I could get."

TWENTY-TWO
KYLE

SOMEONE SHOULD BUY ME A MUZZLE. Maybe then I wouldn't put my foot in my mouth so often.

"Lee," I called out, chasing after her.

She quickened her pace, breaking into a run as she hurried across the quad.

Running away from me again.

I caught up with her and clasped her arm. "Lee, baby, listen. I know you're upset, but the ground is slippery. It's too dangerous for you to be rushing off like that." She stiffened at first and then slowly relaxed. "I'm sorry," I coaxed. "Just let me take you home, okay?"

Nodding stiffly, she turned around. Her nose was red, her eyes watery. "It's a cold. I'm not crying."

I cringed, but kept my expression neutral. She didn't want me to know how she was feeling. I could read her like a book though... Right now she was feeling hurt, raw pain...and it hit me like a bulldozer to the chest.

"Well, let's get you out of the cold before you freeze." I took her hand for the second time and for the first time today she didn't pull away.

"I'm so mad at you, Kyle," she whispered as we walked, ever so quiet that I wasn't sure if she meant me to hear.

I squeezed her hand tightly. "I know, baby."

When we reached the parking lot, I stopped and leaned against a shiny black Mercedes Benz as Lee walked past me.

Noticing I wasn't beside her she turned and frowned. "What are you doing, Kyle? I'm pretty sure you could get arrested for touching that beast," she warned, walking over and pulling on my arm.

I grinned sheepishly. "I probably could...if it wasn't mine." Her mouth fell open as I opened the passenger door and gestured for her to get in. Lee gaped at me and I smiled.

It was cute that she was so surprised I could own a car like this. I could own a car-lot full of them and then some, but knowing she didn't look at me with dollar signs in her eyes made my heart swell. She didn't give a fuck about the money and I hated that I had made her feel like I thought she did. "Get in the car, princess."

She got in and I closed her door. Hopping into the driver's seat, I started the engine and pulled off.

"So you got a new car, why?"

I glanced over at her. She was fidgeting nervously. It didn't settle well with me. "I needed to change." I hoped she heard the unspoken meaning of my words. "You look well today, princess. Are you feeling okay?"

I wasn't sure what the correct terminology was for complimenting a pregnant woman's appearance, but she looked so much more than *well* and *good*.

Lee was sexy, undeniably fucking sexy, and that swollen belly...knowing I'd done that? Well, that made her irresistible to me.

"Yeah, I'm doing well. I still get morning sickness sometimes, but it's less often than before. Apparently, it eases up for some women during the second trimester, so fingers crossed."

She was still getting sick? Was that normal? Fuck, did she need a doctor? Jesus, I was clueless. "And the baby?" I asked quietly, hoping like hell my voice stayed even.

She sighed happily. "Yep, he's great. Dr. Ashcroft is really happy with him."

My eyes jerked to Lee. "It's a boy?" My voice came out all high and pitchy.

"No. I don't know the sex. That's just my own prediction. Cam thinks I'm having a girl, but he feels like a boy to me." She rubbed her bump. "It all makes a lot more sense now."

I looked at her. "What does?"

She clasped her hands on her lap, twiddling her thumbs. "Why I was so sick before the miscarriage," she said quietly.

I nodded, unable to answer her verbally. I hated that word.

Miscarriage.

It didn't mean enough...didn't voice the gut wrenching, soul shattering feeling of purloined life. How could one word define the stolen loss of human life?

But what Lee said made a hell of a lot of sense. She'd been sick, vomiting on and off for months before the miscarriage. If I'd had half a brain, I would have guessed she was pregnant, or at the very least considered that she could be.

The first night I'd made love to her, I'd been careless and ended up taking her virginity as well as getting her pregnant.

I hadn't used a condom.

Not that I was regretting getting her pregnant, just the fact that I should have protected her.

I'd known better, she hadn't.

I'd been rough with her and thoughtless and I'd acted like a total fucking idiot afterwards. I'd been so wrapped up in my warped sense of duty to Rachel, so petrified of my feelings for Lee, that I'd let her down in the worst imaginable way.

My jaw ticked as I nodded towards her belly. "I am so sorry, Lee. I should have known something was wrong with you. Should've figured it out before you...before that happened. I should have fucking been there with you."

I heard her sharp intake of breath and I focused on the road, waiting for her to answer. I hoped I'd sounded calm. The last thing I want to do was to upset her again, but she deserved an apology and I owed her one.

She was silent for such a long time that I thought she was going to ignore me, but then she reached her hand towards me. Her hand squeezed my knee and that small gesture meant more than a thousand words. I watched as a single tear slipped down her cheek. "I don't blame you anymore," she whispered. "I know it wasn't your fault."

I didn't realize how important it was for me to hear those words until they came from her mouth.

I released a sigh–more like a choked sob.

Fixing my gaze on the road ahead I blinked away the tears

that were filling my eyes and covered her hand with mine, holding on for dear life.

The silent absolution that passed between us was so simple, yet so profoundly comforting.

TWENTY-THREE
LEE

I WAS home for two months – two freaking months – and Linda still hadn't scheduled me back to work. I'd tried on numerous occasions to sway her, but she was standing over Kyle's orders.

It was an absolute joke.

Loads of pregnant women worked to full term. I was only twenty-eight weeks along. I had plenty of time before the baby came and an even pathetically larger amount of time to waste.

Being cooped up in the house like I was on my last legs was not winning Kyle Carter any brownie points.

I spent most of my days cleaning the house and vacuuming up dog hair.

I was bored out of my mind, and lonely. I was also incredibly irritated with my housemates.

All three of them.

No exceptions.

Derek was being his usual smart-assed self, and I swear if I heard one more 'preggers' or 'got milk' joke come out of his mouth, I was going to lose it. I knew his jokes were good-natured, but at seven months pregnant, I didn't have my usual patience with him.

And Cam's mood swings were impressive to say the least. If she wasn't smothering me, cooing over me like a mother hen, she was screaming her head off at Derek and accusing anyone who came within a ten mile radius of something outrageous. Cam was behaving as if she was the one with the pregnancy hormones and

I was actually beginning to find her suggestive comments about mine and Mike's friendship both gross and offensive.

Cam and I had been friends our entire lives and in all my life I had only ever been with Kyle. She knew that.

So for her to imply that I was messing around with Kyle's brother, while carrying his baby, showed how much mass she had in my moral fiber.

Just two nights ago, when I got back from dinner with Mike, she'd practically accused me of cheating on Kyle with him, which I found ridiculous for two reasons.

The first being the fact that I wasn't with Kyle in the first place, therefore even if I was seeing Mike – which I wasn't – it wouldn't constitute cheating.

And the second, Mike had mentioned to me that he was seeing someone, which as far as I could gather, was getting pretty serious. Mike still wouldn't tell me who his girlfriend was, but my money was on the new girl in housekeeping he spoke about. The other night when we grabbed a bite to eat at a diner down-town, Mike had droned on and on for over a half an hour about how funny this Karen girl was, so I figured she was a prime candidate for his heart.

She'd started working at the hotel around the time I had my miscarriage, which conveniently was around the same time Mike started dating his mysterious lady. I was secretly delighted that he was into her so much. It made our friendship so much easier, less controversial.

And of course, Kyle was doing what Kyle did best. Avoiding me. After our talk in his car the other week, I'd hoped that we were getting places, solving some of our issues, but nope, I'd been wrong again.

Two days after our talk, I broached the subject of going back to work in my foolish assumption that Kyle was a conciliatory person.

He had shot me down without listening to my argument, which in turn had elicited an even bigger argument. A lot of stuff was said, mostly by me, and we hadn't spoken more than a handful of sentences since.

I guessed he was giving me space, but by avoiding me, he was just making this living arrangement unbearable.

I knew why he was keeping his distance, which at first had

made me feel bad, but now just aggravated me. I was feeling guilty and I was mad at Kyle for making me feel guilty.

Maybe I was clutching at straws, but I needed to hold on to my anger. I wasn't ready to forgive and forget. Or maybe I was and I was angry with myself for giving in too easily.

Out of sheer loneliness, I phoned my father yesterday to check in. Daddy had been happy to hear from me and was recovering well from his heart attack in November. Most importantly, he had sounded sober.

We hadn't spoken for long, just a couple of minutes, but those few minutes had given me a little peace of mind.

To be honest, I'd needed the comfort of hearing his voice. It was a crazy thing to need after eighteen years of hell, but Jimmy Bennett was the only family I'd ever known. As insane as it sounded, I needed to hear my father's voice.

My life had changed so much in the past year that I needed the anchor of familiarity.

———

I'd spent most of the evening outside scooping up Bruno's poop. The sheer boredom had reduced me to pulling weeds and dead-heading the limited shrubbery in our back garden. By the time the watery April sun went down, I was feeling icky and gross and smelled a little funky. I needed a shower. I truly did.

Pressing my ear against the door of the downstairs bathroom, I could hear Derek belting out the chorus of 'LMFAO's *Sexy and I know it.*'

He'd been in the shower for over forty minutes and considering he'd already performed two renditions of '*Take another little piece of my heart*' I figured he was only warming up.

"What are you doing?" Cam asked, as she rounded the corner of the hall.

I blushed and moved away from the bathroom door, hovering awkwardly. "Nothing. I was just checking if Derek was nearly done."

Cam sighed, and shook her head. Grabbing my hand, she pulled me towards the stairs. "Come here, I need to show you something."

Following Cam, I shuffled up the stairs, freezing to the spot when she put her hand on the door knob of the upstairs bathroom. "Cam, I can't go back in there," I whispered, horrified.

I couldn't.

I never wanted to step foot inside that room again and see those tiles, that toilet bowl…I backed away to the far side of the hallway. My back pressed against a cool steel door knob.

"Lee, you know I love your bones, but you need to get a grip on this and face your fears. Come on, this is for your own good."

"I am not ready to go in there," I snapped, anger boiling to the surface. "Back off, Cam."

"You are acting like a baby. You need to get a grip," she said impatiently, stepping towards me. "You have to face this and move on. Just go in there and stop being so ridiculous. The bogeyman isn't going to jump out of the toilet, Lee."

"My life fell apart in that bathroom, Camryn," I screamed, my body heaving in panic. "I collapsed on those tiles, experiencing more pain than a human body should as my unborn child bled out of my body in clumps of blood. How I felt that night…you have no idea what that feels like, so don't you dare judge me."

"And that is exactly why you need to get your ass in that room, so you can get over it." Cam moved towards me and grabbed my hand just as the door I was leaning against swung inwards.

Stumbling backwards, a pair of strong hands caught me and broke my fall. Kyle turned me in his arms. "Shh baby, I got you," he whispered, wrapping his arms around me protectively. "What the hell are you doing, Cam?" he growled, while he rubbed my back tenderly.

I sagged in his arms and held him just as tight. "I can't go in there, Kyle," I sobbed, tucking my face into his chest.

"She needs to get over this, Kyle," Cam screamed. "She was sneaking around downstairs, waiting to use my bathroom. It's ridiculous. She needs to get a hold on this grief. I'm trying to help her."

I felt Kyle's arms tense around me. "She can use whatever the hell bathroom she wants."

The steps of the stairs creaked as Derek bounded towards us, with a towel wrapped around his waist and pink shower cap on his head. "What the hell is going on?" he panted.

"Shut up, Derek," both Cam and Kyle shouted, not taking their eyes off each other.

"Kyle, this isn't healthy," Cam started to plead, but Kyle interrupted her.

Tucking me into his side, he pointed a finger at Cam, glaring violently. "And what the hell do you think forcing her into that room will achieve?" he asked. "Do you think it will automatically wipe the slate clean?" Kyle shook his head. "You don't know shit, Camryn, so keep your fucking self-righteous tactics to yourself. You don't get to force Lee to do anything, you got it? No one does."

Cam shook her head in disgust. "Fuck you, Kyle. I was the one who sat with her day in and day out. I know what I'm doing. You...you are babying her, treating her like a child. She isn't made of glass. She needs to face this."

"I was there, too, Cam," he snarled. "Every fucking night. I never left. So don't pull your condescending bullshit with me."

"Guys, please stop fighting," I begged. "Please, just stop arguing. I can't...I can't." My voice cracked, tears blurred my vision.

Kyle responded to my pleas by tightening his arms around me. "It's okay, baby. We're not fighting. There's nothing to worry about."

"See," Cam said in a high-pitched scream. "This is exactly what I'm talking about. This...mollycoddling. It isn't healthy."

"Jesus, Cam," Derek snapped, moving forward. "Stay out of it. Their relationship has nothing to do with us."

"Oh, you would take his side," Cam hissed as she started to cry.

"I'm not taking his side," Derek said calmly. "I'm making an unbiased observation, babe, and you are out of line."

"Fuck you both," Cam hissed. "She is my best friend. I know what's good for her."

"You don't know shit," Kyle shot back.

"Fine," I screamed, half choking on my tears. Pushing away from Kyle, I staggered towards the bathroom door and flung it open. "Does this make you feel better?" I screamed, stepping inside. My stomach lurched and I dove for the toilet, vomiting excessively.

Kyle rushed to my side and held my hair out of the bowl until I stopped retching. Lifting my head, I looked straight at Cam, who was standing pale faced in the doorway. "Did I pass your test?" I spat, wiping my mouth with the back of my hand. "Am I fixed now?"

Cam shook her head, tears streaming down her cheeks. "Lee, god, I'm...I was wrong."

"Damn fucking straight you were wrong," Kyle snarled as he helped me up. "She is seven months pregnant, Camryn. Do you think this is good for her, or the baby?"

"Kyle," Derek said quietly, coming to stand next to Cam. "Back off, dude. She knows. She's sorry."

"I'm sorry, Lee," Cam cried before turning on her heels and rushing away.

TWENTY-FOUR
KYLE

FURY. Pure fucking rage was coursing through my veins.

I needed to hit something.

I needed to break something.

Ignoring her protests, I lifted Lee into my arms and carried her into my room. No fucking way was I letting her out of my sight. Not now that Cam had lost her damn mind. "Should I call a doctor?" I asked as I sat a trembling Lee down on my bed and moved away to lock the door.

"No," she whispered. "I'll be alright. It was just the shock."

"I can't believe she did that," I muttered, rooting in my wardrobe for some clean clothes. "Cam's lost her damn mind."

Passing Lee an old red t-shirt, I turned my back so she could change and rummaged around for some sweats. "Maybe she had a point," Lee whispered. "I mean, I think I get what she was trying to do."

I jerked my head back to stare at Lee who was standing next to my bed, dwarfed in my shirt. "No," I said as calmly as I could. "Nobody is going to do that to you. Do you hear me? I won't allow it."

"Kyle," Lee sighed. Sitting on my bed, she played with the hem of the shirt I'd given her. "I've been home over two months and for the most part I've been afraid to even walk too close to that door. Cam was wrong in trying to force me, but she was right in what she said. It isn't healthy. I'm not dealing."

I shook my head, trying to take in what Lee was saying. "So, what are you saying? Do you feel like you need to see a therapist or something?" I crouched down in front of her, placing my hands on her knees. "Whatever you need, baby, you tell me and it's yours."

"Maybe a new bathroom?" Lee joked, cracking a smile. "But seriously, I need to take a shower and I think I need to go in there and just...deal."

I shook my head. "You don't have anything to prove, princess. Not to Cam, or me, or anyone else."

"I need to prove it to myself," she confessed, staring right into my soul with her deep gray eyes. "I need to know that I'm strong and what happened that night didn't break me. I need to claim my life back."

I pulled her into my arms, probably squeezing her too tightly, but I needed to feel her in my arms. I needed that proof for myself.

"Will you come with me?" she whispered against my chest, and I couldn't breathe. I didn't dare breathe. She pulled back, looking into my eyes. "I know it's weird and we're not together, but I just...I really need you with me right now."

I nodded slowly and Lee pushed away from me and unlocked my bedroom door. I followed her across the hall with my heart thundering in my chest.

I stopped at the door. "You're sure this is a good idea?" I croaked out.

Lee took a deep breath, pushed the bathroom door open and walked in slowly. Standing in the middle of the bathroom, she turned to face me. "I've never been much good at knowing what's good for me." Lifting the corners of her shirt, she pulled it over her head. "But right now I'm sure about what I need."

I closed the door behind us and made my legs move towards her.

TWENTY-FIVE
LEE

THERE WAS A COMPLETELY new bathroom installed upstairs two days later, reminding me of how much money Kyle had. I stood in the doorway looking in. It looked nothing like the last one. The old tiles had been replaced with gold and white ones, along with a white toilet, sink and glass double shower. There was an additional feature that hadn't been there before. A white oval shaped bathtub sat against the center of the back wall.

Derek joined me in the doorway. "Damn, that guy moves fast." He let out a whistle. "Do you think you could ask for a pool next time, or one of those hula-hula girls with the grassy skirts and coconut bikini tops? Lee, with you around the possibilities for this place are endless."

I laughed. It felt good. I hadn't felt much like laughing since my fight with Cam. I was hurt, confused and really embarrassed.

What I had asked Kyle to do. To shower with me...I cringed thinking about it. He had been so gentle with me. He had held me in his arms, stroked my hair, my back, my arms. We had stood completely naked under the warm spray of water holding each other. It had been one of the most intimate moments of my life. And nothing had happened...Nothing. Not even a kiss.

"Have you spoken to Cam today?" Derek asked, stirring me from my reverie.

I shook my head and headed downstairs. "No, I haven't seen her since the other night." Cam was doing a pretty good job at avoiding me.

"She hasn't come home," Derek muttered. "I'm worried."

We walked into the kitchen. "Has she called or texted?" I asked, as I plopped two slices of bread into the toaster.

Derek leaned against the refrigerator and sighed. "One text, saying that she's sorry and that she needs space."

The concern in Derek's voice was heartbreaking. "It will be okay Der," I said, moving towards him. I wrapped my arms around his waist. He returned my hug and chuckled.

"Hey, look how far you've come," he teased gently. "This time nine months ago, you were afraid to breathe too close to me."

Stepping back, I looked up at his face and grinned. "Yeah, I'm sorry about that. I had a lot going on back then."

I'd been dealing with a very real fear of men when I first moved to the hill. My father's alcohol induced abuse and beatings had given me more than enough to fear, but it was Perry Franklin's attempt at raping me that had terrified me to my core.

All of that seemed so long ago now....

Derek ruffled my curls with his hand. "You got there once." He grabbed his keys off the table. "And you'll get there again. You're a tough little ball of curls. This stuff you're going through isn't even tipping the scales on what you are capable of handling."

I stood there in shock as Derek waved and headed out. That boy could say the nicest things when he wasn't being a douchebag.

TWENTY-SIX
LEE

I PACED outside Kyle's bedroom door.

I'd been doing this for the past five minutes. I didn't know why I was so freaking nervous. Kyle had asked to be involved.

It wasn't a big deal.

I should just knock on the door and say what I had to say.

Moving forward, I raised my hand to the door then quickly retreated. I was such a wimp.

Just do it. Just knock on the damn door.

My thoughts were spared when the door opened and Kyle stood in front of me, wearing nothing but a pair of black boxer shorts.

My heart catapulted in my chest as my eyes fed upon his carved stomach.

Everything on his body was just so pleasing to the eye. From his broad defined sun-kissed chest, to the rippling mass of muscles in his stomach, to those sexy indentations between his narrow hips and that strip of dark hair trailing from his belly button south....there wasn't one unappealing slither of skin on that man's body.

Oblivious to my ogling, Kyle stretched his arms over his head. His biceps bulged as he yawned widely. "Princess, what are you doing banging around out here?" His voice was thick from sleep as he scratched his bare chest and looked around the hall. "All the footsteps...I thought someone had broken in. What time is it?"

"Uh…" I cringed. It was five forty-five. Way too early for the normal people of the world to be up–or at least creeping around outside bedroom doors.

His eyes rested on me, blinking twice before a concerned look crossed his face. "Are you okay? Is the baby all right? Are you in pain?"

He was throwing questions at me quicker than I had time to answer them. "I'm fine. We're fine," I said quickly. "I was just going to… I just wanted to let you know. To ask you really…" I was babbling.

Kyle smirked. Reaching out, he briefly stroked my cheek with his fingers. "Say it, baby. Say what's on your mind."

I breathed deeply, steadying myself. "I have an appointment at the hospital today and I was going to get Mike to take me, but he has work and I don't want to mess his day up. And you said you wanted to be involved. But if you're busy I totally understand. I mean, I know you have a busy schedule and I just dropped this on you…I don't expect you to drop everything. I just…"

Kyle put his finger over my mouth silencing me. "Of course I want to go. I'm not busy. There is nowhere else I'd want to be."

I exhaled a huge lungful of air and nodded. "Great. Good, I mean, that's cool. We have a couple of hours before we have to go, so I'll let you get dressed, or sleep…or shower." I blushed, then scurried away, mortified.

"Hey princess?" I was at the top of the stairs and turned back. Kyle was standing at his bedroom door with his head tilted to one side as he rubbed his hand over his chest.

"Yes?" I asked nervously.

He smiled. "Thank you."

I nodded, blushing before turning around and climbing down the stairs shakily. I thought I heard Kyle chuckle from his doorway.

TWENTY-SEVEN
KYLE

I COULDN'T SIT STILL.

My knee kept jerking as I tried to sit patiently next to Lee while we waited for her name to be called.

My heart swelled up with pride as I sat beside her. She looked beautiful today wrapped up in her khaki coat and tight faded jeans.

Damn, I needed to take my girl shopping.

No fucking way was the mother of my child going to wear clothes too small for her. Of course, she'd freak out if I suggested it. I'd have to tread carefully. These pregnancy hormones were a crazy, unknown, terrifying bitch.

"Are you nervous?" I whispered, nudging her softly. She looked up from the magazine I knew she was pretending to read. She'd been staring at the same page for the past twenty minutes. Chewing on her lip she nodded slowly. I rested my hand on her knee. I felt her stiffen, but I didn't move it and slowly she relaxed.

A burly looking red headed nurse stood with a folder in her hand as her eyes swept across the crowded waiting room. "Delia Bennett?"

Lee raised her hand timidly and started to stand. I stood with her and walked towards the nurse.

The nurse introduced herself as Nurse Swallow–I nearly pissed myself at that–and instructed us to follow her down a clean clinical corridor to the last door on the right.

"You can make yourself comfortable on the bed sweetie. This

will be an external ultrasound, so no need to remove anything this time," the nurse instructed when Lee began to pull her jeans down her hips. Her fingers froze, her face blushed scarlet.

So fucking adorable.

"I'll be back in a jiffy with the doctor." The nurse left, leaving Lee and me alone.

"That was so embarrassing," Lee said, laughing quietly as she readjusted her jeans and climbed onto the bed.

"Nah, I'm sure there's not much that could embarrass Nurse Swallow." I laughed again at her name and Lee joined me. "What do you think her brothers and sisters' names are?" I asked. "Crow and Swan?"

Lee snorted. "Swallow isn't so bad. Her parents could have named her Thrush."

I had to bend over. I laughed so hard. "Well, princess, I hope you don't have any weird animal fetishes because we are not naming our child after a bird."

Lee chuckled, wiping a tear from her eye. "Agreed."

"Out of curiosity, what did she mean by doing an external ultrasound?"

Lee leaned back and made herself comfortable. She folded her arms behind her head and sighed. "I've had to have a few done internally."

I gaped at her. "Internally how? Where?" Call me a fool, but I didn't get it.

Lee pointed down to her crotch and blushed.

I fucking blushed and nearly lost my breakfast.

Jesus Christ, how the hell did that work?

Did they put a camera inside her or something?

I spotted a dildo-shaped microphone thing and a pack of condoms on the tray of the machine next to the bed and cringed.

Ugh, got it.

I felt like cupping my balls in sympathy.

No wonder she hated me. She had doctors sticking god knows what inside of her because of me and my reproductive dick.

The door opened and a white haired middle aged doctor strolled into the room. A middle aged *male* doctor.

I wasn't too sure I was cool with this. Didn't they have any female doctors for this kind of thing?

His smile was friendly and he had honest eyes, but still...I didn't like it.

Not one fucking bit.

The doctor smiled broadly as he came to stand at the other side of Lee. "Lee. How have you been? Settling back into routine?"

Lee smiled, shaking the doctor's hand. "Hello Dr. Ashcroft, I'm doing well thank you. I'm getting there."

The good doctor nodded and raised his head. His eyes met mine and I suddenly felt like I was the one being examined.

Lee cleared her throat. "This is Kyle Carter. He's my...he is the father." She turned to me. "Kyle, Dr. Ashcroft was one of the doctors' who operated on me."

I quickly understood the sudden scrutiny and cold appraisal.

He knew.

Dr. Ashcroft held his out hand towards me. "Hello, Mr. Carter, glad to *finally* meet you."

Stretching my hand over Lee's head, I shook his hand. "Good to meet you too doc. I'm sure we'll meet *many* more times in the future considering you're taking care of *my family*."

I glanced briefly at Lee who was frowning at me. She didn't like me calling her mine.

Well tough. She was going to have to get used to it because she was never going to be anyone else's. That was for fucking sure.

The doc's eyes widened slightly in what looked like mutual respect. "That's good to hear," he said before turning towards the ultrasound machine.

He pulled on some gloves, gelled up Lee's belly and–with what I can only describe as a similar shaped device to one of Cam's huge razors, the one with the soapy shit on it–began probing her swollen belly.

Lee lifted her top up further as the doc placed extra paper towels around her lower stomach. "I thought they had a sonographer for this?" I asked in irritation when his hand slipped under the waistband of her jeans. "Or a female nurse."

Dr. Ashcroft chuckled. "Yes, but Lee's case is quite complicated and I prefer to monitor her myself."

I forced my gaze to the machine. Everything was kind of

black and fuzzy. He fiddled with a few buttons on the machine, moving the wand around until…holy shit, I could see it.

I could actually see it.

"Is that…" I began to ask, but Lee interrupted me.

"Does everything look okay?" Her tone was anxious and I grabbed her hand closest to me and squeezed it. She squeezed back just as tightly.

"Yes, perfect. I'm measuring the size of the baby at the moment…" His voice trailed off as he concentrated on the screen.

Shit, was that good?

I looked down at Lee and she smiled nervously at me. I could feel tears burning the backs of my eyes.

This was incredible.

A baby. A real live baby with hands, feet, a head and a body wiggled on the screen in front of me.

After three long and terrifying minutes, the doctor placed the wand back on the trolley. Handing Lee some more paper towels to clean the gunk off, he smiled at us. "Everything looks good. Perfect size for twenty-nine weeks and the sex of the baby is still clear. As a pregnancy progresses it can become quite difficult to tell. Would you like to know?"

I said, "Yes" at the same time Lee said, "No."

We both looked at each other and started to back track. "We can find out if that's what you'd like?" she suggested.

I shook my head. "No, you're the one doing all the work. We'll do this your way."

I was stupefied as Dr. Ashcroft handed Lee a picture of the baby.

My baby.

She passed it to me and I stared at it reverently. My heart was beating at a hundred miles per hour and I'd never felt more for Lee than I did in that moment. I swear at that moment I worshiped her.

After a brief lecture–not one word of which I heard–Dr. Ashcroft asked us if we had any questions. I'd about a million, but again Lee beat me to the cusp. "How soon can I go back to work?"

I glared at her and then at the doctor who was frowning. "Well, physically you're fit to work. But given your special circumstances, I would prefer you to steer clear of stressful environments and of course no heavy lifting."

I butted in before Lee had a chance to speak. "So a loud and busy hotel environment wouldn't be a good idea? Like housekeeping and waitressing?" I hoped like hell he would agree with me. Maybe then Lee and I could put that argument to rest.

"Most definitely not," the doctor confirmed. "During a normal pregnancy I would say no problem, but due to Lee's ectopic miscarriage and removal of her fallopian tube, I would strongly discourage her from working in that sort of environment."

Relaxing, I looked down, met Lee's narrowed eyed glare and grinned. *Sorry baby, doctor's orders.*

The doctor continued, oblivious to Lee's dark mood. "Lee, it would be more prudent for you to find a quieter, less stressful and strenuous job for the remainder of your pregnancy, if it is your intention to work."

"Don't worry doc," I interrupted, ecstatic and smiling broadly. "Lee won't need to work. I've got her covered."

TWENTY-EIGHT
LEE

THAT JACKASS. He loved this.

Kyle nodded in agreement with Dr. Ashcroft, as they talked over how it would be 'prudent' for me to not return to work.

What rubbish.

If it wasn't for the fact that Dr. Ashcroft had once saved my life, I would be seriously pissed.

I grudgingly nodded at my cues and thanked him before we left. Walking back to the car, Kyle kept trying to talk to me, but right now all I wanted was some damn peace and quiet.

I wouldn't be so mad if it wasn't for the fact that Kyle was reveling in victory, having gotten his own way again. "So, am I supposed to guess what I've done this time, or should I just know?" he muttered as we pulled out of the hospital parking lot.

I looked over at his face and groaned internally. It would be so much easier to stay pissy at him if he was ugly. "I want to work, Kyle. That was bull. I felt cornered there."

Kyle took a deep breath and I figured that he was counting to ten in his head. I did too and reached seven before he spoke. "You're not going back to work. Get it out of your head."

I huffed and turned sideways to face him. "You are such an ass."

He laughed which made me angrier. "Call me what you like, princess," he chuckled. "But you're not getting your way on this."

Folding my arms over my chest, I tucked a leg up on my seat. "I never get my way," I growled. "And don't tempt me." At the end of the street Kyle took a right turn instead of a left. "Where are we going?" I asked. "The house is back that way."

Not even looking at me, Kyle indicated again and drove into the mall parking lot as he spoke, "We are going to go get you some decent clothes."

Pulling into a parking spot, he killed the engine and opened his door. Climbing out, he rounded the car and opened my door. "As hot as you look in those skin-tight jeans, we need to get you some…"

"Don't you dare say bigger," I threatened, climbing out after him.

Kyle stared wide eyed and innocent as he took my hand and led me towards the entrance. "I was going to say comfy. Something more comfortable."

Sure he was.

TWENTY-NINE
KYLE

SHOPPING WITH LEE turned out to be far less painful than I had anticipated.

As unassuming as she was, Lee was still a woman and from my experience they usually loved to shop.

But the discount sweats and plain shirts Lee chose showed just how different she was.

I'd told her money was no object, but from the pained expression on her face, I didn't argue when she chose to shop in the discount rails. I'd forced her to buy some jeans and dresses and she all but forcibly removed me from the lingerie section when she was picking out bras and panties…

"Thank you for today and for the clothes, Kyle. I'll pay you back," Lee said when we got home.

No way in hell was she paying me back, but rather than cause another argument and ruin the best day I'd had in months, I wisely changed the subject. "Thank you for including me today."

She smiled at me as I turned my key in the lock and opened the front door for her.

The minute we stepped inside Cam's raised voice bellowed from the living room.

"I guess she's back," she mumbled nervously. I frowned and nudged Lee into the kitchen.

I was going to kill them. I hadn't uttered a single vowel to Cam since she went bat shit on Lee the other night, but I hadn't forgotten and I definitely hadn't forgiven her. The doc had said

Lee needed to be in a stress free environment and Cam and Derek going fucking nuclear in the front room was setting off red flags in my head.

I felt bad for Derek, but Lee was my priority.

They could take their shit elsewhere.

"Sit down, baby. I'll be right back," I muttered.

Dropping our shopping bags on the table, I walked over to the door, but Lee grabbed my arm and tugged me back. "Don't, Kyle. Let them be. It's none of our business. Stay here with me."

I looked at her nervous expression and channeled a level of calm I hadn't realized I had. Lee smiled and lowered herself into one of the kitchen chairs. "Here," I said, rooting around in one of my shopping bags until my hands found the small rectangular cardboard box.

"What's this?" Lee asked surprised, taking the package from me and opening it. Her face snapped up. "You got me a phone?" She shook her head in confusion. "Why? I mean thank you. I mean, when did you get this?"

"You need a phone, princess. I got it when you were getting your, uh, boobs measured." I grabbed us two sodas from the fridge. "It's all set up and ready to go. Unlimited minutes and texts."

"I've never had a phone before," Lee muttered, staring nervously at the slim white plastic in her hands. "I don't want to break it."

"You won't break it, baby," I laughed. Sitting down beside her, I took the phone from her hands and powered it up. "You've used Cam's iPhone before. I got you the same one as her." I stored my cell and work numbers into her contacts list and handed it back to her.

"Thank you, Kyle," she whispered, shaking her head. "It's amazing." She fiddled around with her phone for a few minutes before jumping up. "Oh, I nearly forgot. Wait here," she muttered, rushing out of the room.

A few minutes later she returned holding a rectangular box in her small fingers.

"I got this for you months ago, before..." Her voice trailed off as she shoved the package into my hands. "Happy belated birthday." Kissing my cheek awkwardly, she came and sat beside me.

"What is it?" I asked, staring down at the fancy wrapping paper and bow.

"It's nothing special," she mumbled blushing, "just something I'd been putting together for you. I almost forgot I had it. I had intended to give it to you on your birthday, but..." *We'd been fighting...*

Tearing open the box, I looked inside and gaped. "When did you do this, princess?" I asked in awe as I took the book out of the box.

Her face reddened. "When we were together, before the...um, it's really not a big deal."

I shook my head at a loss for words. Opening the first page of the brown leather book, I was bombarded with emotions as memory, after memory, of our life together unfolded on the pages.

The movie stub from that god-awful chick flick we went to see was glued to a page, along with the feather from my Peter Pan hat and a Halloween candy wrapper.

There was a Kings of Leon C.D taped to another page, along with two photos. One of us dressed as Peter Pan and Tinker-belle on Halloween and another one of us with our arms wrapped around each other, grinning like idiots, as we stood in front of that ugly-assed tree last year.

I remembered Cam taking the photo of us at Christmas. She'd been snap-happy with her phone when she got home from the club the night Lee and I had put up the tree. But I hadn't realized I'd been snapped in those tights...

"It's a memory book," Lee explained quickly. "I thought... maybe it's silly. You hate it. Here, I'll just take it..."

I held her wrist when she tried to take the book. "No," I said, my voice hoarse. "I love it. Thank you."

"Oh," she sighed blushing. "That's good, I mean, you're welcome."

"Lee, baby, it's just me. You can relax." I hated that she was so skittish. I wanted her to be comfortable. I could have sworn I heard Lee mutter, *"Can I?"* but I wasn't certain, so I got up and made some coffee.

"So, how are you feeling after today?" I asked, placing a cup of decaf in front of her. "Are you tired?"

Resting her elbows on the table, she curled her fingers around her cup and sighed heavily. "Okay I guess. Physically I feel fine. Emotionally I'm a wreck."

I'd been waiting for Lee to talk to me, to open up. Now she was and I hadn't a fucking clue what to say.

She continued quickly. "I am happy you came with me today, Kyle. It felt right, like I'm not completely alone. I mean, I know I'm not, but it was nice to have you with me. It fit, you know?"

Sitting down, I nodded and pulled one of her hands into mine. "Yeah, I really do. I liked it, too, Lee. It felt good to me." I paused for a second, racking my brain for something to say that would fit the situation, yet not entirely freak her out. "You were amazing today, princess."

She snorted and shook her head at me. "Oh yeah, it's such an amazing thing to lie on the flat of my back."

I chose to ignore the sexual innuendos that raced through my brain. "You were," I said. "Seeing the baby on that screen, knowing that my son or daughter is growing inside of you as we speak is definitely an amazing thing. You are incredible."

She had a pained look on her face and I feared I'd said something stupid and fucked it up again, but what she said next took the air right out of my lungs. "I'm sorry, Kyle." She squeezed my hand and continued. "I was unfair to you. I punished you because I was hurt and I used our baby as a weapon. It was wrong of me. I shouldn't have stopped you from coming to the hospital. This is your child, as much as it is mine. It was cruel of me to keep you away from him."

I couldn't speak for a moment while I registered what she was saying. "You think that's why I'm here, don't you?" I asked her.

The look on Lee's face confirmed my fears. I clasped her chin forcing her to look at me. "I want you," I told her. "Not because of the baby, or some twisted sense of guilt. I'm here with you, fighting for you, because I want you. The baby is a bonus that I'm fucking thrilled about. But even if you weren't pregnant, I would still be here with you. I don't want to be anywhere else."

She leaned into my hand. "Why Kyle? I haven't exactly made life easy for you."

I got up and walked over to her chair. Crouching in front of her, I brushed my lips against her shoulder. "Because I'm in love with you, that's why. You think it's all about the baby, but you don't see.

You don't get it. I fucking adore you. I love you so much it burns." I paused and moved closer to her, cupping her cheek. "Lee, when I told you that you ruined me, I meant it. You have. I'm done, baby. You fucking own me. I'm yours. I couldn't be more yours, baby."

Lee looked down at me, her eyes full of tears. She let out a choked sob. "You do?" she whispered.

I nodded. "Yeah, I do. I always have."

"You've never said it." She shook her head. "Why didn't you tell me earlier? Kyle, I've spent months believing that you don't love me. I've based decisions on the notion that you'd never love me."

I shrugged apologetically. "I'm sorry, baby. I'm shit with words."

"But you do love me?" she asked nervously. "You are in love with me?"

"I'm desperately in, I undoubtedly do, and I fervently will, forever."

"You're not shit with words," she muttered, smiling through her tears.

Happy tears I hoped.

Unable to resist, I slid my hand behind her neck and pulled her face to mine. Our lips brushed once, then twice before I deepened the kiss, running my tongue across her lower lip until she groaned and opened up for me.

Her hands slipped around my neck to cradle my head as I put everything I had into kissing her.

Stroking her cheek with my thumb, I wiped away the dampness under her eyes. I pulled back to look at her. "Why are you crying, princess?"

She sniffled as she played with the hair at the nape of my neck. "You need a haircut."

Okay, not what I was expecting…

"I'll get on that," I chuckled, brushing my lips against hers lightly.

Lee sighed loudly and leaned into me. "I just miss you so much. But I'm so scared. My brain is screaming at me to run. And my heart…my heart is saying don't you dare."

I rubbed her lip with my thumb, stroked her hair. I couldn't help myself. "Which one is winning?" I whispered, almost afraid of her answer, but needing it just as badly. I needed a break, just one tiny opening into Lee's heart.

If she'd just let me back in, I could show her, prove to her I was good enough—could be good enough for her.

She sighed. "I should tell you my brain. That would be the smart thing to say." My fucking heart was ripping to shreds from her words. I turned my face away and nodded. Lee placed her palm on my cheek, forcing me to look at her. "But I'm not a liar," she whispered. "So I won't tell you that."

My lips covered hers before she could change her mind. "I still need time," she muttered, pulling away from my mouth.

I nodded and pulled her mouth back to mine. I'd agree to anything as long as she kept letting me kiss her. "I'll give you anything you want," I vowed between kisses. "Just give me a little hope. Tell me there's a chance." Pulling back, I stared into her eyes. "Say it, princess. Tell me you'll try and I'll give you whatever the hell you want."

Lee closed her eyes, as she sighed shakily. "I'll try."

"I won't let you down again." My face broke into the biggest fucking smile ever. "I mean it, baby. I'll never let you down again."

Lee nodded as a small, shy smile crept across her face. "If we are going to do this, Kyle, then we need to take it slowly." She held my hands in hers and then smiled softly. "I love you, too, Kyle. I want to be with you. I just need you to go slow with me. Be gentle, and please, please don't hurt me."

THIRTY
LEE

WE WERE GOING to do this.

I couldn't keep the goofy smile from my face.

Kyle was my boyfriend.

And he loved me.

My boyfriend was in love with me.

His words earlier tonight were still dancing around in my head. I had the strongest urge to get out of bed and sneak into his room. He had that effect on me.

But we needed to take this slowly.

THIRTY-ONE
KYLE

I HAD HOPE.

I had a huge motherfucking pile of hope, churning around inside of me and it was all because of, and directed towards, the girl curled up on my lap.

I couldn't believe how many of the small details I'd forgotten in the months since I'd last held Lee in my arms. I'd forgotten about the small strawberry shaped birthmark she had behind her ear, hidden by her soft brown curls. The small silver scar on her baby toe where she told me she got two stitches as a child. I'd forgotten that, too.

I hadn't appreciated how right, or how perfect her head felt when tucked in the crook of my arm, or the softness of her hair against my chest.

Her skin felt like silk and smelled like strawberries.

Never again would I forget the little things.

Lee stirred and I prayed for her to stay asleep. I wasn't ready to give her up. Since I'd–rather belatedly–told her how I felt last week, we had been spending time together, a lot of time together.

She was trying and I was respecting the hell out of that.

We hadn't done much of anything besides kissing, but that didn't bother me in the slightest. Well, it bothered my dick and I'd had to take a *lot* of cold showers, but this...spending time with her, lying with her, made the whole blue-balls deal completely worth it.

"Hi," she whispered, stretching out her body before curling

back into my side. "I guess I'm never going to get to see the end of that movie."

I grinned and pulled her closer. "Ah, you know what they say, third times a charm." This was the second night in a row we'd watched The Notebook. Well, I had watched the film. Lee had fallen asleep half way through both times–thank god–because I'd wept like a pussy when old-Ally died *both times*…

"I should go back to my room," she said quietly, and I tightened my arm around her.

This was the moment I dreaded each night. "Don't go," I whispered. "Stay with me tonight."

"Kyle," she sighed, pulling herself up on her elbow to look at my face. "That's not a good idea. We're supposed to be taking this slowly. Baby steps…"

"I won't touch you," I promised, cupping her neck. "I won't lay a finger on you if you don't want me to. Just sleep in my bed with me. I need you close right now."

Lee groaned. "I want you to touch me. That's the problem." Shaking her head, she kissed my forehead before throwing off the covers and climbing out of bed. "Goodnight, Kyle."

Groaning, I twisted onto my stomach, pressing my weight down on my hands in a bid to bury my raging hard on and keep my hands from grabbing Lee and dragging her back to my bed.

THIRTY-TWO
LEE

DRAWING on all my courage I made my way down the corridor of the hotel towards Kyle's office.

I'd been hoping to speak to him about going back to work the past few days.

I was feeling good. My feet were a little puffy from the extra weight, but I was certainly well enough to be working. And considering we were on much friendlier terms–*boyfriend and girlfriend terms*–I figured now was the time to strike.

Unfortunately for me, Kyle had been away for the past four days. There had been an emergency with the hotel in New York and he had flown out last Sunday to deal with the problem. He'd called me on my new phone countless times each day, but I hadn't been able to work up the nerve to ask him. He'd told me he was coming home on Thursday, so here I was.

Bracing myself, I smoothed down my blue knee-length dress and knocked on the door of his office. I heard some shuffling before his familiar voice beckoned me inside.

"This better be important," Kyle muttered, leaning over studying the paperwork on his desk.

"Hey," I said when he made no move to look up.

Kyle's head snapped up. Surprise encompassed his features. "Princess, what are you doing here? You okay?" He pushed his chair back and rose to his feet.

"No, sit please," I urged as I walked on wobbly knees to his desk, lowering myself awkwardly into the chair on the other side of his desk. "I'm here on business. I have a proposition for you."

Kyle frowned for a moment, his brow creasing as he stretched his back. "Okay…shoot."

I inhaled a steadying breath, before speaking. "Firstly, I would like to thank you for your hospitality in having me stay with you and for your generosity in paying my hospital bills, but I feel…"

"Hold up," Kyle interrupted me and held up a hand. "You want to thank me for my what?"

"Your generosity and hospitality," I repeated, wanting to get on with my proposition.

Kyle pulled at his tie and shook his head. "Yeah, I thought that's what you said." Standing up, he ran a hand through his hair before rolling his shirt sleeves to his elbows. "Why?"

Why?

I was puzzled, unsure how to answer him. I thought I'd told him.

"Um, for letting me stay at your house and for paying my medical bills."

Kyle shook his head slowly. "No, baby. You're gonna have to be a bit more specific."

Okay, I had no clue of what he wanted to know.

"I'm not following you," I admitted, rubbing my forehead.

Kyle came around his desk to where I was sitting and rested himself in front of me. "I want to know why you've traipsed across town in your condition to thank me–when I happen to be your boyfriend, not to mention the father of your child–for something as fucking absurd as my hospitality."

My back stiffened. "In my condition?" I stood up feeling suffocated and paced the floor, urging myself to calm down. This was not the way this conversation was supposed to go. "I'm not diseased, I'm pregnant. I was trying to be gracious."

"And?" Kyle added, folding his arms across his chest.

I rested my hands on my hips and stared him down…well, up considering our height difference. "And I want my job back."

"Absolutely not," he said with finality.

I gaped at him and resisted the urge to stamp my foot, barely. "You haven't even heard me out, asshat. I'm not expecting to go back to my old position. I have a proposition for you."

"I don't need to," Kyle shot back. "You can talk your sweet mouth off until the cows come home, sweetheart, but it won't change a damn thing." He hissed and waved a hand at me. "You are thirty-two weeks pregnant. You heard what Dr. Ashcroft said. There isn't a hope in hell that I am going to allow you to work."

"Allow me to work?" I asked, outraged. "You are not the boss of me, Kyle Carter."

Kyle smirked. "Actually baby, I sort of am."

"Uh," I growled, throwing my arms in the air. "You are being a damn control freak."

"No," he said calmly. "I am being protective. Taking care of what's mine. There's a difference. You are being irrational, baby."

I balled my fists tightly, trying to resist the urge to push his paperwork off his desk. "You are being old fashioned and incredibly sexist."

Kyle straightened and smirked at me. "And you are incredibly sexy right now, princess," he purred, stroking my cheek.

I gaped at him. "And you are…what ... don't try to change the subject Kyle."

"I thought we were listing each other's character traits," he chuckled.

"I was stating the facts," I growled, slapping at his chest softly.

Kyle caught my hand and pulled me into his chest. "So was I," he whispered, leaning so close his breath blew into my face.

"Kyle," I warned, but it was a weak threat and my voice exposed it.

His hands came around my waist and my pulse raced, my eyes fluttered shut. It was my body's involuntary reaction to his close proximity. He was intoxicating and absolutely lethal.

"You come into my office all pissy and demanding, and expect me to stay calm." He tightened his grip on me, causing me to whimper. "I'm so fucking hot for you right now, princess."

I pushed him away, but somehow my hands found his hair. My eyes were squeezed shut, my chest panting, my body locked in anticipation as Kyle's lips touched my ear.

I knew I needed to push him away. This was not how this conversation was supposed to pan out, but…I couldn't.

My body refused to step away from him.

"I want you," he whispered, nipping my earlobe with his

teeth. I could feel his erection digging into my swollen belly and I dampened between my legs.

"Kyle," I said, this time a breathy moan. I looked into his desire-filled blue eyes and my brain switched off.

I couldn't think straight. He was smothering my senses.

His face in my vision, his voice in my ear, his scent in my nostrils, his body against mine, his hair in my hands...

I was coiled tight with lust, with fevered anticipation.

His lips touched the part of my neck where my pulse was hammering. "I want you so fucking bad I can't think straight, Lee."

He ran his tongue up my neck before planting a kiss on my jaw and in my desire provoked state I cried out, "Yes."

Turning me in his arms, he pressed his front to my back as he trailed his fingers up my sides before circling and cupping my aching breasts. My head fell back against his chest, eyes closed and mouth open. I moaned loudly as his fingers traced the outline of my nipples, straining against my maternity dress.

"What do you want, princess?" he murmured against my neck. His right hand slid down my leg, sliding my dress up to cup my throbbing heat. Squeezing my thighs shut, I was grinding myself against Kyle's hand as the ache to have him inside of me grew into an almost frantic state of desire-driven desperation.

"Oh please," I begged, delirious as Kyle stimulated every nerve ending in my body.

"You wanna come baby?" he crooned, slipping his hand into my panties, teasing my saturated folds with his skilled fingers. "You want me to play with this hot little pussy?"

I whimpered, nodding. "Please," I begged, pushing at his hand with mine.

Kyle chuckled against my neck. "Shh baby, I got you."

And he did.

Thrusting two fingers inside me, Kyle massaged my clit with his thumb. "You like that, don't you, princess?" I sagged against him, my legs weakening as shocks of pure euphoria rolled through me. "You like it when I'm deep inside you," he coaxed as he used his free hand to push my dress up. "My fingers, my dick, my tongue..."

Tearing his hand away, Kyle spun me around and hoisted me onto his desk as he tore my dress off, tossing it on the floor. "It's your lucky day, princess," he growled, pushing me onto my back. "Turns out I'm hungry as well as horny. Spread those sexy legs. Now." My legs fell open of their own accord and Kyle's head descended on me, his mouth feasted on me.

"Oh, god," I cried out and tried to close my legs when his teeth grazed my tender bulb of nerves.

Kyle clamped his hands down on my thighs, spreading my legs wider as his tongue tormented me. "Fuck me, baby," he breathed. "Fuck my tongue with that tight little pussy."

I screamed out his name, bucking my hips wildly as Kyle worked me over with his fingers and tongue. "That's it, baby," he praised, sliding another finger inside. "Squeeze my fingers. You're so tight…So fucking sexy."

My back arched, my thighs trembled and I screamed as my orgasm crashed over me.

Kyle pumped me with his fingers until my body went limp.

"You are so fucking sexy," Kyle husked, breathless as he trailed kisses up my neck. "I can't wait any longer, baby. I need to be inside you. Now."

I groaned, my arousal rising up for round two as I watched Kyle unbuckle his belt. Leaning over me, he kissed my lips before pulling back to look at me. "Pregnant and spread bare on my desk," he murmured, sliding down his pants. "All I need now, is you barefoot in my kitchen,"

Pregnant and barefoot in my kitchen…

"Hold up, Casanova," I said, pushing at his chest, my desire deserting me. "What the hell does that mean?"

Kyle's brow creased for a moment. "I was joking Lee."

"Some joke, Kyle," I muttered. Sliding off his desk, I dressed quickly.

"Lee, where are you going?" He grabbed me. "Come on baby. It was a joke."

I yanked away from him. "Are you going to give me my job back?" I asked, hands on my hips.

Kyle hissed and ran a hand through his hair. "Don't start this…"

"Are you?" I demanded.

"No," he growled, matching my stance.

"Fine," I snapped as I turned on my heels and stormed out of the room. I stopped at the door and swung around to face him. "I *am* going to work, Kyle."

"Over my dead body," he shot back.

"We'll see."

THIRTY-THREE
KYLE

"SHE'S IN THERE?" I asked in disbelief as I stood outside the honeymoon suite on the top floor of my hotel.

"Oh yep. She's in there, kiddo." Linda nodded towards the door of the suite. "She's refusing to leave until she speaks to you."

"How the hell did she get in?" I asked, a mixture of confusion and nervousness washing over me. Since the last incident in my office, I had told security to remove Rachel from the premises.

Yet here she was, in my hotel again. In the bridal suite of all fucking places.

I was actually a little afraid of going in there.

"Karen, the new girl in housekeeping, let her upstairs," Linda said.

Someone was getting fucking fired.

Opening the door, I stepped inside and groaned. "I've been waiting for you," Rachel purred.

"I bet," I muttered, covering my eyes with my hand. I'd seen enough of Rachel's naked ass over the years to last me a lifetime. "What are you doing, Rachel?" I strode over to the window, needing to look at something other than the redhead in nothing but a black thong.

"Kyle, look at me, please," she urged, stepping up to me, grinding her breasts against my back. Slipping her hands in my pants pocket, she stroked my dick which was still in a state of semi-hardness since Lee's visit earlier.

I pinched the bridge of my nose. "Please Stop." Stepping sideways I tried to move away from her, but Rachel predicted my move and pressed me up against the window. Dropping to her knees, her fingers attacked my belt buckle and my hips thrust forward without my brain's permission. "Rachel, you need… to… stop," I groaned, trying to push her head away from my junk.

"You're hard," she crooned, cupping my dick with her hand and my eyes closed.

My head fell back against the window.

Jesus, what was happening to me…?

"You're like a rock," she purred. "Let me put it in my mouth. I'll make it real good for you."

The sound of the zipper on my pants opening brought me back down to earth and I tore myself away from her. "You need to get the hell out of here," I growled, fixing my pants.

"You know you want me, Kyle," she pouted as she swaggered towards me, her tits bouncing. "Why are you denying yourself pleasure and *you know* it will be pleasurable." She smiled. "You remember that thing I do with my tongue, don't you?"

I needed to get the hell out of here, fast.

I shook my head and made a dash for the door.

"Well?" Linda asked as I stormed past her.

"Call security," I muttered.

I needed to go home and take a cold fucking shower.

*

Lee was in the garden playing around with Bruno when I got home.

I knew I should go and speak to her and sort things out, but I couldn't face her.

I was too fucking shaken up.

I'd been *that* close, *that* fucking close to wrecking everything.

Ashamed and mortified, I headed straight for the shower.

I needed to scrub that bitch off me.

THIRTY-FOUR
KYLE

MY OFFICE DOOR OPENED. I raised my head from the pile of paperwork on my desk that I was pretending to read.

"It's over," Derek announced as he strode over to the mini-bar in the corner of my office. "It's fucking over, Kyle."

He grabbed a bottle of Jack from the bar and then proceeded to guzzle it straight from the bottle.

"Do I want to know?" I asked, swinging my chair in his direction.

Damn, he looked like shit.

"I don't know," Derek choked out. "Do you want to know about how Cam has just ripped my fucking heart out of my chest?" He made a sound that I could only describe as something similar to a lion in pain, before taking another gulp of whiskey. "She broke up with me," he continued, wiping tears out of his eyes. He took another slug of whiskey. "After two years, she fucking dumped me and she did it in a fucking text message."

Aw shit.

I stood up and walked over to him, but shit, I didn't know what to say.

I settled on an awkward pat on the back. "You wanna go get drunk?" I asked.

Derek sighed heavily. "Yeah, man. I really fucking do."

THIRTY-FIVE
LEE

I DECIDED TO GO SHOPPING.

I took a cab into the city and spent most of the day browsing around the baby aisles in every store I visited.

It was after seven when I got home with my supplies. I'd bought a small truck load of baby vests and suits and I was still despairing over the price of diapers.

Even though I had shopped in the discount stores, and bought the cheapest brands I could find, my necessary shopping spree had virtually wiped out my savings. I estimated that I had about three hundred dollars left.

A horrible niggling thought emerged from my subconscious; *'What would you have done with two babies? You can't even afford to support one.'*

Trudging up to my bedroom, I tucked the bags of baby clothes and packets of diapers under my bed and then headed across the hall to the bathroom. There was a quailing feeling of despair growing in my heart and I felt stupid for ever thinking that I could raise this baby without Kyle's help.

I needed his help, but I didn't want his money.

I knew that didn't make much sense, but I wanted to be financially capable.

I loved him, desperately, but the thought of asking him for money made me feel icky.

Once I was showered and dressed in my pajamas, I went downstairs in search of food.

I was starving, so I reheated the remains of yesterday's chili-con-carne in the microwave.

I lapped up the silence. I reveled in it.

For once the house was quiet and I ate my meal in peace at the table while making a mental list of all the other baby equipment I needed to get.

I would need a crib, and a buggy. I would need more clothes for the baby and I really wanted one of those changing tables I'd seen displayed in the window of that uppity baby store that I had neither the nerve, nor the bank account to go into.

My stomach knotted up at the sound of a door closing.

Oh great.

Right now there wasn't one single person in his household who I wanted to run into. Well, Derek was fine. It was the other two I wanted to avoid.

Lately, Cam was scaring me and Kyle was on my shit list after his sexist comments. Although, I wasn't too mad with him. He had given me one of the best orgasms of my life yesterday, but I figured he needed to sweat it out a little before I caved, which eventually I would because, let's face it, I always did.

I heard footsteps in the hall and prayed they would stay out of the kitchen.

I had no such luck.

The kitchen door opened and Cam walked in. Her eyes met mine and I was immediately concerned. "What's wrong?" I demanded, taking in her red-rimmed eyes and blotchy face. "Why are you crying?"

Cam snuffled. Her chest quivered. "Can I talk to you, Lee?" she asked in a hoarse voice. Her shoulders sagged as she came to join me at the table. Sitting down, she folded her hands on the table and began to twiddle her thumbs, nervously I think. "I've done something terrible," she whispered. Her voice cracked. "I'm *still* doing something terrible."

I straightened up and reached across to hold her hand. "Cam, you're starting to scare me," I confessed.

She was.

She hadn't been herself in months.

"It's so bad, Lee," she breathed, choking up with emotion. "You won't understand. You'll hate me."

I squeezed her hand. "You can talk to me," I urged. "You know you can tell me anything. You're my best friend and I love you. I won't judge you."

"How can you still consider me your best friend?" she cried, wiping her eyes with her hands. "I've been a bitch." She sighed and grabbed my hands. "Oh Lee, I've been such a bitch to you. You didn't deserve it. You don't deserve the way I've been treating you."

"It's okay," I murmured in a soothing voice. "It's in the past."

"I'm so screwed up right now. My guilt…what I've done, I took it out on you." She blanched and covered her face with her hands. "Oh god, what I did to you, trying to force you into that room…"

"Stop Cam," I begged, not wanting to bring up the memory of that night. "Just tell me. Please tell me what's going on."

Cam lowered her hands and looked at me guiltily. "When you were in the hospital," she sobbed. "I…" The front door slammed and Kyle and Derek's voices filled the house.

Cam leapt up and backed out of the kitchen. "Forget it," she muttered. "Please, forget what I told you."

I watched her retreat, absolutely dumbfounded and irritated. Whatever was going on with Cam, she was about to tell me and those two idiots had interrupted her.

"Wahey, it's the resident incubator. How's the bun?" Derek asked, swaying as he walked into the kitchen.

I groaned and lowered my head in my hands. That's all I needed. A drunk idiot falling around the place.

"Hey, don't talk about my bun, you douche."

My head snapped up and I doubly groaned.

Make that two drunk idiots…

Kyle staggered through the door, taking two steps before slamming heavily against the table. "Whoops," he laughed, sliding onto a chair. Shaking his head, his glazed eyes met mine. A predatory smile crossed his face. "Princess," he purred.

"Dude," Derek said in a joking tone and I turned my head to look at him. He was grinning like a lunatic. "Do you think if you blew into her mouth the kid would pop out?"

Kyle bent over the table snickering. "Pop. Good one, dude."

"You two are disgusting," I snapped as I pulled myself up. "So childish." I pushed my chair in hard and moved for the door.

Grabbing my waist, Kyle pulled me towards him and rested

his face against my belly. Lifting the fabric of my string top, he rubbed his nose against the swell of my stomach. "Kyle," I warned, holding my hands in the air. "Get off."

"Mommy's mad at me, kid," he mumbled, kissing my belly. "But it's Uncle Derek's fault. He's a bad in-flu-ence on daddy."

"Other way around dude," Derek hiccuped, staggering towards us. "You're the one who wanted to go to that last bar."

"Kyle," I whispered, shocked that he was talking so intimately to my stomach. "Come on, let me go and go to bed."

"Now that's what I'm talking about, baby," Kyle slurred, tightening his hold on my hips.

"Alone," I growled, embarrassed that he was making a scene in front of Derek. "I meant, go to bed alone, Kyle."

"Too much information, guys," Derek chuckled as he staggered out of the kitchen. "Night pop. Night bun."

"So beautiful," Kyle mumbled, stroking my belly with his nose and lips. "So incredibly fucking beautiful…" I groaned and Kyle's head jerked back. He stared up at me, wide eyed and looking completely freaked out. "Your stomach just kicked me."

"He's kicking," I chuckled and stepped back, pushing my top back down.

"He kicks?" Kyle shook his head and moved towards me, falling off the chair in the process. Running his hand over my bump, he looked up at me. "Since when has he been kicking?"

I took his hand and placed it low on the left side of my belly. "A few weeks. At first, it felt like butterflies, but he's kicking good and strong now. Can you feel it?"

Kyle nodded eagerly, and pressed his ear to my stomach. "Does it hurt you?"

"No, it's nice. It's comforting."

Pulling his face back, Kyle stared up at me with a strange expression. The blue of his eyes darkened. "Marry me?"

"Come again?" I shook my head to clear my thoughts.

He couldn't have asked me that.

"I asked you to marry me," he hiccuped, staggering to his feet. "Fucking marry me, Lee."

"Okay," I said, stepping around him, heading for the hallway. "You are obviously drunk. I'm going to forget you ever said that." I climbed the stairs quickly.

I reached my bedroom door when Kyle stumbled onto the

landing. "Are you going to?" Kyle slurred as he crawled towards me on his hands and knees.

I begrudgingly turned around and helped him up. "Am I going to what?" I asked, wrapping my arms around his waist. "Jeez, Kyle. Why did you do this to yourself? You can barely stand."

Stepping away from me, he leaned against the wall. "Are you gonna marry me, princess?"

"Don't talk stupid," I snapped. "This is not the time to have this conversation."

Shoving away from the wall, Kyle staggered towards the bathroom. "It's never the right *time* for you," he spat. "That's the fucking problem."

"Sleep it off, Kyle," I growled.

Heading into my room, I slammed the door shut and locked it.

THIRTY-SIX
LEE

MIKE'S PENTHOUSE apartment was situated on the top floor of a swanky apartment complex, twenty minutes from the hill. I sat on his couch in the open plan kitchen/living area and gazed out the large window. I briefly wondered how Mike paid for this place on his wages when he answered my thoughts aloud.

"This was my grandfather's place," he said, passing me a glass or orange juice. "Kyle inherited the bulk of his estate, but grandpa left me this apartment."

"Thanks for this, Mike," I said gratefully, taking the glass. I'd walked to his apartment building and was exhausted. I took a sip of my juice, swallowing quickly, quenching my thirst. "And you really don't have to explain about your family to me. It's really none of my business."

Mike nodded and released a deep breath, sitting down next to me. "Hey, that's my niece or nephew in that belly of yours. You're family now, too. You got that?" I nodded, smiling. Mike returned my smile. "Good," he said, poking my shoulder with his. "So, how's my infamous brother treating you?"

"Uh," I groaned. "The little that is said about Kyle and me the better." I hadn't seen Kyle since his drunken marriage proposal. He probably wouldn't even remember asking me. He'd been wasted. "I came here to get away from all the drama for an hour. Tell me something juicy."

Mike chuckled and brushed his blonde curls back off his forehead. "You know the girl I'm seeing? Well, I think I'm really starting to fall for her."

My eyes bugged and I twisted round to face him. "Spill the beans, Romeo."

"There's not much that I can say," he muttered, not making eye contact. His cheeks actually blushed. "She's very private about our relationship but I care about her, Lee. She's...amazing." I searched his face for the secrets I knew his voice was hiding. He squirmed under my scrutiny. "Stop looking at me like that," he said, clearly uncomfortable.

"What aren't you telling me, Mike?"

Mike didn't have a chance to respond as a key turned in the front door of his apartment and in walked a glamorous middle aged woman dressed in a tailored, soft pink trouser suit and with the shiniest blonde bob I'd ever seen. The man, who stepped inside after her, caused my heart to drop into my butt.

Holy crap. They're so alike.

"Mom, dad, what are you doing here?" Mike asked with a puzzled expression on his face as he stood up quickly.

"Michael, I was worried about you. You haven't stopped by to see me in weeks," his mother crooned in a soft British accent as she placed her clutch purse on the island before closing the distance between herself and her son. "What made you so busy that you couldn't call your mother?" she asked, kissing both of Mike's cheeks, before her curious gaze landed on me.

"Mom, this is my friend Lee. Lee, this is my mother, Anna," Mike mumbled, waving his hand back and forth between us.

"Hi," I muttered, waving awkwardly as I pulled myself up to a stance. "It's nice to meet you Mrs. Henderson."

I held my hand out towards Mike's mother, who after a heart-beat shook it. "Yes, you too dear," she said, smiling kindly at me. "Michael has told me so much about you."

I was baffled for a moment, unsure of what to think.

I had imagined Kyle's father's wife to be...well, to phrase it bluntly, a bitch. But Anna Henderson had kind eyes and a warm smile.

"David, come here and meet Lee," Anna said, waving her husband over.

I watched Kyle's father watch me as he slowly prowled towards us.

David Henderson was every inch the spitting image of Kyle, with the exception of slightly less muscles and a few gray hairs sprinkled on his dark head.

His sharp blue eyes–identical to his eldest son–scrutinized every inch of me before resting on my swollen belly. He raised his brow at Mike in disgust and snorted. "Please tell me that's not yours?" he asked, his voice laced with contempt.

I immediately stiffened and stepped away from the tall intimidating man. I wrapped my arms around myself protectively.

"David," Anna chided, clearly shocked at her husband's lack of subtlety.

"Shut up dad," Mike said defensively, coming to stand beside me. "It's none of your business."

David gazed at me with a look of disdain in his eyes. "What's your game little girl?" he asked me as he pulled out his wallet. "How much will it cost me to make you disappear?"

I gaped at Mike and Kyle's father as he held several hundred-dollar bills out for me. "Oh my god," I gasped, appalled and quite frankly dazed.

"Jesus Christ, dad, put it away. She's Kyle's girlfriend," Mike shouted.

Anna has gone speechless.

So was I.

"That fucking idiot," David muttered, shoving his money back into his wallet. "He has his own money to get rid of her."

I grabbed my coat off the back of the couch, and hurried towards the door.

"Lee, wait. I'm sorry about him," Mike apologized, rushing after me.

I held my hand out, warning him off. " It's okay Mike, honestly. I'm going to go. I'll talk to you later okay?"

I didn't wait for his response before closing the door of his apartment in a state of complete and utter disgust.

THIRTY-SEVEN
KYLE

I PACED the length and breadth of my office holding my phone away from my ear, while Linda sat in a chair with an amused expression.

"Rachel." I spoke in a firm voice as I tried to get her to shut the fuck up for a second so I could speak. "Just listen to me will you?"

"No, you don't understand, Kyle. I love you. I do. I need to be with you. We need to be together," she wailed, continuing with her incessant bullshit.

I rolled my eyes and shrugged off my tie. "Listen to me," I ordered, putting the phone to my ear. "You need to get it into your head that *we* are *not* together."

I heard her sobbing on the other line and shuddered. "Please Kyle. I'm sorry for lying to you about the baby. I am. It was wrong, but I love you. Let me fix this. I will do anything to be with you. Anything."

Jesus Christ. I was losing my patience, fast. "There is nothing to fix, Rachel. I think you need to see someone. Seriously, I'm starting to worry."

"See," she sniffed. "You're worried about me. That has to show you that you still care about me."

I shook my head. "I'm worried about Lee. I care about the fact that I think you're having a breakdown and your behavior is affecting the mother of my child. All of this craziness isn't good for her. You need to back off."

"Ah," she screamed and I had to pull the phone back from my ear. "Her. It's always about your *little princess*," she spat. "If she wasn't pregnant we wouldn't be having this conversation."

"Rachel," I growled. "I am not having this conversation anymore. It is over. I do not want to be with you. Do you understand me? I *do not want you*."

"How do you know the baby is yours?" she shot back angrily. "That hick is awfully friendly with your brother, you know?"

"It's my baby," I seethed, running out of patience. "Lee is not a whore like some people I know."

"She doesn't want you," Rachel urged. "She told me herself. She can't stand you. She hates your guts."

"Get help, Rachel. Go and get yourself some treatment and keep away from Lee." I hung up and threw my phone at the wall.

Dropping into my chair, I propped my elbows on my desk and ran my hand through my hair roughly. "She's fucking crazy," I said to Linda who was sitting across from me. "Insane."

"Do you think you should phone the police?" Linda asked, patting my arm.

I scrunched my brow in disgust. "And say what? My big bad ex-girlfriend is scaring me?" I shook my head. "They'd laugh their asses off."

"I don't know, Kyle," Linda said as she leaned back in her chair. "I feel this has gone too far. She needs to be dealt with."

"I'm handling it," I muttered.

There was a knock on my office door, and I threw my hands up in frustration.

"Oh fucking great," I hissed. "What next?"

The door opened, and in walked the other pain in my ass. "What the hell do you want?" I demanded as I glared at the tall dark haired man in front of me whose blue eyes were boring into mine.

"I'll leave you two at it," Linda muttered, as she excused herself from the room.

"You look a little stressed out, son," David Henderson said as he sat in the chair Linda had vacated. "Care to off-load?"

"Don't call me son," I growled. "And no, there isn't a damn thing in my life that I'd care to share with you."

David smiled stiffly, unbuttoning his suit jacket. "I figured you'd say that," he mused, crossing his legs at the knee. "But bearing in mind the pregnant teenager I just met at Michael's apartment, it would be fair to assume that you've offloaded more than just your problems into her."

I stiffened. "What did you say?" What the fuck was she doing at Mike's place?

David straightened in his seat. "Look, Kyle. I know we haven't seen eye to eye over the years…"

"Damn straight we haven't. Whose fucking fault is that I wonder?" I demanded. I was angry and fucking hurt that he was trying to play the daddy card on me. He had never been any type of a father to me.

In my twenty-three years on this earth, David Henderson had been nothing but a disappointment to me.

And backtracking to his previous statement; why the hell was Lee at Mike's place?

"Just hear me out before you jump in all guns blazing, will you?" I nodded stiffly, holding my tongue as my father continued. "I may not have been the world's best father to you." I snorted, causing David to raise his brow.

Sighing heavily, I nodded my head, indicating for him to continue.

"I made a lot of mistakes with you, and for that, I'm sorry."

There must have been some peculiar fucking funny-dust, zapping around the airwaves.

First Rachel, now my father…

What the hell was happening around here?

I had never heard David Henderson utter the word sorry in the eleven years I'd known him.

"But?" I urged, knowing full well he was up to something. I knew he had a motive for this spurious heart to heart.

David sighed deeply, his expression sympathetic. "Michael told me about your situation, and son, if I was to give you any advice in your life, it would be this…" Leaning forward, he splayed his hands on my desk and looked me dead in the eye. "Take the girl to a clinic or send her home to her family. Let them deal with her. One error of judgment shouldn't determine your future. You might think you love the girl, and maybe you do. She is an attractive little thing. I can imagine that's why you're so caught up with her. But you are young. You have your entire future ahead of you. What you feel now, you won't always, Kyle.

Do not let some adolescent infatuation with that girl destroy your life."

"Get out," I whispered. Shoving my chair back, I jerked up and lunged towards him. "I am *nothing* like you," I hissed as I grabbed his shirt and dragged his face closer to mine.

He smirked. "Oh, give it time," he sneered. "Young girls like her are only good for one thing." Grabbing my hands, he pushed me back and straightened himself. "Look at your mother," he chuckled as he backed away from me. "She was only good for one thing and she couldn't even do that right."

"Fuck you," I snarled as I tried to keep my body behind this side of my desk. "You fucking destroyed that woman's life."

"You'll learn, Carter," he said. Opening the door, he looked back at me and smirked. "One day, you'll find yourself looking at your biggest regret. Like I am now."

THIRTY-EIGHT
LEE

MY SHOCK HAD TURNED into pure outrage by the time I made it home.

I was freezing cold and my coat was damp from a combination of the shower of rain I'd gotten caught in, and sweat. Slamming the front door, I stormed into the kitchen and threw my coat at the table. It slid onto the floor and I didn't bother to pick it up.

I was hopping mad.

Opening the refrigerator, I grabbed the milk and drank straight from the carton, totally backwashing in the process. My mind was fixated on Kyle's despicable father and the wad of money he'd held out for me at Mike's apartment.

"How much will it cost me to make you disappear?"

"How dare he?" I screamed, slamming the carton of milk on the counter as I tore off my hat and gloves, casting them aside to join my coat on the floor.

I kicked off one of my converse, which narrowly missed Bruno who darted out of the room quickly.

"Sorry Bruno," I grunted as I bent down to loosen the lace on my other shoe.

"Calm down, Cruella," Derek joked from the kitchen doorway.

I swung my face around to glare at him. "Don't," I warned. "For once in your life, do not make a joke."

Derek held his hand up innocently. "Jeez, what's gotten your panties in a twist?"

The front door slammed at that moment and Kyle strode into the kitchen. "I want a word with you," he growled, marching towards me.

"You," I screamed as I pulled my shoe off and threw it at him. Pregnancy must have made my aim more accurate because my wet converse smacked Kyle straight on the head.

"What the hell, Lee?" Kyle accused, rubbing his head. "Have you gone fucking crazy?"

I had no idea why I was so angry with Kyle, but at that moment he seemed like a culpable target in my momentary rage. His sexist behavior when I asked for my job back roared to the surface. "Don't call me crazy, you jackass. You're the one with the crazy family," I shot back, furious.

"And you're the one who seems awfully fond of my crazy fucking family," he retorted. "What the hell were you doing at Mike's place today?"

Kyle stepped towards me and I grabbed the carton of milk and tossed it over his shirt.

Yep, I was feeling better already.

Reaching behind me for something to throw, my hands found the fruit bowl on the counter.

This will do, I thought as I launched apple after apple at Kyle's head.

I hit my target twice before Kyle decided to duck and an apple I had intended for him went wildly off target, socking Derek directly in the balls.

Derek fell to his knees, his face red and contorted in pain. "You two are both fucking crazy," he muttered, holding himself. "Grade A lunatics," he growled. Climbing to his feet, he staggered out of the room, clutching his injured area.

Kyle and I both glared at each other for a moment before bursting out laughing at the sight of Derek hobbling down the hall. I quickly masked my features and resumed my glaring.

Sighing heavily, Kyle pulled his shirt over his head and tossed it on the floor before grabbing a towel. "You wanna tell me what that was in aid of?" he asked as he stood in front of me, wiping milk off his bare chest.

Oh god…

"I…I…What?" I asked, unable to keep my eyes from straying

to his rock hard abs.

Kyle chuckled. "My face is up here, princess."

I reddened and reluctantly tore my gaze away from his eye candy naked torso. "Shut up, Kyle."

Kyle tossed the towel on the floor and stalked towards me. I backed up until I felt the cold frame of the counter against my back. "Make me," he challenged, in a husky tone.

Bending slightly, he grabbed my thighs and hoisted me up. Sitting me on the kitchen countertop, he dragged my body towards him and pressed himself roughly between my legs. I could feel his erection, hard and pulsing, probing my wetness. And I was wet. I was so incredibly aroused. My heart hammered in my chest as I stared into the lusty depth of Kyle's blue eyes.

"You won't marry me," he growled. "And now you're throwing fruit at my fucking head and telling me to shut up? Why don't you try and make me, baby?" he taunted, grinding his hips erotically against my aching core.

I ran my hands up his bare chest, feeling every dip, grove and muscle on his perfect body. "You didn't ask me nicely enough," I retorted.

Grabbing his hair, I yanked it roughly, jerking his mouth down to mine. Swiping my tongue across his mouth, I dragged his lip roughly between my teeth and tugged hard. Kyle growled and I lost all grasp I had on my self-control. Tearing off my shirt, Kyle quickly went to work on the clasp of my bra, undoing it with a proficiency that should have worried me.

It didn't.

His mouth found my rigid nipples and I was too aroused to feel anything but the drowning pleasure of his tongue on my skin. "You want me to repeat the question, baby?" he breathed.

Reaching for the buckle of Kyle's belt, I quickly undid his pants before slipping my hand inside his boxers. His erection fell heavily into my palm, huge, hard, and throbbing. "Not yet," I moaned. "Not…ready."

Kyle groaned against my breast, thrusting himself into my hand as I stroked his impressive length. "Baby, fuck…" he hissed claiming my mouth, kissing me deeply as I worked him over with my hand.

I could feel his balls tighten, his cock jerked. I knew he was close and that thought alone drove me wild.

Quickening my pace on his shaft, I slipped my other hand into his pants and cupped his balls, massaging them slowly, reveling in my domination of this powerful, beautiful man.

Kyle trembled, his back bowed, his hips thrust forward as the first signs of his orgasm spilled from his cock in a hot flood of cum. I pumped him until his body sagged and he buried his face in the crook of my neck, panting heavily. "Baby," he groaned. "That…was…I'm…I'm…"

"Scarred for life?" My head jerked in the direction of the kitchen door and I screamed while scrambling to cover myself up.

"Jesus Cam. Fuck off, will you?" Kyle growled, wrapping his arms around me, covering my bare breasts with his chest.

"Good to see you two have come to your senses," she said. "But for future reference, you might want to take it somewhere other than the place we have to eat." She shook her head as she trailed out of the room, closing the door behind her.

"Hmm, princess, that was fucking unbelievable," Kyle whispered as he trailed kisses up my neck.

"I'm worried," I confessed, tucking into his chest.

"About Cam?" Kyle asked, tipping my chin up. I nodded, biting on my lip. Kyle smiled sadly and then his face turned serious.

"What?" I asked in alarm.

Kyle stroked my cheek as he leaned his forehead against mine. "Come upstairs with me?" he whispered.

"I…" My voice trailed off as my brain frantically tried to dissuade me, claiming it was too fast.

I told my brain to shut the hell up.

I couldn't deny this…intensity, this connection I had with Kyle any longer.

My heart was calling the shots now and my heart was screaming *yes*.

"I don't want to fight anymore, baby," he whispered. "I want to be with you, bury myself inside of you."

"Okay," I breathed.

Kyle grinned. Picking up my shirt, he slipped it over my head, covering my nudity before lifting me down. "I'm crazy about you. You know that, don't you?"

I nodded, taking Kyle's outstretched hand as he led me

upstairs.

———

Kyle led me into his room, removing our clothes as we went. By the time we made his bed we were both naked. There was a lot of fumbling because of my big belly. "You're so beautiful," he murmured as he sat me on his bed and trailed kisses over my stomach, up to my breasts. His tongue was driving me insane with want and I couldn't take anymore teasing.

Pushing at his shoulders, I pressed him down on the bed and straddled him. "Go slow baby," he whispered with concern in his eyes. "I don't want to hurt you."

I nodded eagerly as he held his erection and slowly pushed every hard, thick inch inside me, filling me to the brim. He was so big. "I feel so full," I whimpered, sinking down on him. Placing my hands on his rock hard chest, I rocked my hips.

Oh, the feeling was incredible.

So intense…

"Fuck," he moaned, his teeth clamping down on his bottom lip as he ground upwards. "You're so tight, so fucking tight." I cried out. It seemed the only thing I could do. He was stretching me too thin. "Are you okay baby? Is this okay?"

I nodded. "Yes, perfect. Don't stop. I won't break."

The lazy, upward thrust of his hips excited me, thrilled me. My core thrummed to the rhythm of his throbbing cock. I felt myself rising, building. I knew I was close, could taste the sweetness impending on me.

I slammed my hips downwards, spreading my thighs as far apart as I could, urging him. "Harder. Please."

He grasped my hips and taking control of our rhythm he quickened the pace, sliding into me with hard, fast thrusts. "I need you. Don't leave me," he grunted.

I could hear the emotion in his voice. His words were gruff, tormenting. "I won't," I panted.

He ground upwards, rubbing against my clit. "I mean it," he hissed, pumping me hard. "Don't go. I don't need people….I never have. But I need you."

His words caused the tightening feeling to explode, shattering me, completing me.

THIRTY-NINE
LEE

"OKAY, I think we need a night apart," I said as Kyle and I walked up the driveway towards the house. We'd been shopping all day and had bought all the supplies on my list. I'd felt shitty about the money, but if Kyle wouldn't let me go back to work, there really was nothing I could do.

Oh, and he'd bought me the changing table I'd seen in that posh baby store...

Kyle frowned, linking my arm with his. "You see, this is exactly where I disagree, princess. I think we need to spend a lot more time together, on an intimate level."

I gaped at him as he unlocked the front door and gestured me inside. "Is sex all you think about?" I asked. Taking off my coat, I hung it on the rack on the back of the door. "We are supposed to be taking this slowly, Kyle."

Okay, I realized that was a ridiculous statement considering we'd been sleeping together for a month, but still...

Kyle threw his head back laughing as he removed his jacket. "As tempting as taking you upstairs to bed is, I meant intimate as in emotional. Getting to know each other better."

I eyed him warily. "Get to know each other?"

He smiled and brushed a hand against my belly. "I could take you out on a date?"

I snorted. "You're asking me to go on a date with you? To date you? Um, don't you think that's a little backwards?" I asked, pointing at my stomach.

Kyle's smile faded. "I was trying to be romantic," he muttered, running a hand through his wild mane. "Look, forget about it. It was stupid."

He turned to walk upstairs and I found myself tugging him back. "It wasn't stupid, it was just surprising."

Kyle scrunched his brow. "Why do you find it surprising that I want to take you on a date? I love you. I've asked you to marry me on numerous occasions and you're having my kid. Does a date sound so strange to you?"

"Fine, I'll date you, you weirdo."

The smile Kyle flashed me had my heart fluttering crazily. "That's not a very nice thing to call your baby-daddy, now, is it, princess?" He arched his brow as a wide teasing smirk flickered across his face. His dimple puckered in his cheek.

I shook my head and snorted. "Classy title, Kyle. Very original."

Kyle grabbed my hips and tugged me towards him. "Baby-daddy, boyfriend, sex slave, hot stuff… Call me what you want, baby. No, wait, you'll scream it when I'm through with you." His lips dipped to my neck and I lost all power of speech when his hot, wet tongue scorched my skin.

"Is that a threat?" I breathed. My skin tingled with pleasure, burning from his hot, sweet lips.

Kyle chuckled deeply. "Oh, baby, you know my threats are never empty."

I knew that already and from the hungered look in Kyle's eyes, I guessed I was about to be re-educated on that theory.

"My lips," I breathed, I needed to feel his mouth on mine.

Smiling in triumph, Kyle lowered his mouth to mine. "Just so you know," he whispered an inch away from my mouth. "You have the sexiest lips I've ever kissed." Running his tongue over my lip, he pulled it into his mouth and sucked gently. "So fucking sexy," he growled. His hands gripped my hips. "And these hips…" He lifted his head. "Marry me," he grumbled, kissing my jaw, trailing his tongue towards my earlobe.

"It's not time to repeat that question," I all but screamed out as Kyle's hand slid under my skirt and his fingers traced the outline of my panties.

"One of these days," he muttered, stepping back from me. "One of these days you'll ask me to repeat the question."

"So, about that date?" I asked, smiling and changing the subject.

His smile returned. "Could I interest you in the second part of The Notebook, a pint of chocolate chip and my bed," he kissed my neck. "I'll make sure you stay awake the whole time."

Giggling, I pushed him towards the kitchen. "Okay, you had me with the ice-cream." Kyle grinned and went in search of ice-cream.

There was a knock on the front door and I couldn't keep the stupid grin off my face as I went to open it.

The smile on my face slipped the moment my eyes met Rachel's.

"Hello Delia," she said sweetly. "Mind if I come in for a moment?" Not waiting for me to answer she pushed past me, into the hall.

"Princess," Kyle called out from the kitchen. "I can only find one spoon, so you'll have to share with me, or you could always lick it off my…" His voice trailed off when he came into the hall and saw our visitor. Glaring at Rachel, Kyle strode forward and pulled me behind him. "What the hell are you doing here?" he growled. "Can you not get a fucking hint?"

Ignoring Kyle's threatening tone, Rachel dug her hand in her purse. "I came to give you this," she purred, handing Kyle a familiar looking black leather wallet.

Kyle's wallet.

"I found it on the floor after you left the hotel room," Rachel continued, smiling. "I meant to give it to you sooner, but it slipped my mind. It must have fallen out of your pocket when we…well, you know…"

I gaped at Rachel and then at Kyle, who was frowning at his wallet, blinking rapidly.

My body went bone cold as my brain put the pieces together.

It wasn't hard…I wasn't an idiot.

Breaking out of his momentary trance, Kyle swung around and grabbed my arm. "It's not what you think."

I pulled my arm out of his grasp. "Don't touch me." I meant it. I didn't want him anywhere near me.

"I'm going to go," Rachel said, smiling broadly before opening the door. "I'll talk to you soon, Kyle."

Rachel closed the front door and Kyle ran his hand through

his hair roughly as he stared down at me with an incredulous expression. "I can explain that. It is not what you think, baby." He hissed loudly. "Jesus, she is fucking crazy."

I shook my head in disgust, and turned for the stairs. Kyle grabbed my arm again and I pushed him away. "I said don't fucking touch me."

He stepped back, splaying his hands out. "I know the way this must look, but I haven't done anything wrong. Rachel, she must have taken my wallet out of my pocket."

"Why would she have her hands in your pockets?" I spat. "You know what, I don't care anymore. Do whatever the hell you want, Kyle. You always do."

"I didn't fucking touch her, why won't you believe me?" he roared.

I laughed humorlessly. "Why won't I believe you? Is that a serious question?"

"I'm not lying to you, Lee," Kyle growled, following me up the stairs. "Just give me a chance to explain."

Swinging around outside my bedroom door, I poked his chest with my finger. "You are a compulsive liar. Your words mean nothing to me. Do you hear me? You mean nothing to me."

Kyle staggered away, chest heaving. "I'm not bulletproof, Lee. Jesus Christ, I have a heart, too, and right now you're crushing it."

Opening my door, I stepped inside my room, and glanced back at Kyle. My wounded pride and battered heart were what forced the next words to come out of my mouth. "Good. I hope it hurts."

FORTY
KYLE

"YOU REALLY MEAN THAT?" I whispered. "I'm nothing to you?"

Lee nodded stiffly.

I turned around and walked away.

I couldn't look at her. I was too hurt.

The fact that she was so quick to think the worst of me and what she'd said…Well I didn't think I'd get over that any time soon.

She meant it. She never said anything she didn't mean. That fucking bitch had ruined everything again.

She wasn't getting away with it.

My phone rang as I made my way outside to my car.

I pulled my phone out of my pocket and groaned when the number of the New York hotel appeared on the screen.

For just once I wanted a breather from this fucking life.

FORTY-ONE
LEE

"YOU'RE SURE?" I asked the nurse nervously as she prodded my belly with the heart monitor.

"Yes, I'm quite sure. Can you hear that Delia? That's a strong healthy heartbeat," she assured me kindly.

Thank God.

I woke up with twinges in my stomach this morning and came straight to the hospital. The taxi I had paid to drive me here had wiped out my paltry savings, but money had been the least of my worries.

The cramping pain I had experienced was all too familiar to me and I wasn't taking any more risks.

Not with this baby.

"Everything is fine? You're absolutely sure?" I couldn't help but ask. I needed reassurance. I was terrified. I wanted my baby so desperately.

"Honey," the nurse said in a soft voice. "Are you feeling okay? Have you been under any excess strain recently?"

"A little," I muttered, Rachel's name coming to mind.

Checking my blood pressure, the nurse clicked her tongue and frowned. "I'll be back in just a moment," she muttered. "Stay lying down and try to relax."

———

Twenty minutes later, the door of the examination room swung inwards and my mouth dropped open. "What are you doing here?" I asked, scrambling off the bed, adjusting my shirt.

Kyle's eye locked on me and he darted over to where I was standing. "Jesus, baby," he breathed, pulling me into his arms. His voice was laced with concern as he kissed the top of my head. "I got a call from the hospital, saying you were here. What happened? Are you okay?"

I was baffled. Absolutely stunned… I couldn't move a muscle with the shock of him being here.

"I'm fine," I muttered, patting him on the back awkwardly. "I had some pain when I woke up, so I came in to get it checked out." Even my voice sounded confused as I comforted Kyle, whose powerful body was trembling against mine.

"I'm sorry about Rachel. I'm sorry, baby."

I dropped my hand from his back and pushed him away. "I don't want to talk about her. Ever. Don't bring her up in conversation with me ever again."

"Ah, Mr. Carter, thank you for coming so quickly," the nurse who had been treating me earlier said. "I have some concerns about Delia and checked her file. You're signified as her next of kin and the baby's father, is that correct?"

Kyle straightened, and nodded. "Yes, that's right," he confirmed, masking his earlier emotion. "Why, what's wrong with her? Is it the baby?"

I could do nothing but gape at both the nurse and Kyle. Since when was Kyle signified as my next of kin?

I wanted to see those damn files.

"The baby is fine," the nurse reassured him. "It's Delia who I am concerned about."

"Me?" I asked in alarm.

What the hell was going on?

FORTY-TWO
KYLE

"I CALLED you because I'm concerned for Delia. Her blood pressure levels are rather high, not dangerously, but enough for me to be concerned about the level of anxiety and stress she's under."

My heart dropped and my guilt overrode me as the nurse continued.

"As you already know, Delia is only nineteen and has had a traumatic pregnancy. At thirty-six weeks gestation, I can't stress to you enough the importance of a calm and stress-free environment. You may not be aware, but Preeclampsia is a common, but in many cases fatal, medical issue during late pregnancy, in particular to girls as young as Delia."

"But I'm fine though, right?" Lee asked calmly–too calmly– as she picked up her purse from a chair. "I'm fine and so is the baby?"

The nurse nodded slowly. "Your blood pressure is a little high, but yes, you and the baby are well."

"Well then," Lee muttered, moving to the door. "If that's all, I would like to go home."

———

I followed her out of the hospital expecting to have to chase her down the street.

She surprised me by walking silently to my car.

"I don't have enough money to get home and I'm tired," she said quietly.

My heart fucking fell.

Jesus.

I unlocked the car and we climbed in, driving in silence until we reached the house.

"Lee," I sighed, turning off the engine.

"Don't," she warned, climbing out.

I got out and walked ahead of her to open the door.

"Do you hate me?" I asked as she stormed into the kitchen. "Did you mean what you said?"

Lee swung around, facing me. Her mouth was hanging open a little. "My feelings for you haven't changed, Kyle. Don't confuse hurt with hate."

"You still love me?"

Lee shuddered and looked me straight in the eye. "Yes, I still love you, Kyle. And apparently that won't change no matter how many times you betray me, or shatter my trust."

The door opened inwards and Derek hurried inside, closing it and sliding the deadbolt.

"Kyle, where the hell have you been?" he panted out of breath, face flushed, concern etched across his features.

"What's wrong?" Lee demanded, moving towards Derek. "Derek, what's the matter? Is it Cam? Is she okay?"

Derek's eyes slipped from her to me. "I need to talk to you, in private."

———

"What the hell is wrong with you?" I asked, closing the kitchen door on us. "That was really fucking rude, dude."

Derek paced the floor, his movements frantic. "Believe me, Kyle, you *do not* want Lee to hear this."

Okay, now I was getting worried. "Jesus, just tell me already. You're freaking me out."

Derek stopped moving, shrugged off his coat, and I froze.

His white t-shirt was covered in blood.

"Fuck," I hissed, charging towards him. "What the hell happened to you, man?"

Tearing his shirt off, he tossed it in the trash. "I don't know what happened, dude," he whispered, trembling. Moving to the sink, he turned on the faucet and grabbed a bar of soap. "One minute everything was fine and the next he just started pissing blood." Scrubbing his hands, his body shook. "I tried, Kyle. I fucking tried to save him, but the blood…there was so much fucking blood. He went down so quickly."

I stood, frozen to the spot and confused as fuck. "Derek, who are you talking about?"

Tossing the soap in the trash, he grabbed a towel. "I got him in the car, Kyle. I took him to the vet, but it was…too late."

My mouth dropped open.

"Bruno?" I asked, breathless. "Bruno died?"

Oh Jesus, no…

Derek threw the towel on the floor and ran his hand over his shaved head. "He didn't just die, Kyle." Shaking his head, he rubbed his jaw. "He was fucking poisoned."

The kitchen door blew in and Lee stood in front of us, tears streaming down her face. "Poisoned?" she cried. "Who would poison my dog?"

She sank to the floor, and I rushed to her side. "Baby, are you okay?"

"No," she sobbed, curling her face into my shirt.

"I'll tell you who would poison him," Cam hissed, storming into the kitchen, red eyed and raging. "Your crazy bitch of an ex."

"Rachel?" I asked, shaking my head. "No, she wouldn't do that."

"She would," Cam countered. "And she did. She was here this morning. I caught her snooping around in the kitchen. Bruno was fine and after I kicked her out he…" Cam stopped, her voice cracking with emotion.

"Oh my god," Lee wailed. "Of course."

"Hang on guys," I said trying to be rational about this fucked up situation. I stood up and paced the floor. "Maybe he ate some-thing…soap, or washing detergent or something?"

"It was no accident, Kyle," Cam snapped as she knelt beside Lee and pulled her into her arms. "Stop defending her. She did it. And I've called her ass on it."

"What do you mean?" I asked warily, finding it fucking unbe-lievably hard to believe that anyone, including Rachel would poison a dog.

"I called the cops on her crazy ass," she snapped. "Something you should have done a long time ago."

"You okay Lee?" Derek asked, hurrying across the kitchen. I swung around to look at her.

My heart fucking broke at the sight.

She was huddled into Cam's side, shaking and crying uncontrollably.

"Lee," I whispered, rushing towards her.

"Don't," she screamed, staggering to her feet. "This is all your fault. You are the one who brought her into our lives and look what's happened."

"Come on, babe," Cam crooned, wrapping an arm around Lee as they walked out of the kitchen.

I couldn't fucking breathe.

Did she do it?

Was Rachel capable of such a fucking thing?

I didn't know.

I really didn't.

FORTY-THREE
LEE

WE SAID our goodbyes to Bruno on a Sunday morning in April, scattering his ashes in Chautauqua Park as the watery sun shone down on us.

Some people might think it was a ridiculous gesture, but that just showed what they knew.

Bruno had been my best friend and I'd loved him and would miss him always.

He'd protected me from a rapist, kept me company when I was a lonely, scared little girl. He had given me almost thirteen years of unconditional love and loyalty.

There weren't many human relationships you could say that about.

All three of my roommates came to the park to silently say farewell and pay their respects.

None of us spoke.

I stood with Cam,

Derek stood with Kyle.

The cops hadn't charged Rachel because of lack of evidence.

But I knew she did it.

I knew.

———

"You're moving out?" I gasped as I watched from the doorway as Cam piled her clothes and possessions into bags.

"Yeah," she said, sighing. "It's time for me to go, Lee," she said in a shaky voice. "I'm graduating next week and since the breakup I don't...I can't. I just can't, you know?"

Sadly, I did know.

I completely understood what she meant and how she felt.

Cam and Derek hadn't spoken since their breakup, not a word.

He was completely torn up about it.

They tolerated being in the same room as each other, but after a month of tension and unhappiness I could understand why Cam couldn't stay here. "Where will you go?" I asked quietly. "Have you somewhere to go?"

"I have a friend who will put me up for a while," she replied.

"I'm going to miss you, Cam," I muttered.

Cam stopped packing and came towards me. Wrapping me in a massive hug, she squeezed me tightly. "I love you," she whispered. "And I am so terribly sorry for how I have treated you these past few months. I've been a terrible friend to you, but I promise from now on I'll have your back."

"You've always had my back, Cam," I replied, squeezing her hard.

"Will you be okay here, with him?"

I nodded slowly. "I hope so."

"He loves you," she whispered.

I sighed. "He thinks he does."

FORTY-FOUR
LEE

I WALKED AROUND AIMLESSLY for half the day trying to rid myself of the strange swell of guilt, loneliness and neediness inside of my heart since Bruno's memorial.

I found myself sitting on a bench in the campus of C.U watching Kyle as he strolled across the quad, alone and with a deep frown creasing his forehead.

Even in my depressed state, I was aware of his beauty. He made casual look mouthwateringly sexy. His blue over-washed jeans hung low on his hips and his long-sleeved black t-shirt clung to him, pressing against every sculpted muscle on his stomach. When his eyes found me, his frown disappeared, replaced by a nervous smile.

He prowled towards me and I remained perched on the bench, not trusting my legs to be steady enough for walking. Kyle claimed the space between us in a few brisk strides. "Hey princess," he said quietly. Kissing my cheek, he dropped his bag on the bench and sat.

"Hey," I mumbled awkwardly. We hadn't spoken since the day we'd found out about Bruno and I wasn't sure what to say now. Maybe I was a glutton for heartbreak, but I needed to speak to him. I needed to find a common ground. My due date was in three weeks and I was terrified.

I needed…him.

"So, what do I owe the pleasure?" Kyle was smiling. His dimple widened in his cheek.

I shook my head to clear my thoughts. "I was hoping we could take a walk?" I asked, returning his smile with a small one of my own.

"Sure," he said. Standing, he offered me his hand. I took it. We walked for a few minutes before he spoke. "How has your day been?"

"Okay," I said quietly, strolling across the quad, trying to calm my soaring heart rate, as the feel of Kyle's hand covering mine thrilled me. "Kyle, I need to talk to you."

Kyle tightened his hold on my hand. "I thought we were talking."

"You know that's not what I mean."

Kyle sighed, and pulled me closer to him. "Can we pretend?" he whispered as his hand slipped from mine only to find my waist and squeeze me tighter. "Just for a little while, can we pretend that the past two weeks haven't happened and we're deliriously happy? That you love me and I love you. And we are just two human beings, carefree and desperately in love with one another?"

"Kyle," I choked out, overwhelmed by his words.

His eyes searched mine, almost pleadingly. "Please, baby, just for a little while?" His arms came around my waist, holding me close to his body.

Against my better judgment I nodded and stepped closer.

Kyle smiled in relief. Taking my hands, he placed them around his neck. My heart thrashed against my ribs as Kyle tucked my hair behind my ears, trailing his fingertips over my cheekbone, before cupping my cheek.

"You burn me," he whispered. "I close my eyes, you're there. I open them, you're everywhere. Surrounding me. Possessing me. I scorch for you. I breathe for you. I'm drowning so deep in you that I never want to come up for air."

"Kyle, I…"

"I can't cope with the thought of losing you…I can't, baby. It makes my chest squeeze so fucking tight, I can't breathe." Kissing my neck, my jaw, my cheek, he whispered, "Let me back in. Let me love you and I will, forever."

I was drowning in his words, suffocating in the ecstasy of his presence. "I love you," I breathed as I claimed his mouth. "I love you so much," I said against his lips before his tongue slipped inside. "I've missed you so much."

My tears soaked both our cheeks as we clung to each other. "Don't leave me again," he murmured against my lips. "I won't survive you twice."

I shook my head. "I won't. I'm yours." My hands tangled in his hair as he melded my body to his. "You own me."

This was the most exposing, intimate tender moment Kyle and I had ever shared as we claimed one another, possessed each other, reveled in our insecurities and soared.

I wasn't playing pretend anymore.

I meant every word.

"Get your hands off him, you whore. I know what you're doing, trying to pass that the kid off as his when everyone knows you've been fucking his brother."

My blood ran cold.

Panting, I tore my mouth away from Kyle's and glared at the evil bitch-troll who was standing a couple of feet away from us.

I was about to respond, but Kyle beat me to it. "Rachel," Kyle sighed, pulling me close to his chest as if to shield me from his ex-girlfriend. "For the love of god, can you please just leave us alone?"

"I'm not giving up on you," Rachel shot back, eyes glued on Kyle. "I love you, she doesn't. She doesn't love you like I do. No one does. Just me. Just me. I do. I do, Kyle. It's me, just me." Rachel launched herself at Kyle, shoving me away from him. "Please," she cried tugging at his arm, running her hands all over him. "Take me back. Take me back or I'll die. I will die if you don't forgive me."

I staggered away, gaping in horror and shock. "Kyle," I whispered.

He didn't hear me.

His focus was completely on Rachel who was clinging to him like a baby monkey and raving like a lunatic. "Me, me, me, not her."

"Kyle," I shouted louder.

Nothing.

I couldn't look at this for one more second.

This was everything I'd been afraid would happen.

My worst nightmare was coming true.

Unable to stomach the sight of Kyle comforting Rachel, I turned around and rushed away on shaken legs.

FORTY-FIVE
KYLE

"I NEED AN AMBULANCE, C.U CAMPUS," I demanded before hanging up and slipping my phone into my pocket.

"I'm sorry," Rachel cried pitifully. Dropping to her knees, she hugged my leg. "I love you. That's why I did it. She doesn't love you. She is a bad person. She wants to take you away from me. But she won't. You won't let that happen, will you?"

Rachel's body shook violently and I had no idea of what to do.

Going against every instinct in my body, I stroked Rachel's hair. "Shh, it's okay," I soothed. "You'll be okay. I'm gonna get you some help. Real soon."

I hoped the ambulance would hurry the fuck up. Or campus security, where the hell were those guys when you needed them?

There was a crowd gathering around us and even though I couldn't stand Rachel, I didn't want this for her.

She was sick, not a fucking spectacle.

"What the fuck are you looking at?" I snarled, which caused a few bodies to scamper. Tugging off my t-shirt, I slipped it over Rachel's head and then put her arms through the sleeves.

"Is she gone?" Rachel howled, shaking her head viciously. "She has to go. She has to leave. She has to disappear."

"She's gone," I soothed, crouching down beside her.

I couldn't blame Lee for running off.

I'd deal with her later.

I couldn't think about her right now…

I heard the sound of a siren blaring moments before an ambulance pulled up next to us.

Rachel scrambled into my lap, clinging to me. "They want to keep us apart, but they can't. Nothing can keep us apart."

I kept my arm around her shoulder and my eyes on the paramedic rushing towards us. "Shh," I whispered, praying to god they'd hurry the hell up.

"Come on sweetheart," one of the paramedic's said, wrapping a brown blanket around Rachel's shoulders.

"Tell them Kyle," she begged. "Tell them we belong together."

"We belong together," I said in a coaxing voice as I peeled her arms away from me and pushed her into the arms of the medic.

They bundled Rachel into the ambulance and I staggered away, unable to watch or listen to the feral screams coming from her throat.

———

"Open the door, Lee," I asked for the fifth time in a matter of minutes.

Banging louder, I tried the door handle even though I knew it was locked. "Lee please, open this door."

Leaning against her bedroom door, I allowed myself to sink to the floor.

"I'm sorry," I whispered.

FORTY-SIX
LEE

MIKE AND CAM?

I couldn't believe it.

I didn't believe it.

I had come straight to Mike's apartment from the CU campus and I couldn't freaking believe what my eyes were seeing.

"What the hell is going on?" I demanded as I stood in the doorway of Mike's apartment.

Cam stood inside the door, wrapped in a towel.

Mike stood behind her, clad in a pair of boxer shorts.

I really didn't know why I was asking that question.

It was obvious from their guilty faces, and near naked bodies, exactly what was going on…which stemmed my next question. "Let me rephrase my question to: how long has this been going on?"

Cam shuddered. Tears filled her eyes. "Oh, Lee…"

"How long?" I demanded. "Is this a new thing, or…" My words trailed off as my brain put the pieces together. "Oh my god," I gasped in disgust, realization dawning on me. "That's why you were so horrible to me for being friends with Mike," I said, disgusted. "You were jealous."

"Lee," Mike said, but I waved a hand at him.

"Tell me one thing," I asked Cam. "How many months have you been cheating on Derek and lying to all of us?"

"It wasn't like that," Mike added defensively. "We're in love. We love each other Lee…"

"How long Camryn?" I urged.

"Since January," she whispered, lowering her eyes. "It just happened. One night...after visiting you, we went to a bar, we had too much to drink...and then things just happened. I didn't mean to hurt anyone, especially Derek. But I fell in love with him and I can't change the way I feel..."

"Well," I said stiffly. "I guess I know one thing." I glared at Mike as I spoke. "Kyle was dead right about you."

———

Kyle was leaning against my bedroom door when I got home.

"Baby," he whispered standing up.

"Don't," I warned.

Stepping around him, I walked inside and slammed my door. I started pulling my clothes out of my wardrobe quickly and packing them in my duffel bag.

When I first escaped my life in Louisiana, I didn't think there could be any reason or force on this earth that would send me home to my daddy.

I obviously hadn't added Kyle Carter into that equation.

My door flew open, and Kyle stormed in. I ignored him and continued packing.

I was so done.

I couldn't take it anymore. I couldn't. I'd had enough of Rachel. I'd had enough of it all.

"What are you doing?" he asked, reaching out to touch me.

I was having none of it. "Don't touch me."

He balled his fists, his body shuddered. "Why are you doing this to me? You know I love you."

"Just not enough," I sneered, grabbing my underwear out of a drawer and tossing it in a bag. "Not enough to walk away from her." She was the crux of all our problems. Rachel would always find a way to get in between us.

He lowered his head. "You don't get it, baby, Rachel is sick. She is having some kind of a breakdown."

"Oh, I get it, Kyle," I screamed. "I get that you have an irrational need to protect that girl. Maybe it's because you think you owe her, but I can clearly see it's because you love her. You're so consumed in her."

"What the fuck are you talking about?" he demanded, grabbing my arms, forcing me to look at him. "I love you, you idiot. I'm in love with YOU."

"I don't want to see you again," I sobbed, delirious with emotional grief. "I am better off without all of you, than just having a piece of you. I do not want to be anybody's second best. I'd rather do this alone."

He gripped my arm. "Lee, you don't mean that."

I pulled away from him. "No Kyle, I really think I do. I cannot live like this anymore." I couldn't live with the lies or the constant worrying.

"So, what are you saying?" he demanded, his voice cracking. "You don't love me anymore? You're going to let Rachel break us apart again?"

"I'm saying that I am going home."

Kyle looked at me confused. "What are you talking about? You live here."

"I'm going home, Kyle, to Louisiana. I'm going home to my daddy."

"Is that some kind of joke?" he demanded, eyes locked on mine. "Is that some kind of sick, fucking joke?"

I shook my head as Kyle stared at me, seemingly frozen. Finally, he moved, shaking his head. "No you're fucking not."

"Oh yes I am. Now leave me alone."

"There is no fucking way you are going back there so he can use you as a punching bag," he snarled, unzipping my bags and tipping my clothes out on the floor.

"You can't stop me," I screamed as I rushed out of the room.

Screw my clothes. I was getting the hell out of here.

I bounded down the stairs and reached the front door when he pulled me back hard. "You're not taking my kid away from me. You're not taking you away from me. Don't even think about it. It's not happening."

"Well, I'm going," I growled, opening the door. "And considering our baby is still growing inside of me, I most definitely *am* taking him with me."

He pulled me harder. "Lee, I'm warning you…"

"Don't you dare threaten me Kyle Carter. You have no right. Go find your crazy bitch of a girlfriend. I'm going." I pulled from his grasp and ran.

He shouted at me as he chased me down the street. "Lee, Get your ass back here."

"Let me go," I screamed, when he caught up with me and grabbed me from behind.

Kyle wrapped his arms around me and held my back to his front. "No. I love you too much to let you go. You need to calm down. I'm fucking innocent. The only thing I'm guilty of is showing compassion to a sick woman, phoning an ambulance for her and waiting for it to arrive. That's it."

"She killed Bruno...Your wallet...Uh, I don't want to go through this anymore," I screamed. "I don't want this life with you."

I heard him gasp, and he released me.

"Take it," I heard him cry and I turned around. Kyle was on his knees in front of me, tears flooding down his face as he dropped his shirt at my feet. "Take everything I have," he cried as he emptied his pockets. "That's what will happen to me if you leave me, you'll take away everything."

"Kyle," I choked. "Please stop."

"Take it, Lee," he shouted before a fit of crying enveloped him. "I don't want it without you," he cried, his chest heaving. "You are all I have." He covered his face with his hands as he cried. His body was shaking, every piece of him trembled. "I haven't done anything. I didn't touch her."

I lost all resolve and dropped to my knees in front of him as the truth of his words blew through me with the force of a hurricane. I was wrong.

I'd been so terribly wrong...

"I believe you," I sobbed, scrambling on my knees towards him. "Kyle, please, I'm sorry," I whispered as I cradled his head to my chest.

"I can't do this anymore, Lee," he whispered. "I won't." Lifting his head, he rested his forehead against mine. "This is it." He shuddered as tears poured down his cheeks. "You need to trust that I will never hurt you again. You need to have faith in us. I can't keep going through this with you."

"I do," I cried. "I will. I'm sorry."

FORTY-SEVEN
KYLE

"I DON'T THINK this is a good idea," I muttered to my two idiotic fucking friends and my hot idiotic girlfriend.

They were all sitting in my kitchen, trying to plot a road trip.

I had no fucking clue how Derek was sitting so calmly.

Cam was fucking Mike–had been for months. Lee had told me the other night when we had both calmed down enough to speak.

Thank god she'd believed me. I knew Lee had trust issues, and god knows, I'd put them there, but I'd been all but fucking crushed when she said she was leaving me.

Seriously, I'd never felt so afraid and helpless in my life.

Thankfully, we were back on track and moving on from Rachel.

Yep, there would be no more drama.

Drama could kiss my ass.

But the whole Cam, Mike, Derek love triangle? Well, I was disgusted to say the least.

But I was more pissed with Mike than Cam.

He was a sly fucker, always had been, and I'd thought better of Cam than to fall in with the likes of him.

But Lee said, that Cam told her that she was in love with him...But hey, fuck it, as long as he wasn't sniffing around Lee I was happy.

Lee was upset with Cam over the lying, but they made up like they always did.

However, Lee wasn't speaking to Mike over her loyalty to Derek, which made me fucking delighted.

Rachel was tucked away in some facility getting treatment and Mike was out of the picture.

I could finally breathe again...

"Come on Kyle," Lee urged, pulling herself out of her chair and waddling over to me. Yeah, she waddled now and it was so fucking sexy. "Derek said that you guys had planned to take a road trip after graduation. That you've had it planned since freshman year."

That was true. Cam, Derek, and I had always said we'd get the fuck out of this place and hit the road for a few days, but given the circumstances, I thought it was a stupid as hell idea.

"Well," Lee rambled. "You three graduated last week. I think we should celebrate."

"There are two very big problems with this trip, princess," I said agitated, but trying to rein it in. "The first being the fact that those two," I stopped to point at Cam and Derek, who were keeping a respective berth between each other. "Are barely speaking to each other. And the second and most important problem is that you have less than two weeks until your due date."

"Pssh," Lee dismissed. "Cam and Derek want to go, don't you guys?"

They both nodded half-heartedly, obviously agreeing to this for fear of upsetting the pregnant woman.

"Please Kyle," she begged. "Please?"

I groaned. "Fine, pack your shit, we can go."

I needed to grow a pair of fucking balls.

FORTY-EIGHT
LEE

THE CRAMPING in my stomach was definitely contractions.

I was trying to keep calm and not worry the others about the fact that I thought I could be going into labor in a car, in the back ass of nowhere.

Kyle was sitting in the driver's seat of his Mercedes, humming along to the radio and tapping his fingers against the wheel as the Merc ate up the miles on this back road to nowhere. Cam and Derek were dozing in the back and I was about to scream my head off in pain.

I was so uncomfortable that sitting in one spot became impossible.

I twisted in my seat, leaning back before turning sideways to see if that helped.

It didn't.

The tightening started again and I checked the clock on the dashboard.

The contractions were coming quickly now. Two minutes apart.

"Kyle?" I muttered through clenched teeth as I tried to concentrate on breathing slow and deep. When he didn't answer, I snapped, "Kyle. Will you shut the hell up for a sec?"

"Hmm? You don't like my singing princess?" Kyle asked, grinning at me. His smile slipped the minute our eyes met, changing into a worried frown. "Jesus, you're sweating like crazy," he muttered, pressing a button on his door that wound my window down. "Does that help?"

Even though hot sticky air hit me in the face like an oven door opening, it was a relief from the stuffiness inside of the car.

It was so goddamn hot and all I wanted to do was strip my sundress off.

I could feel sweat trickling from my brow as my stomach hardened to a rock.

I grunted in relief as the pain passed and sagged back in my seat.

I wasn't due for another two weeks, so I wasn't entirely sure how this would pan out.

I'd read so many articles in the past few months about first time labor. It was usually long and slow.

The tightening pains had started at home, during breakfast this morning, but I'd been so excited about going on this road trip that I'd just put it down to the usual twinges, or maybe some Braxton hicks. I also hadn't wanted to give Kyle the satisfaction of being right again.

Since then, the pains had gone from mild to crippling and I was struggling to stay quiet and not squirm.

"Yeah, it's good. It helps with the pains," I sighed, wiping the beads of sweat from my brow. Kyle jerked in his seat, turning his head to look at me. "Watch the road," I growled as another sharp swell of pain attacked my body.

I panted, tugging on the hem of my dress so tightly I felt the fabric rip beneath my fingers.

The pain smothered me and I moaned, spreading my legs apart in a bid to relieve myself from the burning pressure in my vagina. The pain in my back was so bad I thought I would die. "Oh shit, they're getting worse," I hissed, grinding my teeth together.

"Worse?" Kyle croaked in a high pitched tone. Veering the car off towards the side of the road, he killed the engine and turned to me with an anxious expression. "Do you think you're in labor, baby?"

I nodded as another stab of pain washed over me. I groaned and tried to hold my breath, but that just made it worse.

"Fuck," he hissed as he unclipped his belt and pulled his phone from his pocket. "Dammit, there's no signal on this motherfucking thing," he roared, throwing the phone at the dashboard violently. The phone shattered into pieces, the battery falling out and landing under his feet.

Oh great, Kyle, really freaking smart.

"Stop shouting at me, asshat," I yelled, clawing at my stomach as the rawest form of agony I'd ever felt washed over me.

Holy shit, I was going to die.

I was going to die on the side of the road, cursing like a sailor, while my boyfriend had a freaking panic attack.

"I'm not shouting, baby. It's okay. It's totally fine," he coaxed, pulling my damp hair back from my face. "We're what, an hour away from the city, max? That gives us plenty of time I'm sure. We'll keep driving until we can get a signal or a hospital." Muttering to himself, Kyle started the engine, tearing off with a speed that on any other day I would have complained about.

But now all I wanted was a doctor, a clean bed and a truck load of drugs.

FORTY-NINE
KYLE

I WATCHED Lee pour the entire contents of a bottle of water over her face. Her face was so red that I wasn't sure what she needed to be treated for first; labor or dehydration.

"Don't waste this one, baby. Drink it up," I ordered, passing her another bottle of water.

I'd been driving an hour since she told me was in labor and fuck if I knew where I was.

I must have taken the wrong turn off somewhere back along the interstate because the only thing around us now was wide grassy fields.

"Don't tell me what to do, you son of a bitch," she growled as she panted breathlessly. "This is your entire freaking fault."

I knew that and right now I was a little afraid of her temper. She was scaring the shit of me if I was being honest. "I'm sorry, baby. I'm just trying to help you. You're burning up." I patted her knee, which turned out to be a bad move on my part.

Lee grabbed my hand, squeezing it with a strength she'd never had before. Her fingernails dug into my palm. "Of course I'm burning up. There's a human being trying to crawl its way out of my VAGINA, Kyle Carter, and you put him there."

I tried to pull my hand back, but she held onto it, with a vice-like grip.

Holy fuck.

I concentrated on the road ahead as I silently practiced my

own breathing techniques to cope with the pain she was inflicting on me.

"Shut the hell up, guys. I'm trying to nap here," Derek grumbled from the back seat, which was a dangerous move for him.

Lee swung around faster than I'd seen her move in months and lunged for his shirt. Dragging him into the space between our two seats, she glared at him. "Don't you dare fuck with me, Derek Porter."

I slipped my hand away quickly while her focus was elsewhere.

Jesus Christ, I couldn't feel my fingers.

Lee whimpered and released Derek's shirt as she began to pant again. "It hurts, Kyle. It really hurts," she cried, clutching her bump with one hand and holding her other hand up for me.

I braced myself for the pain and held her hand through another contraction. They were coming so fast now, I'd lost track of the time in between them.

"Dude, is she having the kid now?" Derek shouted, shaking Cam awake. "Where the hell are we?" he continued, swinging his head around to look out the car window. "Oh great, we're lost. Nice one, Kyle. We're fucking miles away from civilization."

"Not helping, dude," I growled, trying to concentrate on driving with one hand. It should have been easy, but Lee was yanking on my hand so hard I was struggling to keep the car straight. Derek was right though. We were lost. "Check your phone, Derek, see if you have a signal."

"Shit man," Derek muttered from behind me. "I must have forgotten it at home."

Oh, that was just fucking marvelous.

I went to pass him mine, but the battery was under my feet and the fucking screen was cracked.

Goddammit.

Cam, who was now wide awake, leaned forward and started rubbing Lee's shoulders. "It's okay, Lee, you're doing great, babe. How far apart are the contractions?"

"I don't know any more," Lee sobbed. "Less than a minute, I think."

Lee grunted again and hissed. "Oh god," she cried, squeezing my hand tighter.

"What?" we all shouted at the same time.

I glanced over at her red, puffy face. She was biting on her lip, her brows furrowed. "I think my water just broke. That or I've just peed my pants," she panted.

I glanced down at her crotch, grateful for the empty road. If it was busy, I'd have crashed into something by now. Lee's dress and the seat were drenched in a pool of clear fluid.

Jesus fucking Christ.

This was really happening, right here on a country road, in the middle of no man's land.

I'm gonna have to deliver my own kid.

The thought fucking terrified me, but the images flashing in my head were much worse.

We shouldn't have gone this far out of Boulder, not with only two weeks to her due date.

I knew it was a bad idea.

Shit, I should have put my foot down.

I'd been so careful and now here we were. Lee was about to give birth and all she had instead of a medical team was me, Cam and fucking Derek.

"Kyle, pull over the car," Cam instructed in a quiet, but assertive tone.

I pulled over to the side of the road, praying to god that Cam had some clue about delivering babies.

I mean, she was a girl. She had to know more about this stuff than me.

Jumping out of the car, Cam started barking orders. "Kyle, help Lee into the back of the car and make her comfortable. Derek, go and get some towels from my case in the trunk. Oh, and I saw a first aid kit strapped under Kyle's seat earlier, get that as well. We're gonna need scissors."

Scissors?

Following Cam's orders, Derek jumped out of the car and started rooting around in the trunk for towels.

I walked around to Lee's door and crouched down in front of her. "I'm scared, Kyle," she confessed, her gray eyes wide in her face.

I stroked her cheeks, pushed her damp curls back off her face. "There's nothing to be scared of, princess. I won't let anything bad happen to you, I swear."

She nodded, and I eased her out of the seat. "Oh fuck," she

groaned when I got her standing. She bent forward, leaning into my body. "Kyle, I need to...I need to poo."

I froze.

Fucking stunned to silence.

I didn't know whether to laugh or fucking cry.

Was this normal?

"Okay, okay, that's no problem," I said, trying to stay calm. I was freaking the fuck out inside. I'd read something about that in an article in one of those pregnancy magazines at the hospital.

It meant she was ready to push.

"She's bearing down," Cam shouted from somewhere close by, confirming my worst nightmares.

I couldn't see where Cam was.

I couldn't see anything.

I guessed this was what blind panic felt like.

"Get her in the backseat now, Kyle."

Lee whimpered again, clutching at her stomach. I pulled her tighter to my side, stroking her back.

"Come on, sweetheart," Derek crooned, coming over to the other side of Lee. "Dude, let's get her in the fucking car before the kid pops out," he hissed over Lee's head.

I nodded and tried to move her towards the back seat, but Lee wouldn't budge. "Kyle, I'm serious. I really need to go to the toilet," she groaned, staring up at me.

I shook my head at a complete loss. There wasn't a fucking signpost around for miles let alone a bathroom.

I scanned the area, my eyes focusing on a tree.

I was just about to take Lee over there when Cam barged forward. "Oh for god's sake, you guys are pathetic," Cam growled. "She needs to push, not poop and I'd prefer her to do it in the damn car than the side of a road." Coming up to Lee's front she grabbed her arms and pulled her away from me and Derek and guided her towards the car.

Lee crawled onto the back seat trembling. Her whole body was shaking violently and the noises coming from her mouth were fucking terrifying. "Kyle," she cried out.

I could hear the fear in her voice and rushed to her. "I'm here, baby, I'm right here," I said. "Lee, I need you to lie down on your back for me. Can you do that, baby?" She nodded, whimpering as she slowly turned herself around to lie down. "Good, baby, that's perfect. You're doing so damn well," I praised as I crouched at the car door.

"Someone needs to go check for a signal, so we can get some help," Cam said from behind me.

I shook my head.

I wasn't moving more than an inch away from Lee.

"We need to call an ambulance," she repeated.

"Kyle, please don't leave me," Lee begged, clutching at my shirt.

I held her hand tightly and leaned inside the car, kissing her forehead. "I'm not going anywhere," I vowed. "Cam, you go. I got this," I said, finally finding my balls again.

This was my girl lying on the seat and my baby trying to get out.

Mine.

I could do this.

Hell yeah, I could get my baby out if I had to.

Lee smiled at me for a brief moment before her face twisted in pain.

"Okay, I'll be as fast as I can," Cam said as she jogged up the road quickly with her phone held out in front of her.

"Stay with them, Derek. Kyle needs your help more than I do," she said to a dismayed Derek.

Lee cried out, drawing my attention back to her. "I think I need to push," she hissed, scrambling backwards, trying to spread her legs wider.

Oh, holy fuck.

Derek, who'd come back to the car, said the stupidest fucking thing I'd ever heard in that moment.

"Can you like, hold it in?" he asked. "Just until Cam gets back or preferably until we get an ambulance…for me…."

"Shut your face, dipshit. If you can't deal with it, then fuck off," I grumbled as I leaned into the car and hiked her dress up to her waist. "Turn around," I told Derek as I tugged the edges of her panties, tearing them off.

Settling in-between Lee's legs, I braced myself for the unknown, while I coaxed and praised her. "That's it, baby, you're doing amazing. I'm so proud of you." I rubbed her thigh. "You can push, baby, if you feel the urge, you go with it."

My calm voice betrayed my true feelings. "Derek, go to the

other door and rub her back," I instructed, not wanting that douche anywhere near Lee's crotch.

"Dude, I'm gonna be paying for years' worth of therapy after this," he muttered, moving away. He opened the door behind Lee's back, and slid in behind her. "What do I do?" he asked in a choked voice.

"Ahhh, Jesus Christ, it burns," Lee screamed as she threw her hand back to grip Derek. I peeked up and held in a chuckle. She had Derek gripped by the ear. He has gone snow white. In any other situation his face would have looked comical, but the seriousness of the situation sobered me.

"It burns," she yelled once more before she leaned forward and started pushing.

"Great, that's great, princess," I encouraged. "Keep going."

I ignored the blood and everything else, focusing only on getting my baby out and easing Lee's pain. She bore down and pushed and this time I could see something. "Good, baby, I can see the head. Keep pushing."

"You can?" she asked breathlessly, panting. I nodded, not having the heart to tell her that the minute she'd stopped pushing it had popped back up.

Her face reddened as she began to push once again and holy shit, I could see it clearly now. "Great job, Lee. Go for it, push hard, baby." I held her legs apart and scrambled to grab some clean towels. "Derek, can you pass me the first aid kit," I ordered.

Lee screamed and the baby's head popped out.

Holy fuck. Sweet Jesus Christ.

A head of dark hair was all I could see.

Hair plastered in clear, bloody jelly gunk.

I would never eat jelly again…

"Oh, that's the most disturbing fucking image I've ever seen," Derek muttered, tossing the first aid kit at my feet. "Is there supposed to be that much blood?" he continued covering his mouth with his hand. "Dude…I can't. You're on your own." With that, I heard him retreat and a few moments later the sound of loud vomiting.

"Ignore him," I said gently, focusing on Lee. "One more big push, princess. One big one and we'll meet our baby."

Lee whimpered, throwing her arm over her face. "I'm so tired,

Kyle," she cried, tears falling down her face. "I can't push anymore."

Oh hell no, she'd gone so far, she'd practically run this whole show by herself. No way was she going to start doubting herself now. Her cries turned into grunts as another contraction rolled through her.

"Do it now, Lee, push him out."

"I can't."

"You can. I know you can. Push this little guy out right this instant, or so help me, I'll go in there and get him myself."

Lee braced herself, pushing down, growling in sheer concentration.

Everything happened so fast after that…

Lee screamed and there was a gush and suddenly, I was holding a small bundle of blood and goo.

The most perfect creature I'd ever seen in my life, with a head of dark curls and the most beautiful blue eyes I'd ever seen.

"We have a daughter," I choked out, blinking back the tears as my eyes roamed over every inch of my daughter.

"Is she okay?" Lee asked anxiously. Her body trembled from the incredible amount of work she'd just done.

"She's perfect, just like her mother."

With trembling hands, I wrapped her in a towel and leaned over to hand her to her momma. "Thank you," I whispered as I carefully placed her on Lee's chest. Leaning down I brushed my lips over Lee's forehead. "You did it baby. You did it. I love you so much."

"We did it. And I love you more," was her reply and Lee's beaming smile was enough to kick start the tears I thought I had stemmed.

I moved away from them both.

I needed a moment to breathe.

I stood outside the car, my body shaking, bawling like a baby.

I didn't even realize Derek was beside me until he wrapped an arm around my shoulders and shook his head in awe. "You two… are incredible. I'm sorry I didn't do more…"

I slapped him on the back. "You did what you could, man. Thank you."

"Kyle, look at this." I crouched down once more fascinated to find Lee nursing our baby. "She latched on," she said, amazed.

"Oh Kyle...I need to push the rest out," Lee whispered suddenly. "And we need to clamp the cord."

I stared at her dumbfounded as reality slowly dawned on me.

It was one thing to deliver a baby.

I had no fucking clue what to do with anything else.

The sound of a siren coming closer was my saving grace.

Thank you Camryn Frey.

FIFTY
LEE

"LEE, baby, the paramedics are here. They're gonna get you all cleaned up and take us to the hospital," I heard Kyle say from behind me as he wrapped his arms around me, but I couldn't turn my face to look at him.

My attention was entirely focused on my baby lying in my arms.

I felt so many emotions in that moment that I thought I might burst.

The unconditional love, the raw, undiluted purity and strength of my feelings for this tiny person in my arms was almost too much to bear.

I loved her so much in that instant and it was effortless and unequivocal.

She was so beautiful, so tiny and perfect, with wisps of dark curls, eyes the color of the ocean just like her daddy.

I knew babies' eyes changed color, but I hoped hers would stay the same.

I didn't want to change a single hair on her head. She was perfect.

Giving birth in the back seat of Kyle's new Mercedes on the side of the road had to top the list of most terrifying experiences of my life.

The fear I'd felt in those moments had been crushing. But Kyle...Kyle had been amazing.

I had been sure, absolutely certain, that something terrible was going to happen to my baby.

Even when I'd heard her cry, I'd been petrified that the overwhelming sense of euphoria flooding through my heart would be snatched away.

"Say cheese." I looked up at Derek just as a bright light flashed in my face. "Perfect, now how about one with a smile, Kyle?" Derek coaxed before blinding us again with another flash.

I was extremely thankful that Kyle had covered me with a blanket now that it was apparently picture time.

"Jesus," Kyle muttered as he nuzzled my neck. "He's worse than a woman."

I couldn't help but laugh.

"I heard that," Derek retorted, snapping away like a mad man.

"You were supposed to. Now stop flashing that damn thing in my daughter's face. You'll blind her before she's an hour old."

I looked down at her alarmed. Her little face was scrunched up in distaste. I discreetly covered her face from Derek's harassing camera.

"Oh my god, Oh my god," Cam cooed from outside the door. Pushing Derek out of her way, Cam leaned over my legs, gazing lovingly at my baby. "She's so perfect," she fussed, stroking her head and cheeks. "And so beautiful," she gushed. "Oh hey, look Kyle, she has your nose. But we won't hold that against you, will we, gorgeous? No, we won't. Cause you're just too pretty. Who's a pretty girl? Yes, you are. I told them that you were a girl... Derek, give me the damn camera, she's opening her eyes."

I leaned further into Kyle's chest as little tremors of aftershocks rippled through me.

"Hey ya'll, I came to deliver a baby, but I see you guys have had all the fun," a female paramedic with a southern twang–I couldn't place–said, interrupting Derek and Cam's photography session. Her smile was so broad and friendly that I couldn't help but return the gesture.

Cam reluctantly moved out of the way for the paramedic.

"So sweetie, it looks like you and your husband have done a great job, so I'm just gonna get you cleaned up then transfer you both to the hospital. My name's Sarah by the way."

I introduced Kyle, and myself but didn't correct the husband's comment and neither did he. Kyle sat behind me patiently, stroking my arm, kissing me repeatedly on the shoulder and the top of my head, whispering words of praise and love.

Sarah proceeded to clamp and cut the cord. She injected me in the thigh before delivering the after-birth and cleaning me up. It saddened me that Kyle hadn't been allowed to cut the cord, but I guessed the circumstances weren't ideal and I was just so glad that my baby was okay.

I then, rather reluctantly, handed my baby over to be checked over. "Wow, she's a stunner, and look at all that hair. I bet you had a lot of heartburn?"

Kyle chuckled against my neck as I nodded at the paramedic.

It definitely wasn't the easiest of pregnancies, but so incredibly worth it.

Every moment; good, bad and heart breaking was worth it to hold her in my arms.

"Wait, where are you taking her?" I was alarmed as I watched Sarah place my baby in the arms of another paramedic.

"Don't worry, sweetie. Larry here is just gonna check your little girl over and get her cleaned up. She'll be back in your arms in a jiffy."

I sat forward, watching every step Larry took away from me, but Kyle pulled me back against his chest. "It's okay princess. They're just doing their job. She's perfectly fine."

I sighed and waited impatiently as Sarah left to get a wheelchair. Kyle helped me into the chair and again onto the gurney. Those small movements left me shattered and I struggled to keep my eyes open.

The last thing I remembered before my eyes closed was Kyle's soothing voice in my ear. "I'll hold her. I'll keep her safe. Sleep, princess."

FIFTY-ONE
KYLE

IT TURNED out we were only a thirty-minute drive from Jefferson Central Hospital and only two hours away from home.

After both Lee and the baby were examined and checked out at Jefferson, the doctor had agreed–it had taken a hell of a lot of pressure–to have them transferred immediately to St. Luke's Hospital in Boulder. I needed Lee around her own doctors that knew her medical history. Lee slept the whole ride back to Boulder and she'd only woken once in the three hours we'd been back, and that was to nurse.

I was sitting in the chair beside Lee's bed, cradling my daughter in my arms when there was a tap on the door.

"Hey," Cam whispered quietly as she stepped inside and walked over to me. From the way she was hovering over me, I knew she was dying for a cuddle, but I wasn't ready to give her up just yet.

I didn't think I ever would be.

"Have you guys picked a name yet?" Cam asked, stroking my sleeping baby.

I shook my head. "No, we haven't had much time to talk. We had a couple of names picked out, but mostly boy names." I stretched out my legs in front of me, and nestled her into the crook of my arm.

"Hope."

I turned around to find Lee awake and smiling at me.

"Hope?" I asked, tossing the name around in my head.

Hope.

"Hope sounds pretty damn perfect to me," I agreed, smiling.

She pulled herself up in the bed, stretching stiffly. "I mean, it's your decision too of course. But Hope just feels kind of fitting considering everything we've been through. Maybe it's silly, but the name's kind of stuck in my head. Of course, we could go with something else if you would prefer?"

I stared at Lee, drowning in the emotion I felt for her. Leaning over, I kissed her softly before looking down at my daughter. "Hey baby girl. Mommy and Daddy finally picked you a name and it's something you represent to us."

"Oh Kyle, please. I can't wait anymore," Cam whined, holding her hands out to hold Hope. Lee chuckled and nodded encouragingly.

"Fine, but sit down so you don't drop her," I said, standing up carefully. Cam glared at me, but sat quickly in the chair I vacated. "Support her head," I instructed, placing Hope into Cam's arms.

"Wow, overprotective much, dad?" Cam muttered under her breath.

Choosing to ignore her, I settled myself down on the bed, pulling Lee into my arms. She sighed happily as I kissed her head.

"Hello baby girl," Cam crooned. "I'm your Aunt Cam. I'm the cool one. Mommy and Daddy are pretty cool, too, but Uncle Derek is a douche. Yes, he is. Oh, we're gonna have so much fun, Hope Bennett."

"Carter," Lee corrected and my heart stilted.

"You're sure?" I croaked.

Lee nodded and leaned over to stroke my cheek. "Absolutely," she replied. "Besides, look at those dimples. Apart from my hair, she is all you, Kyle Carter."

"I hate to admit it, but Lee's right," Cam added, not taking her eyes off Hope. "You're packing some pretty powerful *genes* in your jeans."

FIFTY-TWO
LEE

HOSPITALS WERE BECOMING a habit of mine. But this time it was for all the right reasons.

Hope had just had her six week checkup with the pediatrician who confirmed she was perfect.

I had to practically wrestle the buggy from Kyle this morning, eventually using emotional blackmail in a bid to get him to go to work.

"Do you not trust me with our daughter," I'd asked, pretending to be upset.

Kyle had immediately conceded, apologizing repeatedly.

It was pretty terrible of me, but Kyle was obsessed with being involved. He was like a clucking hen, fussing over me, as well as Hope.

I also wanted to pick up something special for tonight. Dr. Ashcroft had cleared me with a full bill of health, which meant my man was getting some tonight...

The sun was throwing out some serious heat as I walked down 11th street, towards the hotel.

I'd fed Hope and settled her before leaving the hospital earlier and was looking forward to a coffee and catching up with Cam. We usually met here, since she and Derek were uncomfortable around each other and I refused to go to Mike's apartment. I loved Cam, and couldn't be too angry with her for her choices, but I still couldn't believe that she was with Mike.

It was so crazy.

Derek was so perfect for her. I didn't understand how Cam could walk away from a man who was so deeply devoted to her.

And Derek.

Oh, poor Derek…

Derek was carrying on with things, joking around as always, but I knew he was hurting. I could see it in those lonely green eyes of his. Cam had wrecked him. I didn't know if he would ever get over the betrayal.

I knew how he felt, except that when Kyle had destroyed me, he'd fought for me and he had kept fighting until he won me back.

It was so much worse for Derek because Cam didn't want him back.

I felt incredibly loyal to Derek. Therefore, I wasn't speaking to Mike. I knew it took two to tango, but what Mike had done, first to Kyle, and then to Derek, in my opinion was downright unforgivable.

I couldn't condone what they had done, so I refused to visit Cam at Mike's apartment where she was living…

Plus, I couldn't wait to show off my gorgeous baby at the hotel.

I gushed to myself as I stared at her sleeping soundly in her forward facing buggy.

She looked incredibly cute in a yellow dotted sundress with a matching headband and white socks and cardigan.

I didn't look too bad either. I was still carrying a little bulge around my middle, and I didn't think my hips would ever go back to their not so former glory, but I was happy. So freaking happy right now, that even in my khaki capris and black vest I felt completely at ease with my body.

I guess it didn't hurt that Kyle complimented me every chance he got.

That boy was something else.

I was closer each day to asking him to repeat the question.

Not yet.

But someday real soon…

I reached the entrance of the hotel when a hand snagged me back roughly. "I hear congratulations are in order."

My mouth dropped open in surprise. "What the hell do you want?" I snarled, pulling my arm free.

Rachel towered over me, her face contorted with malice.

I thought she was supposed to be in a hospital?

"It's quite simple really," she said coldly. "I want what you stole from me."

Her gaze slipped from me to Hope. "Well, what you and your bastard stole. You couldn't have done it without the runt."

"Fuck you," I ground out, moving in front of Hope's buggy to block her from Rachel's twisted sneer.

"Walk away," she threatened. "Pack up your kid and get the hell out of Kyle's life, or I will bury you both."

I shook my head in disgust. "My god, you really are sick," I whispered. Stepping forward, I measured up to the red head. "You need help, Rachel. Kyle doesn't want you. He never has and he never will. You need to get yourself a really good psychiatrist because the last one obviously didn't work. If you come within a hundred yards of my daughter again, I will have you arrested and your ass tossed in a jail cell."

"He wanted me before. He will again. Maybe he still wants me and it's my face he sees every time he's with you."

"That's funny," I chuckled darkly. "Because that is exactly what Kyle told me he used to do when he was with you; visualize my face." The stunned look on Rachel's face was priceless as I turned on my heel and headed inside to meet Cam.

The tiniest flair of guilt burned in my conscience, but I quickly doused that feeling.

I had nothing to feel guilty about.

That girl had made my life a living hell for almost a year.

She'd poisoned my dog and called my beautiful baby a bastard.

No, screw my conscience. Rachel could go to hell.

FIFTY-THREE
KYLE

"DUDE, how do you fly around the country, run twenty hotels, babysit the kid and still kill it at school? It's not fucking fair," Derek grumbled as he buried his head down on his text book. "I haven't slept in a month."

God, he was so fucking dramatic.

I'd hardly call the summer cooking class he'd roped me into going to school.

Dropping my culinary studies book on Derek's head, I switched Hope's bottle into my other hand, before continuing her feeding.

"Ouch Kyle, what the hell was that for?" Derek accused, sitting up straight.

"Exactly. What the hell? As in what the hell are you bitching and moaning about? You've clearly stated how easy you have it, so just suck it up, dude, and study," I said quietly. "And by the way," I added. "For future reference, it's not called babysitting if the child is yours. I'm her father, Derek, and taking care of my own baby is not called babysitting, it's called parenting."

Derek waved a hand at me. "Dude, you are so fucking touchy. If I hadn't seen Lee pop her out with my own two eyes, I would swear you grew a vagina and gave birth to Hope yourself."

"Don't say the F-word around my daughter," I warned.

Sitting down at the table, I pulled Hope's bottle from her mouth and set it aside.

She immediately started to cry and scrunch up.

"You gotta slow down, baby girl," I soothed. "Shhh. Daddy's got you."

Setting her on my knee, I leaned her against one hand and patted her back with the other.

Hope answered with a loud burp.

"That's my girl," I praised, shaking my leg a little, she let out another loud milky burp.

I grinned like an idiot.

It was incredible how something as small as getting Hope's wind up gave me such satisfaction.

I couldn't help but lean down and kiss her curly hair. She was so adorable with that milky-filled sleepy look.

She yawned widely and began to doze off in my arms.

Tucking her against my chest, I looked up and caught Derek's baffled gaze. "What?" I asked a little defensively.

Derek held up a finger towards me. "Firstly, she's like six weeks old. She doesn't have a clue what 'fuck' means."

"Derek," I warned.

Ignoring me, he held up a second finger. "And secondly, I can't figure out who has you whipped more, Lee or Hope?"

The front door banged loudly and I winced.

Thankfully, Hope was good with noise. She hardly stirred in my arms.

"Hey," Cam said strolling into the kitchen, looking between Derek and me before settling her attention on Hope.

"How did her checkup go?" she asked, making a beeline for my sleeping baby.

"Great, she's perfect" I muttered, standing up quickly and slipping past her to the door.

Derek beat me to the door, slipping out of the room quietly.

Cam couldn't help herself. She woke Hope up for a kiss and a cuddle every time she visited, and Lee and I were left with a very cranky overtired baby. "I'm just about to put her down for the night."

"Fine," Cam huffed. "But you can't hog her forever, Kyle."

"Can't I," I muttered before leaving the room.

―――――

Switching on the baby monitor in Lee's room, I tucked Hope in before pulling out the door, leaving it cracked slightly.

I couldn't keep the grin off my face as I slipped inside the bathroom quietly. The sight of Lee's naked body all soaped up caused my dick to harden so much it was painful.

"Is she okay?" Lee asked, sitting up in the tub, revealing those amazing breasts of hers.

"Fed, changed and sleeping like a baby," I replied, pulling my shirt over my head as I walked over to her.

I watched her watch me.

Her nipples hardened. My cock twitched. I wanted her so bad. Needed to be in her, buried inside her warmth so deep I'd never resurface.

My desire for this tiny woman was limitless.

She sucked me in deeper with every breath she took.

"Is it time I repeated the question?" I asked, crouching next to the tub.

"Not yet," she teased.

"You drive me fucking crazy," I growled, dipping my hand under the water and running it up her thigh.

"Likewise," she sighed, spreading her legs wide for me, signaling the green light I'd been waiting forever for.

"I love you," I whispered, brushing my fingers over the lips of her sex.

I watched her eyes flutter closed; her head fell back against the tub. "I love you more," she breathed as I slipped a finger inside her folds to touch her heat.

Her back arched as I rubbed the pad of my thumb over her clit in a slow rhythmic circle, sliding in and out slowly. I hoped like hell this was okay for her because I was about to combust with need.

Her mouth fell open, a low moan of arousal escaped.

"Marry me," I whispered, pressing my thumb harder against her tender bulb of nerves, slipping another finger inside her pussy. I leaned over and took a hardened nipple into my mouth, teasing the puckered bud with my tongue before rolling it between my teeth.

"Oh god. Yes, don't stop," Lee cried, bucking and clawing at my back as she tried to pull me into the tub with her.

Kneading one of her full breasts with one hand, I used my

mouth on the other as my fingers pumped her hot little pussy. She squirmed under my touch, pressing her hot pussy against the heel of my hand.

She was close, I could feel it. The walls of her core clenched around my fingers as she thrashed her hips wildly.

I stopped moving before she could come and Lee cried out in frustration. "Why'd you stop?" she asked breathlessly.

Leaning back on my heels, I stared into her lustful gray eyes. "Marry me?" I asked again, my voice thick with emotion.

Lee sighed deeply, shaking her head. Her chest was heaving, her arousal clear. "Is this your new plan? Finger fuck me into submission?"

I raised my brows in surprise and smiled. "Dirty words, princess," I teased, leaning forward to place a kiss against the fluttering pulse in her neck. "If I wanted to fuck you into submission, I wouldn't be using my fingers."

FIFTY-FOUR
LEE

I WAS COILED SO tight I thought I'd explode if Kyle didn't touch me.

I brushed my fingers over his cheek. "I like your fingers," I whispered, feeling bold.

Kyle groaned and thrust his tongue into my mouth, tasting me. I knotted my fingers in his hair pulling him closer, teasing his tongue with mine.

It was the truth though. Kyle had serious skills with those hands of his–with every part of him.

He was so virile.

The sheer size of him, his ripped stomach, broad chest and narrow hips, those thick powerful thighs and the heavy length that hung between his legs…

His body was incredible and Kyle knew *exactly* what to do with it.

"You'll like my dick even more when I'm driving it deep inside your hot little pussy," he growled, his lips brushing my jaw, my neck.

I nodded, pulling his mouth back to mine.

It had been a long six weeks. I couldn't wait to be with him again.

I knew I should mention Rachel's little visit today, but I didn't want to upset the apple cart.

And he was distracting me so much I could barely think straight…

"Say yes," he dared with a teasing lilt to his voice.

I shook my head, returning his smile.

"What are you waiting for?" he challenged.

"I have my reasons," I whispered, then leaned forward to kiss him deeply.

"I may have to resort to fucking you into submission after all," he confessed as he stood quickly, taking me effortlessly with him.

"Please do," I mumbled against his lips as I wrapped my legs around his waist, kissing him hungrily.

Kyle growled and strode out of the bathroom and into his room. Placing me down on his bed, he stripped his pants off before covering my body with his. The weight of him on me was ecstasy. "One of these days princess, you'll be the one asking me to repeat the question."

FIFTY-FIVE
LEE

"WILL you please stay out for a little while longer? Have some fun with Derek," I said into my phone.

Kyle grunted on the other line. "Are you trying to get rid of me princess? Moving a boy toy into the house while I'm out?"

I chuckled. "Oh yeah," I joked. "Because that's all I need in the house. Another testosterone filled man."

"Okay, okay. I'll be back at seven," Kyle sighed.

"Good, thank you. I'll see you then."

"Oh princess?"

I smiled at the teasing tone in his voice. "Yeah?"

"You might wanna check around the house and see if you can find some duct tape."

"Oh really," I said, confused. "Why, what have you broken?"

Kyle laughed hard. "Duct tape for that mouth of yours because by the time I'm finished with you tonight, you'll be screaming the fucking house down."

Oh...

Linda stepped into Kyle's office, and I blushed in mortification. "Okay," I muttered. "I'll get that sorted, bye, love you."

Hanging up before Kyle could make me blush further, I cracked a smile at Linda. "Thanks so much for doing this," I told her as I pushed Hope's buggy over to her.

"It's my pleasure Hun," she said, her gaze fixed on Hope's sleeping body all tucked up and cute...

"Besides," Linda teased. "With Kyle monopolizing the baby, I've hardly had a look in."

I nodded in agreement. "I know, he is ridiculous." *Ridiculously cute,* I wanted to add.

The way he took care of Hope...Uh, it kind of made me swoon...

"I've expressed four bottles, not that you will need all of those. And there's diapers, wipes, cream, her formula, four changes of clothes...."

"Will you go already," Linda smirked. "And stop worrying, it's not my first time, you know."

I smiled apologetically. "Thank you so much," I said, suddenly feeling really guilty. "Maybe I shouldn't..."

"Yes, you should," Linda commanded, shooing me from the room. "We will see you both later. Go and enjoy being young and in love."

I smiled to myself, feeling deliriously happy.

Enjoying Kyle Carter was exactly what I intended to do.

———

Turning my key in the front door of our house, I was thrumming with excitement.

Tonight was the night.

I had it all planned for days.

I was going to ask Kyle to repeat the question.

I was ready. He was ready. It was time.

I ran upstairs and changed into the sexy red baby-doll and matching suspenders I'd bought the other day.

I let my curls down–Kyle loved my hair down, and applied my makeup.

Running downstairs, I went in search of the duct tape he'd told me to get.

I had no intention of using it, but I couldn't wait to see the look on his face when he thought I had...

Bounding into the kitchen, I went straight to the knick-knack drawer and started rummaging.

"Hello Delia."

I spun around and froze, my heart dropped.

"I've been waiting for you."

FIFTY-SIX
KYLE

I GRINNED over at Derek as I turned my car onto Thirteenth Street. "So, what's your plan for after summer?" I asked.

Derek sighed and shook his head. "I have no fucking clue. My original plan was to move back to Idaho. My brother needs help with running the business and all my family is there, but…"

"Camryn," I guessed, knowing full well that Cam was the only reason Derek was contemplating his future.

Derek had his future mapped out clearly since he was eighteen years old. Go to college, get his degree and then head home to join the family construction business.

"I don't know, Der," I said. "Maybe if you give her some time, she'd see what she was missing and come to her senses."

Derek shook his head in surprise. "No dude, you've got it wrong, she's not why I'm thinking about staying. I mean, sure, I love Cam and a part of me probably always will, but I know when a ship has sailed. And me and Cam, well, as good as it was, I can't force her to love me. In a way, I've always known that I wasn't the one for her. Besides, even if she did want to start back up, I don't think I could ever get past the whole…Mike thing."

I didn't understand a word he was saying.

My head couldn't grasp it.

"Derek, you've been miserable for months. You love her. I watched how badly you handled the breakup. I had the fucking hangover to show for it."

"Yeah, I guess I didn't take it too well," he chuckled. "I'm okay with it now though."

"That's good man. I'm happy for you."

I was glad Derek had found some semblance of peace. He deserved to be happy.

"Are you happy Kyle?"

I thought about my two girls and nodded. "Yeah, I'm happy."

I'd never been happier in my life. I had a beautiful daughter and an amazing woman.

Derek patted me on the shoulder. "See, now that's exactly why I'm not ready to move back home. I feel like I've got an investment in that kid. She needs her Uncle Derek around, especially when her parents decide to go bat shit crazy on each other."

I laughed at his comment. "No man, Lee and I are solid now. Nothing is going to tear us apart again. Those days are behind us. But seriously, if you're thinking of staying I'd be thrilled...." My words trailed off as we rounded our street and flashing lights and sirens greeted us.

Our house was surrounded by dozens of vehicles and crowds of people.

Slamming on the brakes, I jumped out of the car and ran.

FIFTY-SEVEN
LEE

IN THE MOVIES, when the villain pulls a gun out, a hero bursts into the room and saves the girl.

I knew that wouldn't be the case for me.

I wasn't going to be saved.

I was going to die.

Rachel held the gun steadily in her hand, pointing the barrel directly at my chest and in that moment my only thought was, thank god I'd dropped Hope off with Linda before coming home.

I was going to die, but my baby was safe.

"Please, don't do this, Rachel," I begged, knowing it was pointless to beg for my life from a woman so intent on destroying it. She had just spent the last twelve months executing attempt after vicious attempt to end me.

But the will to live, the overpowering maternal urge to stay alive for my daughter meant that I would say and do anything to survive this.

"I warned you. I told you time and again, but you didn't listen, did you?" Her voice was cold. The look in her eyes was that of feral triumph. "I gave you a choice, but you chose wrong. You won't leave, therefore you have to die."

She pulled the safety, and my heart rate exploded. "This isn't going to make Kyle love you, Rachel. Killing me will only make him hate you more. You're sick, not thinking clearly, I understand that, I can help you, if you just put down the…"

"I haven't thought of anything else in months," she spat. "My

only regret now is that I didn't do this while you were pregnant."
Aiming the gun straight at me, she smiled. "But not to worry.
When I'm your little bastard's stepmother, I'll make sure I remedy
that."

There was a commotion in the hallway and I didn't have a
chance to say another word before the sound of a gun firing went
off and I collapsed to my knees.

FIFTY-EIGHT
KYLE

YELLOW PLASTIC TAPE surrounded the building.

"Holy shit," Derek cursed, rushing for the house.

I couldn't speak. I was too busy pushing past paramedics and cops.

"Sir, you can't go in there," a police officer told me, holding his hand out in front of my chest. "This is an official crime scene, please step back."

"Fuck you, this is my house. My girlfriend and baby are inside that house."

I slammed against him, but two more officers came over to hold me back.

I listened as the officer spoke into his walkie-talkie. "The owner of the house claims there is an infant inside the building." He paused as he listened to the person on the other side, then huffed loudly. "Move fast, leave nothing unturned."

"What the hell is going on?" Derek demanded. "Will someone fucking tell us something?"

"Young man, step back and let us do our job," the officer said, focusing on Derek.

I shrugged free. "Step back?" I shouted, pushing the cop in the chest. "That's our house. Goddammit, my family is inside that house and you're not telling us shit. How the fuck do you expect us to calm down and stand back?"

A hand grabbed my arm and tugged. "Mr. Carter, can you tell

us who may have a grudge on you and your family?" a female reporter asked, shoving a microphone in my face.

I pushed the microphone roughly away. "What are you talking about?" I demanded pushing forward.

"Sir, if you don't step back and let us do our job, we will restrain you," another officer said as he dragged me back.

"Fuck you," I snarled shoving him out of my way. My arms were jerked behind my back, and I was cuffed, forced to my knees.

"Calm down sir," the officer said sympathetically.

I was just about to tell him to kiss my ass when a thunderous noise erupted from inside the house.

My chest heaved as my brain registered the sound.

It could only come from one thing.

A gun.

FIFTY-NINE
LEE

PAIN.

Pain enveloped me.

I was screaming.

Writhing in the sharpest form of physical torture, but I wasn't dead.

I was bleeding, my hands and my stomach. I could see a river of dark blood spreading over the fabric of my red dress.

In the midst of the red haze and agony I could hear voices.

Someone was here.

I was going to be okay.

Someone was going to save me.

Voices were roaring in my ears. I could make out one voice. It was her.

She had come to save me.

She is always saving me.

"You crazy bitch," Cam screamed and I swung my gaze up to see Cam slam Rachel's head into the door.

Rachel's head cracked against the heavy oak door and her body crumbled to the floor.

Cam rushed towards me. "Lee, hang on, I'm going to get help."

I tried to grab her to warn her. But I couldn't get up. Everything was getting dark.

I was going blind.

"Cam…" I spluttered, blood rising in my throat, spilling from my lips. "Get out of here. Run."

She ignored my protests.

Pulling her phone from her pocket, she dialed and held it to her ear. Her hands were shaking. "I need an ambulance and the police, and a straitjacket. Thirteenth Street, University Hill. Hurry, my friend has been shot." She looked down at me and nodded her head. "Yeah, in the stomach, I think. Okay."

Cam hung up and tugged off her jacket. "Lee, I have to put pressure on the wound. I need to slow the bleeding," she said, pressing her jacket to my stomach.

"You need to get out of here," I coughed. "She could…Wake up."

"Stop talking stupid," she replied, holding me to her. "God, I'm so glad I forgot to pack my swim suit when I moved out. That's what I came over for, me and Mike, we're taking a trip…"

"Cam, I'm scared," I confessed, struggling to get air as Cam wrapped her arm around my shoulders. "Am I dying?"

"You better not be," she warned. "You have a beautiful baby who is depending on you. Do you hear me? Focus on Hope. Put her picture in your head and keep it there. Do NOT lose focus."

I nodded and pulled Hope's face into focus.

I concentrated on her dark curls, her huge blue eyes, the cute dimples in her cheeks…

"Get up." *Oh god, no…*

Through bleary eyes, I watched as a very angry Rachel stood over us, aiming the gun once again. "Get out of the way, Camryn. She has to die."

I feebly tried to shove Cam away from me, but I was weak and growing weaker by the second.

"You don't want to do this, Rachel," Cam said quietly, shielding my body with hers.

"Cam run…please, move," I begged, pushing at her hand. "Do it, do it, or she'll…kill us…both."

Cam shook her head.

"And what kind of person would I be if I did that? Who would I be if I stepped aside and watched you die?" She shook her head again and kneeled up.

"Rachel, if you go now, if you run, you'll have time. Think of your family. You're twenty-two years old and you're going to ruin your life...and for what, a man? Don't be an idiot. The cops will be here any minute. You're never going to get away with this."

I watched in a cocktail of horror and relief as Rachel grabbed Cam by the ponytail and dragged her away from my body.

"Do you think I care anymore?" She screamed. "I have nothing left to lose. She stole everything from me."

I was grateful.

Cam would be okay.

She would live and would be there for Hope and Kyle...Oh god, I didn't want to die.

I wanted to hold my baby in my arms again and smell her soft skin, kiss her chubby cheeks.

And I wanted to see Kyle...

Oh, I wanted to look into those blue eyes right this instant and feel the infallible safety and protection that poured from him into me.

But the knowledge that I was Rachel's only intended victim in a sick way eased my mind.

I watched as Rachel shoved Cam hard, causing her to hit the refrigerator.

Rachel turned to face me and I closed my eyes, unable to watch. I didn't want to see her pull the trigger that would end my life.

"It didn't have to come to this. If you had just left when I told you," she growled. "Goodbye Delia."

I heard Cam scream before Rachel pulled the trigger.

SIXTY
LEE

THE GUN WENT OFF and I collapsed...But I was still breathing, still conscious.

My ears were ringing from the sharp bellowing sound and for a brief moment I thought that surely someone would come.

Two loud gunshots on a busy street; someone was bound to have heard.

I thought I could hear people outside, but I wasn't sure if it was wishful thinking...

The kitchen tiles were cool against my back.

Everything hurt, even my fingernails, but that was good.

It meant I could feel my body.

I was still in my body.

I tried to move, but there was weight, a suffocating heaviness on top of me that hadn't been there before.

Struggling to breathe, I opened my eyes and screamed.

Cam.

Cam's bloodshot eyes were open and staring lifelessly into mine.

The weight of her body on top of my chest was crushing my airways.

Fear escalated through me as I managed to drag myself out from underneath her.

Laying Cam on her back, I hovered over her anxiously. Her body was still, she was too still. "What did you do?" I cried while running my bloody hands over her chest, her arms and her stomach. "What's wrong with her? What did you do?" I screamed as I checked her pulse.

I couldn't feel anything. My hands were shaking so badly.

I couldn't see anything wrong with her.

She looked fine.

She must have passed out, that was it.

The shock must have caused her to faint.

Cam is fine. She is okay. She isn't bleeding.

My eyes roamed over her, and that's when I noticed it; the steady flow of blood coming from the back of her head, staining her golden hair, pooling on the kitchen floor.

"NO." I covered her mouth with mine and tried to breathe air into her lifeless lungs, but…I could barely breathe, blood gurgled in my mouth.

"She shouldn't have bothered to try and protect you." Rachel laughed, and it was an, evil, toxic, bone-chilling sound. "You're not worth saving. You're not worth anything."

I didn't look up at Rachel.

I didn't need to.

I already knew what was about to happen.

I curled my body over Cam's and waited for the sound of a gunshot.

And when it came everything went black.

SIXTY-ONE
KYLE

THERE WAS silence and then another shot went off.

I stared wide eyed at Derek.

"Jesus Christ, somebody do something." I roared as I struggled against my restraints and the officers' who were holding me back.

Somewhere from behind me I heard a voice shout, "They're going in."

I watched in slow motion as the cops kicked in my front door and at least a dozen armed officers' rushed inside.

My phone sounded in my pants and Derek came and knelt beside me.

Sliding the phone out of my pocket, he put it to his ear. "Linda, its Derek Porter." He paused for a moment and then sighed. "Oh, thank god." He turned to look at me. "Linda said our house is all over the news. She's at the hotel. She has Hope. Lee dropped her off a couple of hours ago."

I sagged in relief.

Thank god.

I had no fucking clue what was happening inside my house, but the fact that my daughter was safe with Linda gave me hope that Lee wasn't inside that house.

He turned his attention back to the front door and his face paled. Dropping the phone, Derek clasped his chest as he staggered backwards, landing on the ground next to me.

A silence fell over the crowd and camera lights flashed wildly as the front door opened.

Two officers marched out with their hands clamped around the arms of a woman in handcuffs as several paramedics' rushed past them to get into the house.

"Oh god." I collapsed to the ground at the sight of Rachel.

Any hope I had of Lee not being inside the house diminished when Rachel caught my eye and smiled. "I did this for us," she mouthed. "I love you Kyle."

My worst fears were confirmed.

I knew, I *knew* this was bad.

I knelt, frozen on the ground, eyes locked on Rachel as the officers' bundled her into a police car and sped off.

Two male paramedics stepped out of the house next.

My eyes trailed down to the person lying on the trolley they were pushing, and my heart stopped, my entire body trembled.

My body buckled, but I forced myself to move. "Lee," I roared, trying to stand up, pushing past the fear of seeing her underneath that white sheet.

I needed to know it wasn't her.

I had to check.

I fucking had to...

The officer clamped his hands on my shoulders, forcing me down.

"Get the hell off me," I shouted, struggling to break free and get to the ambulance.

Another stretcher was pushed out the door and rushed quickly to the ambulance.

Five paramedics surrounded that one and I couldn't see who it was.

"Please," I begged. "My girlfriend...I think that's my girlfriend."

The officer seemed to waver for a moment before nodding.

Helping me to my feet, he unlocked my handcuffs and walked with me as I staggered towards the ambulance. The officer explained to the paramedics who I was.

And then my entire world came crashing down on me as I was faced with the hardest decision of my life

"They are both female's in their early twenties. Which one, son?" the officer asked me and I didn't know.

Two ambulances with two females... I didn't know which one she was inside of, or who the other girl was.

I didn't know, and apparently, neither did the paramedics.

"We have to go, sir," the female paramedic said as she began to close the doors. "Are you coming?"

I looked at one ambulance and then the one next to it, willing my gut instinct to kick in.

Thankfully, Derek came to my side taking the choice away from me. "Kyle, I'll go in this one, you go in the other," he said, striding toward the paramedic.

I didn't stop to think about it, I ran to the back of the other ambulance and climbed inside.

The engine of the ambulance roared to life, taking off, siring's blaring.

"You need to sit down, and buckle up," someone informed me, but I wasn't listening.

My heart had stopped dead at the sight before me, and I couldn't think past anything but the sight of the sheet covered body lying on the stretcher in front of me.

Ignoring the paramedic's protests, I stepped closer to the stretcher.

With trembling hands and a grief-stricken heart, I pulled the sheet back.

"No," I whispered as my eyes took in what my brain refused to register.

My body quavered and my legs gave out.

I crumbled to the floor as the cruel and torturous agony of grief washed over me.

SIXTY-TWO
KYLE

AS DEREK and I sat silently side by side in the corridor of the hospital's I.C.U unit, I was hit by the overpowering stench of hospital disinfectant.

I welcomed the smell, prayed it could somehow clear my airways of the smell of blood...Of death. I wished for it to clear my mind...

It couldn't. It wouldn't, and I deserved no less punishment.

This was my fault.

I knew it was.

I may not have been the one to pull the trigger, but those bullets had been entrenched in their bodies because of my ignorance, because of my inability to protect them... This was all on me.

I was the one who'd brought Rachel into our lives. I was the one who chose to ignore the signs. I was to blame.

And now, all I was left with was a deep seeded feeling of guilt, remorse and unbearable pain.

"How long have they been in there with her?" Derek asked and I cringed.

"Forty five minutes," I whispered. Seven hours of surgery and forty-five minutes of waiting since they'd pushed her body through that door and told us nothing.

Leaning forward, I rested my elbows on my knees and pressed my thumbs into my eyes.

I couldn't look at Derek. "Did you call her father?" I croaked out. "Did you…" I stopped to catch my breath. "Did you tell him she's dead?"

"I contacted both of them," he said in a hoarse voice and I felt his body shudder. "I called Linda, too, told her what happened… She said Hope is fine and she'll keep her for as long as you need her to."

I exhaled heavily. "Thank you."

"Why did she do it Kyle?" Derek asked, his voice cracking as his emotions spilled out. "How the fuck could she do that to them?"

"I don't know."

"I want to know, I need to know, Kyle. I need to fucking know. She fucking butchered them. Look at me will you?"

I lifted my head and looked into the tear-stained face of my best friend. "I'm sorry."

Derek shook his head. "Why are you sorry? This isn't your fault, Kyle."

The door of the hospital room swung open and we both stood quickly. "Is she okay?" I demanded. My legs shook with every step I took towards that door.

"There were complications," the doctor said, gesturing for one of us to come in. "Which one of you is her next of kin?"

Derek nodded at me to go ahead and I stepped forward.

"I am."

SIXTY-THREE
KYLE

I COULDN'T REMEMBER the last time I blinked, let alone slept.

I knew it had to have been more than a few days since I slept, less than a week? I wasn't sure.

Time meant nothing to me anymore.

There was a fear inside of me, a deep rooted, panic stricken fear, that if I closed my eyes for too long she would disappear.

I kept my eyes focused on the machine next to her bed that was monitoring her heart rate and comforted myself with the knowledge that in spite of the oxygen machine that was pumping air into her lungs, her heart was still beating.

My beautiful princess…

Lee's pale, withdrawn face, her lifeless body lay in a hospital bed, rigged up to more wires and machines than I'd ever seen.

And Cam…

Oh god, she was lying on a slab in the morgue with a hole in the back of her head.

I had to sit here. I needed to be with Lee. There was no other place I could contemplate going.

I hadn't eaten, but I didn't care.

I had no doubt that if Lee didn't pull through this, then I would want to be with her.

I didn't think I could live with the guilt, or live without her.

I wasn't going to live without her.

It was that simple.

"Mr. Carter, you should go home and get some rest," one of the nurses said.

I didn't know which one. My eyes were glued to that machine.

"I'm not leaving," I said, or at least I think I said it.

I didn't know if I spoke the words or just thought them.

She didn't understand, none of them understood.

How did they expect me to walk out of this room? To eat, sleep and live like the world was still turning was beyond me.

Because my world wasn't turning. My world was dying in that hospital bed.

How the fuck did they not understand that?

Tightening my hold on Lee's lifeless hand, I turned my gaze on her. "Baby, it's me. I'm here, I haven't left. I'll never leave you again."

The skin on my cheeks felt dry and brittle from tears.

"You need to wake up, Lee. I need you to wake up and get better. I can't do this without you."

I kissed her hand and lowered my head to her bed, resting my forehead on our joined hands.

"The baby needs you. I need you. I can't...I won't survive without you. I don't want to be here without you. I don't want a life without you."

"Mr. Carter...Kyle, this isn't doing any good, for either of you..."

"I'm not going anywhere," I shouted, moving closer to Lee's lifeless body. "Leave us be."

I needed them all to fuck off and give me two goddamn minutes to make a plan.

I needed a plan.

There was something...There had to be something someone could do to fix her.

I'd asked the surgeon who operated on Lee that very question when she'd come out of surgery.

And he'd filled me with bullshit. Bullshit and sheer fucking terror.

"Mr. Carter, your girlfriend's condition is critical. Whilst we were able to remove the bullet and stem the hemorrhaging in her stomach, and

repair her bowel without removing it, I'm afraid the wound in her back has proved far more serious.

She was shot directly in her left kidney, ravaging the organ, rendering it unrepairable. We removed the left kidney during the surgery and curtailed the spread of blood, but I'm afraid we found large amounts of shrapnel in her right kidney, which has caused severe damage to the organ, reducing its rate of function to an alarming eleven percent, too low for Delia to exist on.

We have equipped her with kidney dialysis, but, to be frank Mr. Carter, without a kidney transplant as soon as possible, Delia's prognosis, to put it mildly, is bleak."

"Have they found a match yet?" I asked.

I knew the nurse hadn't left, I could hear her breathing from behind me.

"Not yet, I'm afraid."

I swung my head around to glare at her.

"How hard can it be to find a fucking kidney? People die every second of the goddamn day. Surely, someone out there is compatible?"

"Mr. Carter, you know it's not that simple," the nurse said calmly as if she heard that question a dozen times a day; in her line of work she probably did.

But this was different. Lee was different.

She needed to live.

I knew that was a selfish way to think, but I didn't give a fuck.

All I cared about was getting that kidney for Lee. I'd been tested myself. I wasn't a match.

"Why hasn't she woken up yet?" I asked, again knowing the answer, but needing the reassurance of a medical professional.

"You know this Mr. Carter. Lee's body has weakened. Her kidney is under extreme demand. The doctors have put her in an induced coma to allow her body to repair itself and lessen the strain on her."

I turned back to Lee, ignoring the rising swell of panic that threatened to smother me. "Do you hear that, baby? They're going to make you better and then you can come home to me. Please Lee, I'm begging you, come back to me, baby."

*

"Your cocoa sucks, baby. I mean it, it's really fucking disgusting," I mused, as I wiped Lee's face with a washcloth.

This was day five of coma-induced Lee and I was getting pissed, and seriously considering buying a kidney online.

I heard they sold all types of shit on the internet.

"And don't get me started on your taste in books." I combed her hair as gently as I could while thinking up as many insults as I could to try and get a reaction out of her.

I didn't know why I was bothering, considering she was in, what I referred to as, a 'doctor coma.' But I needed a response from her and pissing Lee off was usually the best way to get one.

"Do you remember when we were in Louisiana, and you asked me where I got those bruises? Well, I didn't tell you then, but I kicked that punk Perry's ass."

Lee moved her hand, or at least I thought she did.

I couldn't be sure if she was actually moving her hand, or if I was losing my fucking mind.

I suspected the latter, but I rambled on anyway.

"I loved you then, you know. Long before it actually, but that was the night I knew. I watched you from the corner of the bar. You were all alone on the dance floor in that crummy bar. You were wearing that skimpy ass denim skirt, shaking those sexy hips of yours and all I could think of was... Damn, this is her. This is my woman. That was the night when my future attached itself to yours."

Leaning down, I kissed her freshly combed hair, before sitting down to continue my vigil.

My phone went off in my pocket, but I ignored it.

I didn't want to talk to anyone.

I'd been ignoring all my calls for days, avoiding everyone.

Mike had come by the hospital, and Anna, even my father... But I'd told the nurse on call at the time to send them away. The only person I could handle right now was Derek.

Derek had told me the cops had cleared our house, and that Mr. and Mrs. Frey were staying there while they organized the funeral.

If I had my way, I'd take a match and a gallon of petrol to the whole fucking place, but I guessed they needed to be close to where their daughter had spent her final years.

I wasn't sure if I could ever go into that house again, or face those people. Hell, I couldn't even face my own daughter.

I hadn't seen Hope since the evening Lee was shot...The evening Cam was killed.

I couldn't see her...couldn't look at her.

If I did, I would break. It would be too real, it would become my reality.

I felt guilty as shit for thinking like this, but the longer I put off seeing Hope, the longer I could pretend that this was some fucked up nightmare.

If I saw Hope, the veracity of Lee not recovering would wreck me.

I couldn't raise her on my own, I wouldn't be able to.

There was a knock on the door and I sagged in relief.

"Come in," I said, thankful to have a distraction from my thoughts.

"Hey man," Derek said, closing the door quietly. "I brought you some clean clothes, a toothbrush, and your charger," he said, passing me a small duffel bag.

"Thanks man." I stored the bag under my chair. "How is...everything?"

Derek sighed and plopped into a chair on the other side of Lee's bed. "Fucked up as hell, dude, Ted is in bits. Mora is worse. She keeps crying and asking for you."

My head snapped up. "For me?"

"Yeah, she keeps demanding that she talk to you, and says she has something important to tell you. Something you need to know. She rambles on and on about how the truth has to be revealed for a perfect match. Ted is at his wits end with her. He's stopped her from coming here. Poor woman, the grief is driving her crazy."

"I bet." I had a fair idea of what Mrs. Frey wanted me to know, and her telling me how it was my fault Cam was dead couldn't make me feel any worse than I already did.

"They were sitting in the kitchen, looking at some brochures of caskets this morning, and...they asked me to...Oh Kyle, I couldn't look at it man." Derek shuddered and slumped forward. "They kept asking for my opinion on things, like her favorite songs, and which flowers she preferred. I couldn't deal, you know. I told them I had to come check on you."

"Are you dealing, Derek?"

Derek looked up at me, his eyes full of tears. "I'm dealing," he said in a gruff voice. "It would be a lot fucking easier if they went and asked Mike about shit like that."

I didn't know what to say, but my heart fucking bled for my best friend.

Derek loved Cam, he always had, even when she went and screwed him over.

I couldn't imagine what it felt like to have to sit in a room with the parents of the girl who had left me for another man, broken my heart, and have to help organize her funeral.

"You can stay at the hotel if it's easier," I offered.

"Thanks man, but I have to face this. I need closure." Derek shook his head and cleared his throat. "Speaking of facing things…"

"Derek, don't," I warned, my shoulders stiffened.

I couldn't deal with this right now.

"Linda has been calling me non-stop. You're gonna have to see her, Kyle."

"I can't," I growled, blocking out the feeling of guilt in my stomach.

"You have to," he pressed. "She is your daughter."

SIXTY-FOUR
KYLE

THE DOOR OPENED, and I stiffened.

There was only one person who came into this hospital room without knocking, and that person made my skin fucking crawl.

"Morning Darling," Jimmy Bennett said as he walked over to Lee and kissed her on the forehead.

I had to hold onto Lee's hand a little tighter to keep myself in my chair.

Even though I'd paid for him to fly here, I still struggled with keeping my cool around him.

The man was built like a brick shit house, and the knowledge that he used this strength to wield control over Lee as a child caused my body to thrum with rage.

Every time I looked at his beefy arms, and huge mother-fucking chest, I was hit with an insane urge to return the beatings he'd given my girl.

"Carter," he acknowledged, nodding in my direction as he pulled up a chair on the other side of his daughter and sat, eyes narrowed, directed at me.

I nodded stiffly. "Jimmy."

Jimmy didn't like me. He didn't have to say it. It was obvious in the way he moved around me, or the way he watched me like a hawk with those cold gray eyes of his.

It was a fair assumption to presume that the angry energy I had pulsating towards him, was being returned in waves.

"Any news?" he asked, and I shook my head.

I knew what he meant. Jimmy had been checked as a donor.

"You're not compatible. The doc told me this morning."

"Well shit," he muttered, pulling off his baseball cap and wiping his sweaty brow. Running his hand across his gray stubble jaw, he leaned closer to Lee. "Now, don't you worry bout a damn thing, darling. Daddy's here, and he's gonna get you all fixed up." He pulled her hand to his mouth and kissed it, before glaring at me. "I see you still aint put a ring on my daughter's finger, boy."

"Her choice, not mine," I said through gritted teeth.

I'd asked Lee to marry me more times than I could count. She was the one with the reservations.

Jimmy let out a whistle. "Well damn, that girl's smarter than I gave her credit for," he said, looking straight at me. "If she aint gonna marry you, there ain't no reason for her to stay here." Turning to face Lee, he smiled. "You're gonna come with your daddy, ain't ya darling, you and that grandbaby of mine?"

I shoved my chair back and stood up quickly. "Over my dead body is my daughter going anywhere with you. Lee might have forgiven you, but I sure as hell haven't forgotten what you did to her. Lee and Hope are staying with me."

The chair I was sitting on crashed against the wall behind me, but I didn't move to pick it up.

I remained stock still, glaring at the gray-headed child beater holding my girl's hand.

Lee was going to get better, and then we would go and collect Hope together...

"That's real fucking hypocritical, kid," Jimmy snarled. "Considering, you're the reason that crazy redhead bitch put two fucking holes in my daughter's body."

Those words took the air right out of my lungs and I staggered back.

"Don't like hearing the truth, do ya boy?" Jimmy continued. "I never claimed to be a good father. I sure as hell know I screwed things up in the past. But I'm better now, and I'll be damned if I sit back and watch you destroy my baby girl's life." He leaned his elbows on the side of Lee's bed. His biceps flexed as he focused on me. "This is what's gonna go down, son. My baby girl's gonna get better, and when she does, I'm gonna be taking her and the baby home to Louisiana with me, where I can keep her safe, where I can protect them both, because god knows, you've done a real fucking stellar job at it so far."

"I didn't know…"

"I don't give a rat's ass what you didn't know, Carter. I don't like you, not one fucking bit, and I ain't taking no more risks when it comes to Delia. God knows how many more skeletons you got waiting to jump out of the closet. She's nineteen years old for Christ's sake. She's just a child herself. She's my child. My teenage daughter, who you went and got pregnant, and now you've got yourself a baby girl of your own as a result. Put yourself in my shoes kid. Think of what's best for them."

"You're not taking them."

Jimmy shrugged his shoulders. "We'll see," is all he replied.

I had to get away from that man or they were going to need another bed in that room, real fucking soon.

"I'll be outside," I growled, as I stormed out. I had to get away from him or I would lose it.

———

Running my hands through my hair, I rushed from Lee's room, needing to get a little space and breathe for a moment.

I was not prepared for the welcoming party that awaited me.

"There you are, kiddo. I was wondering when you were going to come up for air again," Linda said. "You know…With all that self-pity you seem to be bathing in."

I closed my eyes and went back inside Lee's room, but she grabbed my arm, yanking me back.

"Look at her Kyle," Linda demanded.

I shook my head. "I can't."

The sounds of her babbling were slitting through me. "Please Linda, just take her and get her out of here."

"I'm afraid I can't do that, Kyle," she replied firmly. "This little girl needs her parents. And since her momma can't take care of her, her daddy sure as hell will. Look at her, Kyle. She is your flesh and blood. Open your eyes. Don't let your fear of the future be the cause of you making the biggest mistake of your life. Take your child now."

Shuddering, I opened my tear filled eyes as Linda placed Hope into my arms.

The feel of her, the smell of her in my arms...It was too much. "Linda, I'm scared."

"Since when did fear ever stop you, Kyle Carter? You've been feeling the fear and doing it anyway since you were twelve years old. You can do this, and you will get through this."

SIXTY-FIVE
KYLE

I STOOD at the edge of the cemetery, behind the crowds of mourners and reporters who had shown up to watch Cam's casket being lowered into the ground.

Derek stood stiffly by my side.

Using one hand to rock Hope's buggy, I placed the other on his shoulder.

This was harder for him than me. I knew that and I empathized with him to no end.

It was too hard for him to stand at her grave and watch Cam's burial while Mike stood side by side with the family he'd once been a member of.

I comforted myself in the knowledge that whilst nine days had passed since the attack, and the doctors hadn't yet found a kidney donor, the love of my life wasn't being placed in the ground.

She was still fighting, and she was still alive.

We stood there silently until the priest excused himself and the crowd dwindled.

"You ready to go, man?" I asked quietly, tucking Hope's blanket around her sleeping body.

Even though it was July, the air was cold in the cemetery. My heart swelled in my chest at the sight of Hope and I stroked her cheek as I silently thanked Linda for helping me come to my senses.

I was ashamed of myself for denying my daughter.

The fear of living without Lee, the depression...I hadn't wanted to see Hope because I knew that when I did, I would have to carry on.

Those first few days after Lee's surgery I had –in my delirious state of grief– decided that if Lee didn't make it then I didn't want to...

I had selfishly blocked Hope out of my life in a bid to ease my conscience, knowing that once I saw my daughter I would have to live, regardless of what happened...

It had been an unforgivable thing to think, and to be honest, at the time I hadn't been thinking.

I hadn't considered Hope's future, or thought about what Lee would want. I'd been too caught up in my guilt and grief to think straight.

I was now though, and I wasn't going to let my family down again.

Derek wiped his eyes with the back of his hand and nodded.

I clasped the handles of Hope's buggy and walked towards the exit.

"Kyle, wait," a voice shouted from behind us. "I need to talk to you."

I cringed.

If I had to tell one more reporter 'no comment,' I was going to lose my shit.

I swung around and my heart hammered in my chest.

Not here...

Mora Frey stood five feet away from me, red faced, and panting.

"Mrs. Frey," I acknowledged quietly. "I'm so sorry about Camryn." I didn't know what else to say to the woman. In truth, there was nothing else I could say. Nothing could bring Cam back. No one could rewind to that night and press pause.

Mora kept moving towards me and I braced myself for the slap I was sure to get.

I could not have predicted what happened next.

"Kyle," Mora sobbed, wrapping her arms around me tightly. "I'm sorry, I'm so terribly sorry."

I wrapped my arms around Cam's mom and held her, unsure of what the hell to do.

I glanced over at a baffled looking Derek, then down at

Mora's grief stricken face.

Why was she sorry? Why was she apologizing to me? This was all happening in reverse.

"I'm the one who's sorry..." I started to say but she didn't give me a chance.

"I've been trying to contact you." Her voice quavered as she slipped her hand into the pocket of her skirt. "I hope it's not too late."

She handed me an old wrinkled piece of paper, folded many times over.

I stared down at it, my brow creased.

"I don't understand," I muttered. "Too late for what..."

I was interrupted by the appearance of Cam's father. "Mora dear, please stop this. Let the boy be," he said to his wife as he tried to free her grip on my arms.

He looked at me with dead eyes. "Kyle, please ignore my wife. She hasn't been herself since...Camryn's passing," he said, choking out Cam's name. "She doesn't know what she's saying. She isn't thinking clearly."

"I am thinking clearly," Mora screamed, shrugging away from her husband. "For the first time in nineteen years, I am finally thinking clearly." Turning to me, her eyes filled up with tears as she asked, "How is Lee? Have they found a match?"

I shook my head. "No, she's still the same, the doctors said... why? What's going on here, Mora?"

Cam's mother burst into tears and pointed at the sheet of paper in my hands. "There's your answer. Go there, you'll find a match for Lee."

"Jesus Mora, you can't keep doing this," Ted hissed. "Don't you think that boy's going through enough?"

Ted began to pull Mora away and I kicked into action.

"Derek, will you take Hope home? I won't be long."

Derek nodded, took hold of Hope's buggy and headed towards the exit.

I was confused as fuck.

Mora sure as hell sounded like she knew what she was talking about.

And I needed to know.

Unfolding the sheet of paper, I stared at it, confused for a moment.

"What is this?" I called after her, but she was gone.

"Mora?" I shouted, jogging after them, towards the other exit.

"Let it go Kyle," Ted warned as he bundled Mora into his car. "Go back to Lee. Sit with her and pray for her. Hold her in your arms. I don't want my wife to be upset any further."

I shook my head, ignoring Cam's dad. I focused on her mother. "What did you mean when you said I'd find a match? Are you talking about Lee?" I demanded frantically. Excitement bubbled to the surface of my heart. "Is that it?" I asked. "Do you know someone who can help her?"

"Did you hear what I said?" Ted snapped, as he slammed Mora's door closed and rushed around to his side of the car. "Go home," he said as he opened his own door. "You're chasing a dead end. Tear up that piece of paper and go back to your life and forget this conversation ever happened. Nothing good will come from it."

"What life?" I demanded, at wits fucking end. I threw my hands in the air, gesturing wildly. "My entire world is slowly dying in that hospital bed." Leaning down, I put my hand on the window of the car. "Mora, if you know something, anything that can save Lee, please, please just tell me."

Mr. Frey slammed his door shut and started the car.

"Wait..." I shouted, slamming my fist on the window as the car pulled off slowly. "You buried your world, don't make me bury mine."

The car slowed and the window rolled down. "Go there," Mora sobbed, pointing at the piece of paper in my hand. "Find that address and you'll find Delia Bennett."

I shook my head. "I don't understand?"

"Lee's mother," Mora whispered. "She's alive."

———

The smell was the first thing that hit me when I got home.

"Dude, where the hell have you been?" Derek demanded, when I walked into the bedroom.

"Sorry," I muttered, loosening the knot on my tie. "I got a cab to the hospital. I needed to check on Lee."

"Any change?" he asked.

I shook my head.

"I gave Hope her night-time feed...I used the formula in the white tin, that's the one she's supposed to have, right?" Derek said.

I nodded in amusement as I took in the carnage.

The floor was covered in wet wipes, clean diapers and stuffed animals.

Hope was kicking around on Lee's bed and Derek's face and shirt were covered in baby powder as he held a dirty-diaper away from his body. "Thank god," he said in relief. "I thought I'd poisoned her, but nope, your daughter is just plain nasty," he accused, throwing the diaper at me. "That's her third number two in an hour. She's like a machine."

Hope babbled contently, and I felt myself smile for the first time in nine days.

I tossed the diaper back to Derek, who darted out of the room, holding it away from his body as if it was a bomb ready to detonate.

Shrugging off my black suit jacket and tie, I rolled up the sleeves of my white shirt and walked over to the bed. "Come here, baby girl,"

Hope gibbered, her tiny hands and feet splayed wildly.

"What did Uncle Derek do to you?" I crooned, as I adjusted her back-to-front diaper and redid the poppers on her onesie. "You missed daddy, didn't you, gorgeous?"

Dimming the light, I picked her up and rocked her gently in my arms until her eyes began to flutter.

"Sleep tight, baby girl," I whispered as I lay her in her crib and tucked her up. "Daddy's got a plan."

I leaned down and kissed her tiny head of brown curls.

"Mommy's gonna be home, real soon."

———

After settling Hope down for the night, I joined Derek on the couch.

"I need your help with something," I said, popping the cap on a bottle of beer Derek had set out for me.

"Kyle, it's been a really long fucking day," Derek groaned as he stretched his legs out in front of him and laid his head against the back of the couch. "I'm exhausted. I'm not a nursemaid for

Christ's sake. Besides, I still smell like shit from the last favor I did for you."

"I found out something today," I said quietly, taking a sip of my beer. "Something big."

"Don't wanna hear it, man," he said, closing his eyes. "I need a quiet night, just one drama-free night."

"Lee's mother is alive."

Derek's eyes shot open, beer squirted from his mouth. "Holy shit," he muttered, wiping his mouth with his hand before chuckling. "Good one Kyle. For a second there I thought you were serious. Pretty sick joke, dude."

I placed my bottle on the coffee table and twisted on the couch to face him. "I'm not joking around, Derek. Mora told me that Lee's mother is alive." I pulled out the sheet of paper and handed it to him. "And, apparently, she has been living right under our noses."

Derek read the address on the note. "Denver?" he asked, confused. "I thought that Lee's mother died when she was a baby?"

"So did I. So did Lee for that matter."

"So, what, she's come back from the fucking dead or something?" Derek jumped up and paced the room.

"That's all I know Derek, well, that and the fact that she's living only a twenty minute drive from here."

"This just keeps getting better, Kyle." He ran his hand over his shaved head. "A miscarriage, a poisoned dog, a gun attack from a fucking psycho ex-girlfriend, a murdered ex-girlfriend and now a reincarnated mother...What's next, is Elvis gonna join us for a spot of tea in the kitchen?" He stopped ranting and stared at me. "And Cam's folks told you this?"

I nodded.

"Fuck," Derek hissed. "So, what, they've known Lee's mother is alive and has been living in Denver all these years, and said nothing? Shit Kyle, do you think Cam knew?"

I shook my head. "No, I can't imagine Cam keeping something like that from Lee. She loved her too much to hide that kind of a secret from her."

"Well," Derek urged. "What the hell are you waiting for? Go get her and drag her ass to the hospital."

I leaned forward. "My sentiments exactly."

SIXTY-SIX
KYLE

"DUDE, YOU LOOK LIKE A FUCKING KANGAROO," Derek sniggered as I sat Hope face forward into the baby sling on my chest. She fussed a little as I secured the buckles, hating the restraint of the pouch.

"You have a lot of growing up to do, Derek," I muttered, as I adjusted her sun hat and picked up her polka dot changing bag.

I had a lot of fucking pink attached to my body right now, and Derek's smart comments were doing wonders for my masculinity.

"You're sure that's the house?" he asked, pointing at the white painted cottage.

I nodded, re-reading the address on the page in my hands. "That's the one."

Derek sighed. "You want me to come with you?"

"No," I said and then looked down at Hope. "We'll do this together, won't we baby girl?"

———

I walked up the narrow flowered-filled path and knocked on the door.

Nothing.

Well screw that, I wasn't about to give up now.

I walked around the back of the house and peered over the garden gate.

"Can I help you?" a short, attractive brunette in her early forties asked from behind the garden fence.

Here we go.

"Yeah, I'm looking for someone, Delia Bennett?"

The woman's face paled as she moved backwards. "No, no, no, I don't think so." She shook her head. "What do you want? Did he send you? Does he know?"

I opened the gate and followed her into the yard. "My name is Kyle Carter. I'm here about your daughter, I need your help."

"I'm sorry, I don't have a daughter," she hissed as she slipped inside her back door.

I stuck my boot in her door, stopping her from slamming it shut. "Please," I begged. "She's sick. I need your help. I'm desperate."

The woman's eyes lowered to Hope and her hand shot up to her mouth. A startled cry burst from her throat.

"I'd know those curls anywhere," she whispered looking up at me. "She is yours?"

I nodded. "Yes, she is my daughter, and your daughter is her mother."

"He doesn't know you're here?" she asked again, desperation in her voice and fear.

It didn't take much of an imagination to guess who she was referring to...

"He has no idea," I said.

I found myself wanting to reassure the tiny woman in front of me.

"And I promise Mrs. Bennett, if you help me, he never will."

She seemed to ponder that for a moment, before shaking her head.

"You better come in. And I go by Tracy Gibbons now. Never call me that again."

———

"Shot?" Tracy gasped, appalled at what I had told her.

I didn't know the woman, and she had abandoned Lee as a baby, but there was something about her that made me relax and I'd ended up telling her the whole story instead of the version I'd rehearsed.

She was harmless.

I'd known that the moment I'd set eyes on her.

She had a sadness about her, a lot like the air of sadness that had surrounded her daughter when I first met her.

It didn't take a wild guess as to who had caused this sadness in them both; Jimmy Fucking Bennett.

"Yes," I replied, concentrating on the topic in hand. "And without a kidney donor, then…"

"I'll do it," Tracy burst out. "Of course I'll do it. If I am a match that is."

I sighed, the biggest fucking sigh of relief.

I hadn't expected her to agree so easily. But Jesus, I was grateful.

"Thank you," I said, my voice thick with emotion. "Thank you so much."

Tracy nodded and busied herself with making coffee.

She would be okay. Lee would get better. I couldn't think about Tracy not being a match…She would be and that was that.

So many emotions rushed through me that I felt a little light-headed.

"I know what you must be thinking," she said as she handed me a cup of coffee.

I lowered myself and Hope onto her small beige couch and watched as Lee's mother paced the floor.

"You are probably wondering how I could leave her with him."

I shook my head. "Actually, no, no I'm not. I've met the man. Believe me, I get it."

She seemed surprised with my response. "I tried," she choked out. "I tried to take her, but he…" She stopped and covered her mouth with her hand. "He hurt me. He hurt me so badly that one day I broke." She wiped her tears with the back of her hand. "When she was three months old, I'd tried to get us out."

"It's okay," I said quietly. "You don't have to explain."

"He must have known I was going to leave him," she rambled, ignoring what I'd said. "I had all the things I could sneak without him noticing, hidden at Mora's house." She frowned as she remembered. "But the day I was going to take her, he told me to go to the store…said he needed more whiskey and I was to go alone."

"He cut the brakes in my car, I know he did," she said angrily. "My brakes failed, and my car went off Benny's bridge into the creek."

Holy Fuck.

"I was pulled out by Ted. And he and Mora...helped me disappear. I knew that if I went back there, he would kill me. Mora and Ted promised they would watch her. I didn't have a choice."

Holy fucking shit balls.

I was speechless.

I had no clue what to say to the woman.

"I must ask you," Tracy whispered. "Has she been harmed? Did he ever harm her?"

I didn't know how to respond to that.

If I told her the truth, it would obviously kill her. If I didn't, she'd know I was lying.

"She has a good life now," I said finally.

"And you, you're her husband?" she asked looking from Hope to me.

"I am, or at least I will be when she eventually decides to say yes. She's a little stubborn, your daughter. She's making me work for it."

Tracy cracked a smile and I could see the longing in her eyes to hold Hope so I decided to use it to my advantage.

I took Hope out of her sling and stood up.

Tracy's eyes widened as I offered her my child. Tears filled her eyes as she took Hope with trembling hands.

"Hope, say hello to your grandma," I crooned, stroking her curls.

Yep, I was using my baby as a pawn...as collateral.

I was a shithead.

"Hope," Tracy whispered. "She is so beautiful. There is so much of you in her. But she has Lia's curls."

My head snapped up. "What did you call her?" I asked.

"Lia," Tracy confirmed. "He called her Delia, but she was always Lia to me. My beautiful little Lia Rose."

"She hates to be called Delia," I murmured. "Her friends call her Lee."

"And what do you call her?" Tracy asked as she cooed at Hope.

I smirked to myself. "I call her princess."

SIXTY-SEVEN
LEE

THE WORLD IS *dark and I am the darkest element. My heart, my soul, my inner being and core… Everything is dark. I can't break into the light. There is only one thing, one piece of brightness, in this inescapable pit of despair. That light has a name. His name is Kyle Carter.*

"Lee baby, can you hear me? Come on, open your eyes, sweetheart."

I could, oh, I could hear him.

I heard him every day.

His voice kept me company in the darkness. His voice kept me from falling into the darkness.

"Kyle," I croaked.

My eyelids were heavy. They felt like they'd been sewn shut.

My entire body ached.

"I'm here, princess." He sounded excited.

I felt my lips twitch into a smile. Oh good, at least I had some facial function.

For a moment, I'd thought I'd broken my head or something.

A hand clasped mine and then another stroked my forehead.

I knew both hands belonged to Kyle. I knew his touch. I'd pick it out of thousands.

I tried to open my eyes again and this time, thankfully they did.

Strong sunlight blinded me and I had to blink a few times to focus on the face leaning over me.

"Hey, sleeping beauty," Kyle said, his voice breaking a little. "Long time no see."

He brushed his lips against mine lightly.

"So, my cocoa sucks, does it?" I croaked.

Kyle jerked back, eyes wide in shock. "Holy shit, you heard all that?"

I nodded. "Bits and pieces...not everything. Some stuff is fuzzy."

Kyle shook his head.

"Well shit," he muttered. "I kinda feel like I need to do a mental recap on all that I said."

"Where's Hope? Is she okay?"

"Yeah, she's having some one-on-one time with her Uncle Derek."

Kyle smiled funnily and I was instantly suspicious. I watched his face. He was hiding something.

"What aren't you telling me?" I asked.

He blushed, and ducked his head for a moment. "I have some news, baby," he whispered.

"Okay, shoot," I said.

Kyle flinched, causing me in turn to cringe.

"Do you remember what happened to you?" he asked.

I nodded.

I remembered being shot, and I remembered Cam passing out...

It was blurry after that.

"Well baby, you got hurt...real bad. They removed one of your kidneys," he whispered. "But the doctors had to put you in an induced coma while they waited on a kidney donor for the other."

"Oh my god," I whispered.

No wonder every part of my body was aching. I'd been shot twice and had surgery on my organs *twice*.

"Oh, that's not the best of it," Kyle muttered. "Lee, I...I'm really not sure there's any way to tell you this other than to just come right out and say it..."

"Just tell me," I snapped.

"Your mother is alive."

"No," I whispered, shaking my head. "She's dead. Daddy told me she died when I was a baby…when she was giving birth to me. You must be mistaken."

Kyle sighed heavily.

He ran his hand through his hair. "She's alive, Lee. She is alive and breathing. I've met her. She's the one who saved you, baby. She gave you a kidney…."

"Stop," I screamed, needing Kyle to shut the hell up so I could process what he was telling me. "Just stop a second." I exhaled harshly and it hurt. "I can't…I don't…What do you mean you've met her?"

"She's nice, baby," he mumbled. "She's a real nice lady."

"No," I snapped. "I can't deal with this right now."

I was in no fit state of mind to even humor this crazy fucked up conversation.

Personally, I didn't believe it…

"Baby, if you'll talk to her, you'll understand everything. Your father, he's….Oh, Lee, she's so fragile…"

"No," I warned. "No Kyle."

Kyle sighed heavily, and nodded in defeat.

"Where is she?" I asked suddenly, as the fear caused my body to shake. "Where's Rachel?"

Kyle leaned forward and held my face in his hands. "She's gone princess," Kyle whispered, staring straight into my eyes. "She was arrested. She is being charged with a multitude of charges. She won't be getting out any time soon."

"Are you sure?" I asked weakly, needing to be certain that girl was gone.

"Lee, she is being charged with first degree murder, attempted murder, breaking and entering to mention a few. That bitch will be rotting in prison until the day she dies."

Memories suddenly started to flood through me.

Her lifeless eyes.

The blood…The blood soaking into her beautiful hair

First degree murder.

Cam.

"She's dead?" I asked, praying to god that Kyle would say no.

He didn't say anything at all, just nodded his head, confirming to me that my best friend was in fact dead.

I closed my eyes and screamed.

SIXTY-EIGHT
LEE

THERE WAS A MOMENT, a brief, selfish, fleeting moment when I saw the small timber cross engraved with Cam's name and a part of me wanted to crawl into the ground beside her.

Kyle's tight grip on my waist was the only thing keeping me from collapsing.

Everything he'd done, good, bad and downright stupid, had all been for me.

I could see that now.

But the thought of my beautiful, brave best friend lying cold in the ground was crushing the air out of my lungs.

It could have been me.

It should have been me.

Cam wasn't supposed to die. I was.

Rachel had orchestrated everything so perfectly.

She'd been watching the house, and had known I'd be on my own.

If Rachel's plan had gone to par, it would be me in that grave.

But Rachel hadn't anticipated Cam.

Cam...

My breath caught in my throat. My body shook violently.

I didn't bother to wipe the tears away. They deserved to be shed. Cam deserved my tears.

She'd protected me my whole life and was lying in a box, under six feet of earth, because of my inability to protect myself.

I knew it wasn't my fault, or Kyle's.

But it didn't stem the feelings of guilt and responsibility.

From the moment I'd woken up and Kyle had told me Cam was dead, all that had gone through my mind was that it should have been me.

I was beyond grateful that I'd survived.

Hope needed me.

But the unfairness and anger I felt over Cam's stolen life ate through my heart, blackening it with nothing but the sense of vengeance.

"Hey Cam," I sniffed, taking a step forward before sinking to my knees.

"Princess," Kyle said, moving towards me quickly, but I held up my hand to warn him off.

"I need to do this."

Kyle nodded and took a respectful step back, giving me privacy.

"I still can't believe this has happened to you," I cried. "It's not fair. You're so young, so beautiful. You're my best friend Cam. What am I supposed to do without you? What's Hope going to do without her Auntie?

"We had so many plans, remember? You were going to take Hope shopping for her first training bra. Help her to pick out her prom dress. Laugh at Kyle's reaction when Hope went on her first date, and now I'm going to have to do all of that alone."

I wiped my eyes and nose.

"Why did you do it, Cam?" I whispered.

That was the answer I needed more than anything.

Why had she valued my life more than hers when she stepped in front of that loaded gun?

I asked the question, knowing the answers were buried with my best friend.

I trailed my hand over the upturned earth of her freshly dug grave, and pulled the tiny silver bird charm from my pocket.

"Do you remember when you gave me this?" I asked her.

"I was twelve and you gave it to me the day you came to tell me you were moving away."

Sniffing, I rolled the charm between my fingers.

"I asked you why you were giving me a bird charm, and you said…"

I paused, catching my breath. "You said that you'd always

envied the freedom of a bird and as long as I kept that charm close to me, no matter what happened in my life, no one could clip my wings."

With trembling fingers, I placed the delicate charm beneath the cross.

"So Cam, today, I want to return your wings. Fly pretty girl, soar and be free."

I stood slowly, accepting Kyle's hand.

"Goodbye Camryn Frey. I'll love you forever."

———

"Did it help?" Kyle asked as we drove back to University Hill.

I looked over at him.

His face had taken on a few worry lines, but his eyes were alive, so full of life that it shook my heart.

"I think so," I said quietly. "But I know something you could do that would definitely help."

Kyle clasped my knee, squeezing gently as he drove. "Name it. Whatever you want, just name it and it's yours."

I covered his hand with mine, reveling in the feel of his warm flesh.

I sucked in a deep breath before I spoke. "I think you should repeat the question."

Kyle jerked his face toward me, eyes wide.

I felt a tremor run through his hand as his throat bobbed.

Slowing the car to a crawl, he veered off to the side of the road. Killing the engine, he unclipped his belt and turned his body to face me. "I don't think I should, princess," he said quietly. His voice was gruff, thick with emotion. "You're grieving and I don't want to take advantage of you when you're vulnerable."

He stroked my cheek with one hand, and clasped my hand in the other. "And truthfully, I don't think I could bear the thought of you agreeing for the wrong reasons. I love you, I'm not going anywhere. I can wait for your answer."

Unclipping my belt, I pulled my knees under me and grabbed his face. "Well, I can't wait any longer to answer you," I told him truthfully. "I love you Kyle Carter...I have loved you from the moment you handed me that shot glass in your kitchen. I was lost, lonely and confused. And you were cocky, slutty and arrogant as hell, but something inside of you called to me and I couldn't keep away."

I smiled and stroked away a tear from his face. "You've made me laugh, you have made me cry, you have made me mad as hell sometimes, but I wouldn't change a single second of the time I've spent with you.

"I've never known the love of a man before you and I never will again, because for me, you're it. To me, you are everything. I am not asking you to ask me out of guilt, or grief. I am asking you to repeat the question because I don't want to live another second of my life without joining my soul to yours. I'm only whole when I'm with you." I leaned in and kissed him lightly, before pulling back. "So ask me the damn question."

"Delia Rose Bennett."

I wrinkled my nose at the sound of my full name, which made Kyle chuckle.

"Sorry baby, but I gotta say it right for this, it's important."

I nodded my head, smiling through my tears as I urged him to continue.

"Princess, I have screwed up so many times in my life, it's like second nature to me," he said, stroking my hand.

"And to be brutally honest, I never cared before I met you. I was alone in the world and that's the way I liked it. I screwed around a lot. Treated women like objects, used them as a temporary distraction from a lonely, empty life. I never thought that would change and I was okay with that. Glad even. Until the night you stepped through my door and made me question every aspect of my life."

He shook his head and pulled me closer. "You changed everything. Without even realizing it, you made me see how twisted and conceited my life was and for the first time in my life, I felt something.

"I had looked into the eyes of someone filled with such purity, such compassion and goodness, that it made me feel naked and exposed. I felt it the instant our eyes met. You have the ability to see into my soul Lee, right through all the bullshit. I was hooked and couldn't get enough. I wanted you with a desperation bordering on insanity."

He smiled and stroked my cheek. "And by some small miracle you wanted me, too. I know I've fucked up enough times that I don't deserve to ask you this, but I'm going to ask you anyway because I'm a selfish man and want to claim your heart, body and soul because, baby, you own mine."

Kyle shook his head smiling as he jumped out of the car. Coming around to my side, he opened my door before dropping down on one knee.

"Delia Rose Bennett. I want a life with you. I want to wake up with you in my arms every morning and hold you every night. I want my last name behind your first and I want to be the reason your gray eyes sparkle. I want a lifetime of arguments and making up with you. I want to celebrate your happiness with you and console you through your sadness. I want to make lots of babies with you and raise them together. I want all of your kisses and I want to be the one to wipe away all of your tears.

"It's pretty simple really, I just want you. I promise that I will love you more than anyone else, today and for every day that follows. You, our daughter, and any other children we have will always come first to me. *You* will always come first. So please, please marry me?"

I threw myself into his arms with such a rush he fell back, landing on his butt. "I want all those things with you, too. I want you Kyle. Yes."

———

We sat on the side of the road, silently holding each other until our bodies were numb and Kyle's cell phone beeped.

"It's Linda," Kyle muttered, checking his text message. "She says that Hope is awake and having a ball wooing all the staff."

I smiled and rose from Kyle's lap. "Reality beckons," I joked, climbing back into the car. Kyle joined me and started the engine.

"This is gonna be good, baby. You won't regret this, I promise," he vowed, taking my hand and claiming it with a kiss.

"I know." And I did.

We had a long road ahead of us. Nothing would be smooth or perfect. There was still so much hurt and sadness, so many unknown elements.

We still had to deal with Rachel's murder trial, my mother's return from the grave, Kyle's meddling father and all of our own insecurities and doubts.

But for the first time, in what felt like forever, I had a plan, a map for my future.

And all roads led to Kyle Carter.

THANK YOU SO MUCH FOR READING!

Kyle and Lee's story continues in
Fall on Me,
available now.

Please consider leaving a review on the website you purchased
this title.

OTHER BOOKS BY CHLOE WALSH

The Pocket Series:

Pocketful of Blame

Pocketful of Shame

Pocketful of You

Pocketful of Us

Ocean Bay:

Endgame

Waiting Game

Truth Game

The Faking it Series:

Off Limits – Faking it #1

Off the Cards – Faking it #2

Off the Hook – Faking it #3

The Broken Series:

Break my Fall – Broken #1

Fall to Pieces – Broken #2

Fall on Me – Broken #3

Forever we Fall – Broken #4

The Carter Kids Series:

Treacherous – Carter Kids #1

Always – Carter Kids #1.5

Thorn – Carter Kids #2

Tame – Carter Kids #3

Torment – Carter Kids #4

Inevitable – Carter Kids #5

Altered – Carter Kids #6

PLAYLIST FOR KYLE & LEE

Check out Kyle and Lee's full playlist on Spotify here.

2WEI – In the End
Grace Carter – Wicked Game
Aidan Martin – I Blame You
Black Honey – Bad Friends
Hillary Duff – Beat Of My Heart
George Ezra – Hold My Girl (Daryl about Molly)
The Black Keys – Lonely Boy (For Rourke and Mercy)

ABOUT THE AUTHOR

Chloe Walsh is the bestselling author of The Boys of Tommen series, which exploded in popularity. She has been writing and publishing New Adult and Adult contemporary romance for a decade. Her books have been translated into multiple languages. Animal lover, music addict, TV junkie, Chloe loves spending time with her family and is a passionate advocate for mental health awareness. Chloe lives in Cork, Ireland with her family.

Join Chloe's mailing list for exclusive content & release updates:
http://eepurl.com/dPzXM1

Made in United States
Troutdale, OR
04/04/2024

18945221R00159